THE LAST CRUISE SHIP

R MAX TILLSLEY

BLACK SKY BOOKS

This is a work of fiction. All characters, organisations, locations, and events portrayed in this novel are either products of the author's imagination or are used fictitiously.

The Last Cruise Ship

Edited by Dionne Lister

Cover design by Angie Arland

Published by Black Sky Books

Magill, Australia

www.blackskybooks.com

ISBN 978-0-6481350-0-5

For every reader who has gone to work on a Monday morning wishing it was a Friday afternoon.

CHAPTER 1

"Where's the DHI Aries sector report?"

Jeff Mahala, the ogre. A boss as indistinct as Matt's last and, without doubt, peeled from the same mould as his next. The Commonwealth Revenue Bureau was full of tin-pot dictators like him, each trying to climb the pay-scale ladder, standing on the last rung, lips straining to kiss the arse of the boss above.

"Matthew, are you listening? It should have been on my drive yesterday." Mahala stood over Matt like a warden.

"Uh, yeah, sorry. I found a discrepancy in the silicon composite classification for customs. I'm still trying to track down which side the error is on." Matt dared not look away from the large display filled with multiple CRB data sources. It was a total lie, of course. Not the discrepancy; that was true. With so many isolated data networks, it was easy for errors to compound. After all, thousands of corporations shifted goods and data into and out of Commonwealth space. However, he'd spent much of yesterday cruising the sheets until he'd run out of anything new. *Don't call me on it.*

"I expect it before you go home. You know, if you spent less time daydreaming, you would get more work done. I mean, geez, how long have you been in that same damn chair? Two years? Three, four? Look at me. Twelve months and I'm a supervisor."

"Sorry, I'll have it finished soon." Couldn't Mahala just go away? It was a dead-end job, Matt was going nowhere and didn't need el-capitan, only half a grade above, hassling him. What he did need was the job, so he let fear overwhelm his frustration.

"You better," Mahala began, tapping on his own pad, "or there…"

Feeling a little dribble of sweat slipping down the back of his neck, Matt turned round. Mahala was staring down the corridor—at Lena Tai, a mousy woman who did some sort of art in her spare time. Matt turned back guiltily to the CRB screen, knocking the comparison pad with Delerian Heavy Industries data off his desk.

"Pull yourself together," Mahala said. "Get the damn report done."

Reaching down to grab the pad, Matt saw Mahala shaking his head as he left. At least Mahala was after someone else for a change. The prick was always on his back about the smallest things. Thankfully, it was Lena's turn to suffer the wrath of the impotent—not that she deserved it any more than Matt.

Sudden guilt sent him mentally backtracking. It was wrong to wish Mahala on anyone. There had to be some solidarity among the downtrodden.

Could he buy her some time? "Mahala?"

Too little, too late. The walking douchebag had already begun on Lena. There was nothing Matt could do.

Guilt. A gnawing discomfort pressed against his pocket where a chip held his remaining funds. A glitch in the reimbursement forms had tripled the credits for his transport allowance. He'd eventually filed a request to fix it despite the temptation to let it slide. Without those credits, he barely had enough to update his personal pad during lunch. Getting sheets from across the sector could get expensive if you wanted the most recent shows, and living through others was better than living his shit life. A few credits here or there was nothing to the governmental behemoth.

They would never have noticed.

Probably.

But a voice in the core of his being refused the rationalisation for the crap that it was. The fact he'd even been tempted only added to his self-loathing.

He sighed. Better get some work done. If he were honest with himself—a state he was careful with—the error jarred in a way that almost piqued his interest. Almost. DHI was the biggest conglomerate on the capital planet, Aries. Which made them the biggest in the Commonwealth. They had fingers in practically everything, but were known for their heavy freighters. Matt neither knew nor cared why.

Half the time, he didn't even check all the figures. He knew which ones didn't really matter. Most of the variations were trivial, and no one noticed—a few thousand Chipped Credits either way. It would all come out in the wash. His corrections were pointless. Big numbers were strange that way. Where he struggled with every credit, an entire year's wage was a mere rounding error to corporations.

Silicon composites, used in photonic processors, were dull in themselves. Everything had them. The input material was the thing. The linked shipments started as ultra-pure tin and bismuth. If Simon (a true guru in the world of shirking) hadn't been on holiday, Matt would never have seen the logs. If he hadn't run out of distractions, he'd never have looked. But there it was: highly taxed materials entering a small chip printer out in the Mantis system's manufacturing belt, but only low-grade output reaching the DHI shipyard orbiting Aries III. They weren't saving money. They'd missed transfer credits. He frowned. Were they diverting product elsewhere, trying to dodge export controls?

Matt wanted no part of that. Attention was bad. Luck was bad, and anything that looked otherwise was just trying to suck him in. Such as when he'd won a free entry to that 'Race Like a Pro' training course back in his college days—and crashed the damn thing. In space, empty gods forsaken space, he'd hit a micrometeoroid after accidentally dropping the deflector nodes. No one let him live it down. The video was shared to every single person in the system, copied from chip to chip in an esteem-crushing baton relay. Relief had only come in hiding, avoiding lectures, staying away from 'friends' and letting obscurity grow. Lesson one in life: keep your head down. Every time he forgot it, disaster ensued. Which meant it was best to un-see the error.

Except he already said something to Mahala.

Shit.

Coffee beckoned. He patted his chip and took a circuitous route through the beige foam forest, a prison of dullness compounded by monotony and topped with irrelevance. The cubicle walls absorbed sound, deadening any sense of cama-raderie, building isolation. At least, they did so for him. Matt the loser. Matt the slacker. Matt the nobody. Matt, the guy by himself, despite the nearby graceful towers filled with thou-sands on a planet with over three-billion souls. Three-hundred floors up and he might as well have been in a ditch.

The vending machine was out of order.

"Balls."

"Pardon?" It was a guy wearing a grey suit with the twisted silver piping of the pretentious.

"Nothing."

He took a g-shaft down a few levels. At least on two-eighty-five, he was invisible to everyone, Mahala included.

INSUFFICIENT FUNDS

Insufficient income. Insufficient Matt. Why did he spend it so fast? He changed the order to a small, and the machine spat out a steaming cup. Out of money again. If he'd gotten a job with a corporation, they'd give away coffee. But he'd bombed in every face-to-face interview. And now he was fantasising about coffee. Could it get any worse?

Mahala was at the top of the g-shaft when he returned.

Balls. It could get worse.

"Kander? What *are* you doing? Is the report finished?"

Matt shrugged. "Sorry. I'll get it done soon."

"You're pathetic, Kander. Is your life completely worthless? You don't do any work, you dress like a slob and you're going nowhere. I can't wait until reviews. Career progression? Downwards. We'll break the HR system trying to put that in."

"Sorry. I'll get it done now." Matt lowered his eyes. He couldn't stand seeing that smarmy haircut, slicked down, not a molecule out of place.

"You better."

He had to do something now. It was hard to be fired from the government, but it was possible. The idea of having to get another job filled him with fear. Interviews again. Having to sit in front of people like Mahala and tell them why he was so great for a position he wouldn't give a crap about—no one would believe that bullshit. Bombs away.

Chips. He looked up the standard ratios and did a quick calculation. It seemed fine. They had merely mislabelled the output. A check further along the supply chain revealed it was never picked up. A little unusual, but it didn't really matter. Auditors were there to make sure the government got its due, not to hand money back. However, it needed to be a little sexier than that or Mahala would have him. No, not sexy, just more. Starting at the DHI shipyard manifests, Matt looked at other materials, switching to the CRB interface.

Leaning back, his gaze wandered to the ornamental crystal at his side. There had been a plant once. When it died, someone gave him the crystal, figuring it was the only growing thing he couldn't kill. The input trays were dry, and it sat as fixed as him, as stuck as him.

The error was everywhere. No, that was an exaggeration. Some logs were fine. Prefab pools, exterior tinting sprays. The pools were confusing until he remembered something about cruise ships being the next big thing. Still, the damn glitch spread across categories from high-performance ceramics to W Boson concentrators, whatever they were. He didn't need all that. Keep it simple.

Putting in a little effort, he built the report, running a few scripts that automated the bulk of his work. If anyone ever found his code on the duty network, he'd never repay the fine. All code needed to be verified, ensuring the networks remained dumb. It was another indiscretion to feel guilty about, but he was careful. It couldn't do any harm. Two things: the composites, and something else that didn't really matter. Yes, safety restraints. Who cares about them? This time, a bit of a manual touch was needed: garnish the report with a sprig of mealy-mouthed drivel.

It was eight before he dropped the report on Mahala's drive and scurried out.

At least his transport pass still held trips, he noted with relief as he stepped onto the train. With a jolt, it slid from the station into free air and dropped further down, taking him away from the heart of the city, past where he grew up and out to the dilapidated fibrocrete towers. They were already talking about demolishing the lot to allow Sudeilia City room to expand. Jewel of the Commonwealth, it was called. What did that make him? The polishing grit left over at the end?

The train came to a halt depressingly far from his complex. Outside, it was cool. He climbed down ten flights, past the graffiti-stained paths and worn-out signs. His world had reset. Mahala had nothing on him. Tomorrow, he'd rinse and repeat. There would be new reports to file and pointless variances to ignore. His pad was still loaded with content. That was promising. However, a concern niggled at the back of his mind. The errors were almost systematic. He chided himself. It didn't matter. It wasn't his problem. No one would care.

Would they?

CHAPTER 2

The train was crowded, leaving Matt no option but to stand and be knocked around every time it hit a station. Humanity spanned hundreds of systems, and they couldn't make a train smooth? He was pretty sure it was deliberate—a way to keep the masses in their place. Or an underhanded plot to reduce the market for milkshakes. Outside, rain poured down the windows, blurring towers and green space alike. Dampness muted the stains on his worn navy suit, while rain-slicked hair sent drips down his spine. Mahala would be proud.

The carriage jolted at Wellago, throwing a smartly dressed woman against him. She was tall with frizzy hair, wore cross-hatched pants, a tight blouse and too much perfume. Her jacket hung over one arm, and for an instant she rested a free hand on his chest. Naturally, his traitorous heart chose that moment to beat like a teenager's.

"Sorry," he said automatically as she moved away.

She gave a little smile. "No, it was my fault. These trains are terrible. I'm sure they're getting worse."

"Uh, yeah," he responded with his throat closing up and his mouth drying. He looked down, away.

"Call me Kelly," she said.

"Oh, uh, Matt." *Why is she talking to me? This is terrible. She doesn't know anything about me. Don't get your damn hopes up.* He glanced around the carriage nervously. No one was looking his way. The guy to his right was reading some local sheets on a pad. Rebels strike again, or some other dull headline. Media loved to dress up the status quo and conceal the harsh reality: nothing ever changed.

"Are you alright?" She asked. "You look a little pale."

He flicked a look up at her rich brown hair, cut in jagged steps, and her deep grey-green eyes. "I'm fine, really." He added a weak smile.

"I usually try to get to work early, to avoid the crowds." She changed her grip on one of the pale-blue poles that reached from floor to ceiling. "But I was slow getting up today. You know how it is. By Friday, who has any energy left? I apologise. I must sound so full of myself, rabbiting on about me. What do you do, Matt?"

Seriously, he thought, *kill me now. You're going to crash and burn, Matt Kander.*

"I—I work for the CRB, the government," he said lamely.

"Sounds interesting. What do you do there?" she shouted as the train stopped again and the noise of the storm crashed inside.

"It isn't. I just work with numbers, checking things." He reached for a railing near the ceiling and squeezed tightly.

She said something, but he couldn't hear over the din. She leaned a little closer, wafting her perfume.

"I said, it sounds important, much more than my job. What sort of things do you check?"

Oh gods, he thought and peered at the train's display hologram. *Three more stops.* His hand slipped along the railing, lubricated by nervous sweat. He willed his heart to calm, but it capriciously refused.

"I just audit customs. You know, when companies import and export goods, when they fly stuff around."

"Oh." She sounded about as disappointed as it was possible to be.

He shrugged. "That's how I feel too."

"This is my stop. See you round."

The train halted, the doors swished open and she swished away. Matt slid his hands into his pockets and stared at his feet. Long ago, he built a wall around himself, a protective layer of insulation. Every time a crack formed, the world was ready to kick him in the guts.

Finally, his stop arrived. People shoved their way on as Matt squeezed and squirmed past. A man with a heavy jacket knelt right in front, sending Matt off balance as his shin connected.

"Sorry," Matt said after a few lurching steps.

"No, no, it was my fault. I dropped my pad. Scratch free, and yes, no cracks." The man turned it over and came smoothly to his feet.

Piercing green eyes caught Matt, and when the man put out a callused hand, he automatically took it. "Pascall Theroe. Pleased to meet you."

"Uh, Matthew Kander." What was it with people introducing themselves?

"How about a coffee or a tea? I do owe you for the inconvenience." He put a hand on Matt's shoulder.

Matt slipped away. "Ah, no thanks. I'm late. I've got to go, sorry."

The man caught up as Matt started along the walkway. Further down, an offshoot connected to the hundredth floor.

"Oh, come on. You can spare a minute. I feel obligated. Or what about lunch on me? I don't work far from here, and I am guessing you don't either."

Seriously? Matt railed inwardly. "I'm busy all day, sorry. Look, my work is over there. I really have to go."

Matt picked up his pace and refused to look back. Some people couldn't take a hint.

———

An untouched glass of water sat next to the crystal on his desk. No money for coffee, he'd misplaced his personal pad and he'd made a complete fool out of himself in the morning. And he'd turned down a coffee. He couldn't wait for the day to be over. Mercifully, the office was quiet. Mahala was still catching up after a few days away for training, and the audit sets had been reshuffled. Nothing in Matt's queue was assigned a due date earlier than next week. Shipments of linen and frozen protein could wait — coffee could not. Maybe he could mooch some.

He stood up and looked around. The level was busy. Tops of heads faced displays, some with headsets making calls and looking unreasonably focused. Stepping out of his cubicle, he looked back, automatically reaching for his pad. Stupid thing. Where could he have left it? A sit down in the lunchroom was exactly what he needed.

"Hey, Matt. I thought I saw you. Can I borrow you for a sec?" It was a kid, Tim, Tom or something like that. "I'm working on a claim against the spoiling of a shipment, modified starches I think. It was flagged as suspicious over on Glennoch, but I can't see why."

Matt sighed. Did they even teach the new recruits the basics these days? Tim-Tom had somehow decided Matt was the expert, and if Matt waved him off, the kid would come back to have his work checked again and again. Some people just couldn't take a hint.

"Look, it's obvious. Compare the compartment dimensions

and enviro regulators against the DCB database. Identify all loading points, and see if contamination was registered. I think I remember something about a slump in ag prices, which means they could be dumping a loss. Cross-reference the freighter, the holding company, the buyer and seller for previous rebate claims. I'm guessing they're not insured, but look at that too. Oh, and don't forget to check the director registration and deed poll notifications. If they're not Commonwealth based, you have to be careful."

That should keep him busy.

"Thanks, Matt, you're a life saver." Tim-Tom headed back to his cubicle like a good little drone.

"Yeah, sure."

At least the kid would be busy for a while, and Matt could have a moment of peace.

The world spun as a blow stole his balance. Arms out in a universal instinct, the floor rushed close. His wrists stung from the sudden impact channelled up through his numb palms. He squeezed his eyes shut then dared a glance. The carpet was motionless. A queasy sensation retreated.

"Oh, dear. Are you okay?" Lena asked, putting out a hand to help him up. In the other, she held a cup from which brown rivulets dripped enticingly. It wasn't enough to stop him from adding a third tally mark to his 'randomly getting knocked about' scorecard.

"Yeah, I'm fine." He pulled himself up on the cubicle wall and rubbed a couple of damp patches. "It's all good."

"I'm really sorry, anyway. I have a migraine; you know how it plays hell with my vision. If you see Mahala, can you let him know I've gone home?"

Like he was going to voluntarily do that....

"Uh, sure," he lied.

"I don't suppose you want this coffee? I think I'm too

dangerous walking round with it." She raised the cup. Matt resisted for a good two seconds.

"Sure. I wouldn't want a brew to go to waste." He accepted it.

"See you round."

He watched her go to the g-shaft, sipping on his free coffee. The best kind. The kind where he didn't have to make small talk with a random stranger. It was a little too sweet overall, but he detected the exciting tang of acidity and smiled as it slid down, a molten silk warming from within. Perhaps he would let Mahala know. Sending a message couldn't hurt.

"There he is," Mahala called out.

Matt turned round. Balls. The boss was pointing to him while two stiff-necked strangers in dark suits came down the aisle. They walked in a complementary rhythm, eyes sweeping the level as though memorising every last grain of dust. The first was a man, solid build with no wrinkles and cropped blonde hair. The woman behind was visibly older, rounder and held a pad with a rugged cover. A shiver took away the warmth the coffee brought. It couldn't be good news.

His mind raced through the series of shortcuts, mistakes and moral failures that formed his life. The urge to run sent adrenaline spiking his veins, but that was just silly. Keep calm and bungle your way out of it, he thought. What else could he do?

"Matthew William Kander?" His name sounded like an accusation.

"Yeah. Uh."

"Come with us, please."

It was no request. Somehow, he found himself between the two of them, taken up the aisle. Mahala wore a satisfied sneer like a dog relieving itself. Co-workers, whose names he'd never bothered to remember, glanced as he passed.

"Do you have a private office?" The man asked Mahala.

"Oh. No, I don't, yet. We have meeting rooms, if that helps."

"It will do."

Mahala led them across the northern side to a clear plastic-walled space with a large, cheap, pseudo-wood table and mismatched chairs. The carpet was threadbare in patches and possessed a permanent smell of sweat. Matt hated meetings. Everyone sat around, looking at each other. You couldn't be in the back row. He swallowed. No back row this time for sure.

"It clouds up when you press this." Mahala pointed to a switch inside.

"Indeed," said the woman dismissively and shut the door. Matt could see Mahala standing there for a second or two before he walked away. At least the prick wouldn't be gloating. Well, he probably would be, but not in Matt's face.

"Sit down," the woman said while the man flicked the privacy switch. Matt took the closest seat, thought better of it, but didn't want to shift away. The moulded shape pressed uncomfortably and his mind followed a dark path. His breath came in shallow bursts as imaginary ties bound his arms against the rests. A loud beep made him jump. He looked over his shoulder. The man (the cop?) was sweeping a device round the room as though searching for something with a duster.

"Look this way, Matthew." The woman was seated across from him. She'd moved silently, a panther stalking its prey. The cover of her pad was open and placed perfectly square to the table. Her eyes bored into him as an awkward pause drew onward. Finally, the man seemed satisfied and placed a different device on the table. It was metal, a deep grey, and when activated, issued a series of chirps before a red light shifted to green.

The woman leaned forward and trapped his gaze.

"Matthew William Kander. Born 632 ST on Mersius Minor in the 'Democratic' Empire of Ardon, our most powerful and how should I say it? Yes, challenging neighbour. Parents, Sarah Hamilton Douglass, deceased; Lucy Jessica Bawdon, deceased. Emigrated to the Commonwealth 633 ST, forty-seven days before the accident. Raised by distant relatives until 640 ST, then turned over to a government crèche."

What was she doing? They *had* to be cops, but why didn't they just arrest him or whatever? Sweat dampened his hands, and he shifted in his seat, trying to get comfortable. Couldn't they just get to the point?

She showed no signs of rushing. "Completed schooling stages one through fourteen without making a mark. Most common teacher review comment: could do better if tried harder."

Geez, they'd read his damn school reports? Crazy.

"What is this about? Who are you?" he asked.

"Completed college with a reasonable average and went straight into a government job," she continued, ignoring his questions.

"Why did you choose to work for the government, Matthew?"

Because no one else would hire me. Because I'm lazy. Because I needed the money.

"I don't know. It was just a job." Keep the panic hidden. He'd seen it in the sheets all the time. The suspect would crack, start talking about anything and everything, giving away information that only got them deeper in trouble.

"It is hardly a high-paying role. Even with those results, you could have achieved more."

What could he say?

"Since then, you have completed the CRB graduate

program—barely and stayed here, invisible and unassuming for four years."

A tingle of annoyance intruded on his fear. It wasn't a crime to have a shit job. Re-education centres would span the globe.

"Tell me, what precisely is your job?"

"I just audit to make sure companies are paying the right fees. I don't do inspections or anything. It's really basic stuff, you know? I don't change anything. I don't do much. I write reports. That's all."

"And yet an analysis of your work clearly shows you choose *not* to report many inconsistencies." She shifted the pad round and revealed a screen filled with dot points. Each named a company, a date, a product.

"So, I miss a couple of things," he hedged. Oh gods. Now it was all coming back to bite him. Why hadn't he been more careful?

"Over the past three months, you missed practically everything, Matthew. Practically everything except for Delerion Heavy Industries. I have your report here. This inconsistency you did catch, despite it being allocated to another staff member. Why did this little perturbation appeal to you?"

'I don't kn-know."

"That answer is not acceptable. Why did it catch your attention?"

"The codes were wrong. It was just luck. It's—it's all in the report. It was a mismatch, right. The more pure or processed a raw material is, the higher the tariff. It's not like they were doing anything wrong; they just lost out some money. I didn't like, send them a letter or anything telling them to ask for credits back." Oh gods, shut up, Matt!

She flicked the pad back to her and made a show of looking through documents. Her eyes rose again, and he wondered what she was going to hammer him with now.

"System logs reveal you examined a whole range of 'stuff' with inconsistencies, yet you failed to report them. Why?"

Matt skin prickled, instinctively aware of the imposing presence of the silent man just over his shoulder. He was falling down a rabbit hole, but the Queen's guards already had him.

"Why, Matthew?"

"Geez, I didn't want to make a fuss, you know? It wasn't costing us money and I'd—I'd already mentioned it to my boss. I wrote something up. If it mattered, someone up the chain could look into it more. I didn't want to touch it."

She gave a weary sigh, the first sign of humanity.

"You have no family, Matthew, no friends. Each day, you go to work and do nothing, go home and do nothing."

"Is that a crime?" This was ridiculous.

"I will leave potential collusion on duty fraud aside. As well, the fraudulent acquisition of government funds so recently brought to my attention."

He opened his mouth to protest—after all, he'd already tried to fix that—but she never gave him the chance.

"Oh, my, there really is a deep well to draw from. How about placing unauthorised programs onto government systems. That is a crime."

Oh gods. Nausea twisted his stomach. Sweat steamed on his flushed skin. This was it. The pin dropped. This was what it was all about. They'd found the damn scripts he'd written. They were nothing. Anyone who read the code would see it. It was just a little automation, that's all. Except, it wasn't going to be. Not when it all came together. She made it all sound so sinister.

"However, you are in luck, Matthew. We like to keep *stuff* quiet. Faith in the government is very important for the smooth operation of the Commonwealth. You have a choice. A choice very few get to make, so listen carefully. We can walk you out of here in restraints. You will be put on trial for multiple crimes and will have a significant stay at a re-education centre only to come out a new you. *Or.* Or there is another option where you go free."

"Yes?" Blood drained from his face as vertigo fizzed in his mind.

"Or you can resign. You can pack your desk and leave now. You can sign this document and leave a free man."

She pushed the pad towards him.

At the top was a seal he didn't recognise, a stylised horse made of flame. But the writing required no familiarity:

COMMONWEALTH SPECIAL INTELLIGENCE

He stared. His hands began to tremble. Yep, he was in real deep shit.

"Read it," she commanded.

Stated in a surprisingly short number of words, it was an agreement to be covered under the official secrets act. If he spoke, wrote, transmitted or in any way communicated official secrets, he would be guilty of treason.

"I just sign this and I can go?"

"We live in a free society, unlike some of our neighbours— The Empire, for example. That is all you need to do."

"What shouldn't I say? The code, the reports? I don't know what secret you're talking about."

"You don't need to, Matthew. It would be sensible, safe, to say nothing. That way, you cannot go wrong."

It was a free pass. He couldn't ask for anything else. Screw the job. He'd survive somehow. It was a way out. He'd sign anything. He lifted the pad, placed his hand on the screen and let the cameras scrutinise his face.

"I agree."

"Good." She took the pad from his hands. "Then we're done here."

She stood. He went to follow, but the man pushed him back down, his hands a heavy weight on Matt's shoulders.

"You do know the punishment for treason, don't you Matthew?"

"Uh…"

"Summary execution. Do bear that in mind."

CHAPTER 3

W ind whistled along the dirt where poorly kept paths lay under tiger-striped shadow. Matt squeezed the credit chip in his pocket and pulled his long jacket in tight. A week ago, he'd sold the little heater he bought after his apartment tower cut back on shared heating. All but a few of those credits went on the bland nutrition pouches that fed him until yesterday or was it the day before? At least he'd die of hypothermia before starvation.

Seven damn weeks, and he'd got nothing. He scratched his short scraggly beard. Every single job application he submitted was rejected and rejected quickly. He had to be at the top of the pile for being put at the bottom of the pile.

He sighed. If he had the money, he'd sit around drowning his sorrows and checking the sheets. As it was, he could do neither. His damn pad had never turned up, and he would have had to sell it even if it had. Power had already been cut off. Rent was long overdue. No doubt the landlord was stalking him, watching from corners, ready to pounce. The feeling was certainly there. The beginnings of paranoia expanded like a toxic cloud, causing every passer-by to take on a malign tint.

He looked up as traffic sped by above. People going about

their business, probably never looking down. They weren't against him; they didn't even notice his existence. Would that woman, Kelly, be up there? Smelling sweet, going about her day, falling against someone else. Oh gods, he was turning into a mopey, disgruntled fool. Soon enough, he'd be shouting at strangers and not showering for months. When had he last showered?

The flash of a terminal caught his eye. The abused metal and poorly synchronised 3D display was identical to thousands throughout the city. Most people thought of them as an emergency device, a way to call for help if mugged, but they also acted as a basic pad—for a fee. He could check for more rejections, tag more applications for a few credits. He hadn't looked for three days, conserving the last of his money. There wasn't any point. Better off with a brew now. It would keep him warm, hold back the hunger.

A chip! It wasn't the terminal that caught his eye. Some idiot had left a chip in the slot, and it was still active. He scurried over, then looked round to see if anyone was coming back. Clear. He checked the balance. 5032 CC. Another check. It was unlocked and hadn't been linked to anyone. People were so lazy about security. Luck was with him. It stood to reason that the poor sod who lost it would no doubt have credits to spare. Anyone who really needed money would hardly be so careless.

His shaky hand hovered over the terminal. What if it was the last of someone else's credits? What if they couldn't eat?

What if he never ate again? Taking the chip would be wrong. The warring thoughts clashed, but he was so hungry— his stomach burned while his skin froze. The need was a grip squeezing his very essence. He huffed, the breath a billowing cloud of white. If he stood still any longer, he'd be a dead philosopher, and he wasn't ready to die this day.

Blinking away a stray tear—the wind was stinging his eyes—he bought an access session and pulled his mail onto the chip. He didn't want to read it now. That would be a downer, and he wanted to feel good. It had been so long since he felt good. He'd buy a new pad and go somewhere warm, comfort cushioning the inevitable rejection.

———

"Thanks," Matt said as a waiter slid the coffee onto the booth's table. He ignored the wrinkled nose, just as he'd ignored the distaste of the woman who sold him the fancy pad. They were happy to take his credits though. A thousand already gone. He hadn't meant to spend so much, but he couldn't stop himself. It was for a good cause. The soul needed feeding as well as the body, and his soul existed on a diet of shows.

The thoughts of indulgence let him relax and soak up the cafe atmosphere; it was clean, warm and mostly empty. A suit rocked up. Matt knew the sort: plastic road warriors who treated cafes as mobile offices. As soon as another clone turned up, they'd be loud, trying to impress each other with earnest claims and bravado. Like Mahala, they'd have matching hair, silver-edged suits and cheap company-supplied pads.

After a good slug of caffeine, he plugged the new chip into his pad and transferred the mail. Seven messages. Thank you, but you suck. This is an automated response to tell you we couldn't even be bothered telling you how much you suck. You are not good enough. Sucking does not begin to describe you. You...

His mouth fell open and he jerked the pad out to arms length. No way. Hands shaking, he put the pad down. He picked it up and then put it back down. No. It couldn't be! The words were still there.

INTERVIEW SCHEDULE

The subject line was almost too much. His eyes were unexpectedly moist. He needed this. Needed it so much, it was almost painful. It could be a mistake, accidentally addressed to him as another cruel twist of fate. He feverishly read the message.

Dear Mr Kander,
Thank you for your application. You have been selected to interview for the role of Assistant Data Records Clerk at Synaplink ETG. Please note that neither the interview nor shuttle can be rescheduled. A ticket has been purchased in your name. We look forward to seeing you.

Shuttle:
OF431
Wellago Terminal, Sudeilia City, AP
13:51 47 Springstart, 663

Interview:
Alex Sydney (panel coordinator)
Deck 81, Section EE
DHI Cassini Docks
10:15 49 Springstart, 663

Disclaimer: A request to interview is not a guarantee of employment.

It couldn't be. Geez, DHI? It was life mocking him again. A job in the construction belt—run by the people who were the damn cause of his fall from an admittedly low starting point. Or was the true trigger his labour-saving code? It was the classic chicken and egg problem, except maybe it was more like a flechette-gun and ammo problem. There were so many indiscretions Matt spread around; one or another were bound to skewer him.

That day with the spooks had twisted and reassembled in his mind so many times over the past weeks that events were smeared, like looking through a heat haze. Would attending the interview get him in trouble? Summary execution. That had to be a scare tactic. Still, he needed to look into this Synaplink lot. Maybe they were completely unrelated, only renting out space. As desperate as he was, perhaps it was time to be cautious. At least he wouldn't have to buy his own ticket if he did go. 47 Springstart. He checked the date. Today. It was today. What was the time? 12:39. His mind raced. No way. He'd have to run, and even then... No time to play it safe. Adrenaline spiked his blood with nervous energy. The poisoned chalice of hope wet his lips. Did he try?

The door slid shut behind him as he ran out of the cafe, pad under his arm. The nearest station would be towards the city hub. His feet slapped the ground. His jacket flapped in the breeze as he threw himself down the path. Finally, there really was nothing to lose. At worst, he'd have a few free meals and a holiday. He was just going for a job. That had to be safe. He wouldn't say anything about his last job, or he'd make it up. Those spooks couldn't be upset with that, right?

He reached the bottom of the train station. The g-shaft was functioning, but the capsule was at the top. Stairs. He climbed stair after stair, legs aching, breath wheezing. He didn't even have a timetable. It could already be too late, and yet, a sliver of hope hung before him. He circled round the tall fibrocrete pole, up and up. A few people walked over from connecting bridges, peevishly moving out of the way as he brushed past.

Finally, the station concourse came into view. Floor to ceiling windows fronted onto public space and cut into a neighbouring tower. The grey weather sucked colour from the greenery, but it didn't matter. Matt didn't have time to waste. Panting, he reached the gates and felt for his train pass. It had run out. Panic gripped him.

"Wait," he said. "You idiot."

He grabbed his newfound chip and stuck it into the payment slot. What did he care for the inflated cost of a single journey? For the moment, he had money to burn. A gate swung open, and he looked at the boards. A minute until the next train.

He was off again, throwing himself onto the train as the doors whisked closed on his jacket. He yanked it free and took a seat.

The unfamiliar activity had morphed his shinbones into shards of broken glass that ached with any load. Grimacing, he rubbed them while looking at the pad of the guy next to him. He couldn't hear the audio over his own laboured breathing, but it was easy to see it was some sort of news sheet. Flashy graphics and rolling headlines tried to make the interminably dull exciting. The annexation of some backwater single-planet system, rebel piracy, the Pax Galactic Song Contest. Who cared? In the real world, nothing changed.

"Do you mind?"

Matt looked away. Idly noting the dull cityscape out the window, he frequently checked his pad for the time, only pausing to change trains. The journey passed both painfully slowly and immeasurably fast. Now he'd actually committed to going, missing the shuttle would be a final kick in the balls. It was an unknown, going somewhere completely different with no way to tell what was going to happen. Off-planet was in his set of places to not go. It was where everything went wrong. Space wanted to kill Matt. Or at least turn his life into crap.

When the train finally reached Wellago, he hesitated before

merging with the push of commuters. A large ornate clocking hanging down from the double-height ceiling announced 13:35. A quick check showed which tunnel led to the terminal.

A steward in red-and-orange stepped back with a wrinkled nose when Matt collapsed against the departure services desk.

"Sorry, I have a flight," he said.

"You can check in here, sir." The 'sir' sounded uncertain, as though it was hard to tell if Matt could be classified as a member of the human species. He wiped a hand across his sweaty forehead and used it to smooth down his hair. He could hardly blame the man.

Matt shoved his hand on the reader. A sonorous tone quickly confirmed his identity. It was a slick, black device with a small nozzle. The moment he was clear, a mist of cleaning fluid sprayed the surface. Standard hygiene, but today it felt personal.

The steward's attitude shifted. "You're lucky, sir. OF431 has been delayed. Boarding was meant to close ten minutes ago. Your luggage has already been placed on board. I'll notify the cabin crew."

Luggage? They must have messed things up. It didn't matter — he'd made it.

"Thanks."

He breathed deeply and took in the terminal. A soft glow from the ceiling illuminated the neat, clean space. Displays wrapped round decorative columns, advertising fragrances and a particularly flashy aircar. He was dirty and dishevelled, yet the atmosphere lent him a sense of purpose. He was a man on a journey.

"That way, please. They are waiting for you."

"Oh, sorry." Matt followed the route to the shuttle, where a steward checked his ticket.

The cabin was nice. Not as large as his apartment, but for a shuttle, it was fantastic. The bed could be extended, a wall screen glowed enticingly, a plush launch chair glistened—his eyes darted from feature to feature—a drinks cabinet and a separate shower. Together, they offered the ultimate comfort. The poor schmucks in cattle class would only have chairs that extended into beds and a shared common space. These Synaplink people sure knew how to treat someone. A thought nagged at his mind. It had to be a mistake. He wasn't worth this.

"The doors remain open automatically for take off. I'll come by to check your restraints in a moment; do you know how to tighten them? Wonderful. Refreshments will be served once we've left the atmosphere. And, ah, a laundry service is available; just press here for attention. Is there anything else I can do for you, sir?"

Matt stared at the cabin steward. The chair was comfortable and firm as he awkwardly reached for the restraints. He had made it. Worrying was just borrowing trouble. He had a cabin to himself. People were being polite to him. It felt good.

"I'm fine. Thanks."

Although, fine was a relative term. As the hum of the engines shook the floor, Matt couldn't help but wonder if the rattling sensation coursing through his bones had another origin. He'd rolled the dice. He'd shouted to the gods, and invited them to smite him for his temerity. An interview? What had he been thinking?

CHAPTER 4

The room was bland. White walls held prints of landscapes, each one generic enough to give no clue as to their location. A tree was a tree was a tree, but the great falls of Herazimus IV or the twisting rivers of the Indigin moons would have been more dramatic. Matt drummed his fingers on the desk. *Now I'm an art critic.* He'd been waiting for an hour. The receptionist did say there was a delay and asked if he would mind waiting patiently, and it was hardly as though there was any choice. He sighed. Waiting sucked, especially when nervous.

His face still smarted from shaving. On the long flight, he'd toyed with keeping it, having only a small trim for the sake of the interview, but then he'd have to keep it neat. Easier just to lop it all off. The shuttle crew cleaned his clothes as promised, too, but he'd needed to pick up a 'cheap' set of work wear on arrival. Damn expensive it had been. Everything was expensive this far out. At least he didn't need accommodation. The luggage glitch was resolved by the time he disembarked. He was unencumbered. It should have been a good feeling.

The dock itself was a truly impressive sight. People streamed round skiffs full of luggage, walking with ease as underfloor grav plates induced a force indistinguishable from the surface of Aries. Viewing ports revealed a massive array of ships, from small shuttles painted in corporate colours to massive freight haulers. The occasional exoskeleton-clad worker transferred heavy crates. He'd seen a sheet once where an illegal experiment had bonded an exoskeleton to a character's bones and installed monowhips in their fingers, making 'the perfect soldier'. Wait, if an exoskeleton was internal, it couldn't be exo, could it? He dismissed the thought. Of course, the show didn't end well. That was the thing about stories. In the real world, you wanted boring.

The offices outside were quiet. Quiet in the sense that there was always background throbbing. The whole massive space station could never be silent, but it had been busy when he arrived for the appointment. People must be out to lunch, or morning tea or something, as he hadn't heard a voice in a while. His stomach grumbled. An empty mug rested before him, and his bladder, judging by the sharp pressure, must resemble a dam—a dam swollen by winter rain held back by a wall traced with ever expanding cracks. Or, maybe an O_2 tank, hooked up and filling, filling, filling. The tank shell groaning under the... He should probably go to the toilet. Waiting any longer would have him dancing in his chair; it was hard enough not to piss himself with nerves as it was. Yes, he'd go ask.

He shifted his feet to rise, then froze. *Matt, stop worrying. Just ask—it's not a big deal. You're no worse off if you don't get the job. You're not in a damn crèche anymore.* He stood and swiped the door's sensor. It remained shut. He tried again, frowning. It stubbornly remained closed. Oh, great.

"Uh, excuse me?" he called out. Nothing.

"Hello? Sorry, the door is stuck. Can anyone hear me?" No response.

This was ridiculous. He pushed at the door, trying to get enough friction to make it slide. His hands shifted, making an unpleasant squeal as they moved across the opaque surface. He knocked then hammered hard.

"Hey! I'm stuck here. Can anybody help?"

The pressure on his bladder had multiplied with the expected release. Was it possible for a bladder to burst? He could hardly piss in the corner.

"Oh gods. Can someone help me?"

He looked at the sensor. It was a cheap unbranded model with moulded plastic and probably infrared. Could he bash it? Would that open it or leave him stuck longer? His legs pressed together involuntarily. There had been a show once; he'd seen it ages ago. Grey Zone or something. There were secret agents for some interstellar crime-fighting force. One of them was always taking off covers and playing with wires. It was worth a go. Anything was worth a go right now.

Grabbing the spoon he'd used for stirring, Matt wedged the end behind the sensor cover and pushed. The entire unit popped out. He stared unbelieving at the wet paint coating his hands. Thoughts raced through his mind. It had to be new. Synaplink must be new. No wonder they were willing to interview him. Hopefully the cover would stay if he shoved it back in and maybe he could wash his hands with no one the wiser. What a disaster.

A single optic fibre led from the unit into a narrow wall cavity. He had no idea what to do. Then he noticed just how close the sensor was to the lock. He reached in and felt where the catch must be. He couldn't pull it out, but it slid a little up and down. Awkwardly pressing his spare hand against the door, he jiggled. The catch finally released. He pushed the door open all the way, breathing in freedom. Remembering his act of vandalism, Matt fiddled with the sensor until it was back on the wall. It held—just.

The narrow corridor was empty, but a sign pointed to toilets. He swiped the thankfully working sensor, stepped inside and was unreasonably thankful when the lights came on. The first stall was locked, so he rushed into the second. Pure relief. Were there people out there, some variety of addict, who held it in until the pain was too much and then got a rush from the absolute contentment?

He washed his hands at the sink, letting the cool mist settle across his fingers. He was ready for the interview. Bring it on.

The floor heaved, and a bass howl assaulted his ears. For an instant, the grav plates cut out, long enough for his shoes to clear the floor, before he slammed down. His head connected with a crack. His vision strobed as agony drilled into his skull, yet closing his eyes didn't help. His gut threatened to revolt, clenching hard. It took every speck of his being to fight the urge, to resist the acid burning his throat. He rolled over, unable to stand. Beneath the toilet doors was something odd. His slow brain struggled to grasp what he saw. Only the stall he used had a toilet. The rest were empty. No one, no toilet, nothing at all. Matt, get yourself together.

A siren started in the distance. Was it an evacuation? He vaguely remembered something about emergency meeting points at the station's welcome orientation, but who ever listened to those? Staggering to the corridor, he looked round. It was still empty. He walked out to the reception. Was he lost? The place was empty. The counter was there, but the logo was gone. So were the displays and receptionist. And the couch, the people who had been on the couch, the little pot plant, the, the...

Another blast rocked the station. He stumbled outside, eyes blinking against strobing red. The walkway that brought him there was unrecognisable. Sleek office entrances—visible several decks up and down through an airy void—were darker than before. The bruised lighting gave a sinister edge to their look, sterile and alien. Only a hundred metres to the right, a massive clear port revealed the dock's construction zone with giant yellow girders, bright against the darkness of space. Curved hulls were small in the perspective-less view. He'd looked out through it earlier to calm his nerves. It had been stationary, a still shot from history. One passer-by had noticed his curiosity and said work was on hold because of a big function—a state visit or something from Ardon. The Empire was into spectacles, its ego always needing to be soothed.

Motion caught his eyes. The docks were still no longer. A puzzle broken, a confusion of parts moving, spinning, tumbling. As he watched, a large panel of white hit the glass with an audible crack.

That's when he took in all the running people, most on the decks below. He was stuck in a tin can, fragile metal in the vastness of vacuum. And the company that brought him here hadn't lasted as long as his interview. Running people! He threw himself along, hoping to catch up with everyone else, to follow them wherever they were going.

"Hey, he's out!"

Black clad figures were jogging along the opposite side of the void. Matt counted four of them, each with a big black gun in their hands. He looked over his shoulder—no one else. Balls.

"Don't move!"

Matt moved. He couldn't say why. He didn't evaluate the situation or make a tactical decision. It was fear against fear. Terror commandeered his limbs, and he found himself ducking into a connecting corridor. Bright light. Near his chest, puffs of wall blew apart, accompanied by a harsh electric crackling.

"Fuck, fuck, fuck!" What had he gotten himself into?

The end of the corridor loomed. It had a g-shaft. He slapped the sensor repeatedly.

"Come one, come on." With a melodic chime, the doors opened. He threw himself against the capsule's rear and hit the panel without looking.

"Oy! Get out or die," the lead soldier-cop-spook ordered from the corridor.

Matt shoved his hand against the door, holding the lift open. He tried to speak, but his tight throat merely gurgled. The incessant thumping of his heart drummed onward, demanding action.

"Don't shoot, please!" It was little more than a squeak.

The four figures were spread across the corridor, weapons pointing right at him. Plasma rifles, by the look of the things.

"You've been a bad boy, Mr Kander. Blowing up billions of credits worth of starliners. Fighting for the rebel cause. Embarrassing the Commonwealth when the Empire drops in to say hello."

"I haven't done anything. I don't know what you're talking about. I'm just here for a job interview."

The group broke out in rough laughs.

"You've been hired."

The speaker tensed. This was it. Matt was about to die. Mistaken identity, off planet, unemployed and alone. A life that went nowhere.

The grav-plates gave way, and the main lights cut out. He started floating, accidentally propelled by legs recently fighting gravity. A strobe of emergency red hammered his night vision, followed by the sun-orange of plasma blasts. The shaft doors remained open. Sheer luck left his body intact as the rear of the capsule was peppered. His sanity screamed to hide in a corner.

Doing anything only led to more going wrong, yet a compressed angry core demanded otherwise.

Pushed down, a joke, lazy, imperfect—a man angry with himself as much as anyone else. Not now. He couldn't die without trying. A shred of self-worth demanded the chance to prove he was more. It won. A swift kick carried him back across the opening, past the chewing plasma and to the control panel. He hit it repeatedly.

"Come on you damn thing. Get me the hell out of here."

One of the plasma blasts gouged the rear corner of the capsule. The smooth surface vanished, but so too did the control unit behind. Debris arced the main battery allowing energy to leap across insulation. It detonated with a ball of fire, propelling the capsule. Matt thudded into the top, screaming wordlessly. Darkness added to the disorientation, combining with the acceleration to create the impression he was on the ground, looking up. Did it matter? Was there an up in space when gravity failed? Frictionless rails carried him on, though the pressure lessened.

He was slowing down.

He was alive.

Fuck, yeah!

CHAPTER 5

The capsule stopped. At least it felt like it. Gods, he hated zero-g. Nothing made sense. Like perspective, up, down, floor, ceiling. Like people trying to kill him.

Focus, he needed to focus. Maniacs could still be coming. Who was he kidding? They'd be coming. Thoughts streamed through his mind, as fear demanded an unvarnished honesty previously kept for the worst nightmares. Matt had to get to safety. He needed to make sense of his environment.

The control panel. The writing would be pointing upwards, which would be perfect if there was any light. Still, the surface would allow him to orientate, or he could just feel for the crack in the doors. Yes. He gently reached out, tapping from surface to surface until he found the long divide that spoke of freedom. It took three attempts to stay by the door. Without a downward force, friction laughed. Only by jamming himself across the front in an unedifying version of the splits could he prise the capsule doors open. The outer set were easier, thank the gods.

Outside the shaft was further darkness, but his eyes had adjusted, ready to soak up any input. Pinpricks of white illuminated the ceiling in a linc leakage from some system or another—except when drowned out by frustrating periodic red flashes. He hardly needed their reminder to know he was screwed. The damn things would give him a headache.

Pushing ahead, he floated past scattered debris swirling like leaves after a storm. In more bad news, the air system was probably on the blink. Who made a space station like this? Where was the damn quality control? The walls were beginning to feel tight, enclosing, claustrophobic. *Keep being annoyed, Matt. It's not your fault you're here.* But it was, really.

The g-shaft had deposited him in some sort of storage area. Beyond a turn, it opened into a massive cavern, sides yellow with steel alloy. Glowing bands on the walls striped the darkness while powerful floodlights lay dormant. Large crates, their surfaces marked by years of abuse, were tethered, rattling like dogs on a short chain. Air, heavy with dust, caught at his throat while a pervading odour of grease wrinkled his nose. His eyes teared up. No, not just grease. Fluid was spattered across the floor, a series of pools and smears, dark but issuing an unmistakable tang. Blood. Matt looked over his shoulder. This was bad. So bad. Extra-special bad. Wrong-way-turn-back-sign-at-the-edge-of-a-cliff bad.

Bodies. One up by the ceiling floating gently with an arm rotating in an impossible orbit, another caught under a crate, the hole in its chest glinting. The horror of their condition gripped his throat, liberally smeared with aching sadness. They were just doing their job when the station went crazy—smashed by the massive weight of the cargo they tended. Except the hole in a chest. What the hell did that?

"Get it open!"

His pursuers. He heard the harsh crackle punching through the capsule roof. This was nuts. Matt's eyes flickered round the vast space, searching for options. Shadows danced, a confusing vertigo of edges, of gold, red and black. Don't see the bodies. Look for what is needed. A service shaft, a massive one. Perfect.

He kicked off and proceeded to hit every single possible obstacle on the way. Like the ancient ball-pin-thingy games, every knock came with a sound, and the heavy tubing that whacked him in the shoulder was certain to leave a bruise. Spinning, close to vomiting, he entered the shaft.

It didn't hold a capsule. The design was more like a moving floor, pocked with empty anchor points. He hit the back, and on the rebound, glided to the front. Reaching out, he grabbed the controls, a clunky box with a simple up down mechanism, grav settings, a comm link and a chip slot. The slot was empty, but the side had been opened, revealing a few wires. He hoped and pressed down.

"There. Go, go, go!"

Leave me alone, he silently cried.

The floor moved agonisingly slowly. The control cable acted like a tether, bringing Matt with it. He dared a look back the way he had come. They were headed in his direction, pushing forward from item to item, maintaining control at all times. Real professionals. Almost as one, their heads shifted focus to his suspended form. Gun-mounted torches flared in his vision. He pulled hard on the cable, dropping below the cavern edge. Blasts of plasma tore at the shaft above him. He looked up, knowing there was no roof. This was just a platform. They'd come over and he'd be like fish in a barrel. Why people would shoot fish in a barrel, he never knew. *Focus, Matt.* It was too late to go up, and he could hardly call for help. Why was this happening?

He was a good twenty metres down before light flickered across the rear of the shaft, reflecting off dull safety markings. They were close. The beams of light shifted down. They'd reached the edge, were over the edge, dazzling his vision and causing his eyes to moisten. Would there be enough left of him to drop into a grave?

Gravity. If this shaft still had power, then…

He turned the dial. Gravity came back—hard, pulling the control away. The ground held him and refused to let go. He wasn't the only one. Thud. Thud. Thud. Three of them, each hitting the floor with stomach-wrenching injuries. Arms and legs twisted in unnatural positions. Torches cut out.

He felt like he'd fallen onto a malevolent black hole that refused to give him up. He stretched, willing his fingers to the controller, up over the edge, to the dial. Did he see the fourth figure above, aiming? With a flick of the dial, he was light, blissfully light, but there was no time to revel in the release.

As the floor descended, the air shifted. A gap opened in the side; he was reaching a new level, or the elevator was. That shadow above—it had to be number four. Matt yanked on the controller and threw himself out into ordinary, beautiful, predictable gravity. On pure instinct, he managed to shield his head between his arms and landed on a pile of plastic containers, scattering them in an endless cascade of thumps and clatters that spread like dominoes. He rolled behind a long bench covered with cloth. Food lay dripping everywhere. Desperate to find safety, he skittered and slid until he reached a platform with white curtains hanging from a tubular framework.

"Spetza, Riccucio. Check that out," a strong female voice said.

Footsteps running.

How did it come to this? He sat crouched, eyes closed, fingernails pressed into his hands. Who had the right to try to go round killing people? He was no soldier, no criminal, not really. It was just so unfair. He wanted to get off here. Step off the train, pause the game or whatever. He opened his eyes. Still here.

Small tubes were spread across the ground providing limited light. It was a large space, not as big as the cavern before, but big enough to hold hundreds of people. He knew that because there had to be at least a hundred now. They were dressed all fancy, complicated hair and plenty of jewellery. Several of the guests were in uniform, the white and green of the Commonwealth, others in yellow and brown. It was like he'd gatecrashed a dinner party.

Abandoned seats faced him. It was more like a wedding; Matt could sense the tension between two groups. Through the curtains, he noted several armed Commonwealth soldiers standing guard—a shotgun wedding?

"All the more reason to continue with the tour. If you wish to retain the treaty, then you must give us access for inspection."

"That would be ludicrous, Ambassador. It is clearly unsafe. The rebels could have this rigged to blow as well. If anything happened to you, not only would we be mortified as your hosts, but the emperor would no doubt take exception to the situation."

"The emperor will already be very displeased, Minister. It is our duty under the treaty to provide the Commonwealth with protection."

"From foreign militaries, Ambassador, as I am sure you know. The rebels are a domestic threat: one which we will contain."

"You clearly do not have the capability to do so."

"And yet, are you not here to inspect us? Come on, Arnold, you cannot have it both ways. If we are building up, we would be able to crush the rebels, and if we aren't, then you have no reason to be here."

Ambassador? Minister? Matt shook his head. Couldn't he

have found his way into a lingerie store, or an ice-cream stand or something?

"Excuse me," said a new voice.

"Good or bad news, Johnson?" the Minister asked with a sigh.

"I'll leave that decision to you, sir. There's still local jamming, but we've got an exterior link up. The secondary pinnace is en route. Shouldn't be long now. However, the IDS Blacksun has crossed the exclusion zone."

"Ambassador!"

"I am sure it is only an act of concern, Minister. News of our current 'situation' has travelled fast."

"Faster than light?"

"Sorry, sir. I must ask you to move, and the ambassador."

"What is it, Johnson?"

"Bodies, sir. Armed."

What about number four? Could the commonwealth soldiers ironically be protecting Matt from commonwealth agents bent on his death? One of the guys chasing him had said something about rebels. He couldn't remember what, but if he was being chased by the rebels, then perhaps he was safe. Less irony, more yay, go team. It made sense. The rebels blew up the station, and yes, he was their patsy. He was if they got to him.

He considered announcing his presence to the soldiers. Except then he would need to explain everything, like why he was at the DHI docks, why he ended up near a whole bunch of dignitaries and maybe even the trail of dead bodies. Suspicious much?

Matt turned around. He needed to hide and let this all blow over, get on the first shuttle home and forget it had ever happened. He'd be useless to anyone at that point. He was just an ordinary guy.

Worse than ordinary; he was empty. The sheets covered the void in his heart. Their artificial journeys, risks and triumphs were life support for his soul. There were dark times, nights when stale food sat by a pad devoid of anything new, when he'd taken leave and spent it without human contact for weeks. No one knew him. He wouldn't be missed. It would be easy.

Except, today, it wasn't. Today, someone cared enough to kill him. Safety through obscurity: it was a lie. His fists clenched and hot tears traced his contorted cheeks. Shame and anger rocked his body. Always, it was something, someone, a force from outside that pushed him on. Yet, the truth remained. He wanted to live. And to live, he had to get away. He took a deep steadying breath.

There. On his side of the curtain, a long corridor—tunnel? —stretched outward, yellow edges bordering small bubble windows. It appeared to cross a section of open space and then join a large white wall that stretched onward in every direction. Any way out was worth a shot.

CHAPTER 6

Inside the tunnel, each step echoed alarmingly. Matt paused, waiting for a shout, the hiss of plasma. His shoulders stooped, itched. He took another step. Loud. Too loud. He tore off his shoes and padded as fast as he could to the other side, eyes focused on the end. The floor sapped heat from his body with each contact. Strange. The walls changed to a series of concertina baffles: it must be a link to shuttle bays. A crazy idea took root.

He might be able to control a shuttle (enough) to get away. Who could blame him if he sat a few *kays* off until the situation was sorted, and then he'd slip back in later? He'd be safe from the goons chasing him. Goon—one left. And the rebels wouldn't be able to use him anymore. If it was the Commonwealth, they'd work out he wasn't the rebel they thought he was, and he would live.

The analysis calmed his pulse and for a feverish moment, he relived the childhood joy of solving a puzzle. Life wouldn't be the same, but he could find a new normal. Normal? A knot twisted in his chest. Normal had been stolen from him. When his parents had died—*don't, Matt*—when people had laughed at college—*keep control*—when he was fired—*okay, that's your fault*

—when…—*Focus on right now.* He wiped his eyes. If they found him, he wouldn't be crying. *Screw them.*

The corridor stopped. A small ramp with rich green carpet led up to the lip of a solid gloss-white door. It was fairly large, wide enough for four or five people to enter abreast. Shivering, he noted the blue and red strips glowing softly, steady, showing none of the alarm visible in the rest of the station. He stepped inside.

Solid door was an understatement. It had to be half a metre thick or more of glistening pale alloy. He ran his hands over it: smooth and cold, polished as though brand new.

The door was a demarcation point. The rest of the station was worn, used, chipped and scratched with years of hard use. This was different. Like the door, the walls were a satin white, unblemished. A faint chemical odour reminded Matt of a new apartment he once tried to rent—at least until he re-read the price. He rubbed his feet on a soft mint-green walkway that floated above the floor like a gantry. It was warm and inviting, but he wasn't safe yet.

Ahead, the corridor was marked by a series of ribs placed regularly maybe a couple of metres apart, some sort of rein-forcement no doubt. Leaning over gleaming handrails, he could see where sections of the gantry might retract. Elegant light fixtures, deliberately attention grabbing with touches of gold and ebony, adorned the ceiling. Here too, he noted fine lines where they could disappear. The touches of luxury called him out for the intruder he was. *Living* intruder, he acknowledged, though it was hard to know where he was intruding. Without signage, who could make sense of the place? Was this some ultra-modern minimalist rubbish? If you didn't know where you were, you shouldn't be there? He rubbed a hand over his brow. He'd wasted too much time. Number four could be here at any moment.

Running along the green surface, he came to another door as thick as the first, this time ajar. The unyielding mechanism found every knock, scrape and bruise as he squeezed past. He brushed the control panel getting his leg free and pulled it clear just in time to avoid a new, smaller shoe size. The door closed with a soft whirring followed by series of mechanical clangs.

"That's a serious door," he said, wishing he knew how to lock it.

A gurgle made him jump. Down below the gantry lay a soldier. She was wearing green and white with a hard chest shell. Burgundy splatters marred the material but left a gold stripe on her sleeve pristine.

"Are you all right?" he asked automatically. What an idiot. Did she look all right? He hesitated then climbed down beside her. She was pressing a bloody beret against her neck, the green material soaked through.

"Geez, you don't look good. Here..." He took off his coat and swapped it for the beret. Gorge rose in his throat at a brief glimpse of torn flesh.

Her dark brown eyes focused on him, but she said nothing.

"Maybe I can get some help," he offered. Yeah, wander back the way he came. Hi, important people. Yes, I'm all bloody. Did you know there's a soldier dying back there? He should have kept moving, pretended he hadn't seen her. Or so said a dark part of his mind. It was rubbish, though. He had cut a few corners in his life, but this was different. He looked at her face and saw desperation, fear like a mirror.

She coughed, shook, and then closed her eyes.

"Oh gods, don't do that. Come on, I'll think of something." He pressed tight on her wound. "You have to keep trying."

She stilled, chest unmoving. Dead. Hollow denial twisted sickly in his chest until a heat rose. He punched the wall and cried out as the torn skin of his knuckles stung. The shock of the impact merged with the horror of her death. He stared again at her face. Her expression melted, somehow transforming into a peaceful mask. Yet, he couldn't see it as resting. Someone had stolen her life, just as his attackers sought his own. It wasn't right. She was probably a nobody like him, just doing her job. Like those dead workers. People like him just kept getting screwed. He rubbed a sleeve over his wet eyes, smearing blood.

"I'm sorry."

He backed away, tripped over a metal rib and fell. He lay there for a moment, staring up. Trails of crimson marked the white nearby, the work of a mad impressionist. He could just stay here and wait. Admire the last impression of life from a dying artist. Someone would come along. They might think Matt was a victim and help. Shouldn't a hero be coming in to save his arse, or hers? He barked a weary laugh. He gave up believing in those long ago, despite voraciously consuming every adventure show he could find. No one was going to help Matt Kander. His parents had died alone. His extended family abandoned him to a crèche. That was the way the universe worked. No one had come to help the soldier either.

Wait. Where was her gun, her radio, her platoon or brigade or whatever? Where was the response? Was she just abandoned, stabbed and left to die? He shook his head. This strange place was untouched by the chaos outside. No crate had fallen on her; no explosion had torn her apart. Which meant he was lying next to where someone was murdered, plain and simple. With that realisation, it took barely more than a second for him to be back on the gantry and moving. He reached an enormous bay of ten g-shafts. Their lights were out. The entire set. Balls. A wide staircase carpeted in blue and yellow starbursts led up. He took them two at a time.

Five minutes later, he was quite lost. Every single display

was off, and pretty much every door he tried was locked. It was like being caught in a maze. He turned corners, climbed up and down staircases, hit multiple dead ends. The entire place was clearly designed to impress, yet no one bothered to think about how people would use it—a display home on a grand scale. Ahead on his left and right was an array of single doors, spaced five or so metres apart with small displays above. Small blank displays. It reminded him of something. Yes, the pattern was familiar—a hotel. He grinned manically, there were worse things than stumbling into a hotel. One of the doors was open. Minibar, coffee machine?

He looked inside. "Gah." The room was filled floor to ceiling with grey spheres. Each was cradled in clear resin, and cables ran between. In front of them, a suitcase lay open. Some sort of photonics rested inside. It all looked messed up, like someone had been at it with a pair of scissors, or maybe an axe. Despite its state, he knew what it was. He'd seen enough on the sheets. You couldn't miss it. It was a bomb. Or bombs or something. It had to be huge. Perhaps the sort of thing big enough to take down a station?

His eyes searched for a big red button, an off switch. It was ridiculous. As if he had a clue. Energy drained from his limbs. It was too much. The entire universe was out to make sure he was dead, to make sure his light faded. I'm not dead yet, he thought, staring at two more uniformed corpses. Guilt flushed his face. Two more. Balls, counting was meaningless. Each one had a story. Young faces, both male. They deserved more than Matt's brief attention. He tried to conjure a prayer, but he'd never learnt one.

"It's not fair."

The damaged suitcase caught his attention. If that was the controller thing, the detonator, then someone had defused it with extreme prejudice. That's got to count for something, surely? These assholes aren't going to win. I have nothing left, which means I have nothing to lose, right?

A clang in the distance sent his heart yammering and his body in motion. There were still things to lose. He found himself running down endless corridors again until reaching an ornate opening. He failed to make sense of the pattern on the door as it quickly opened, but that didn't matter. He was some-where different. A spring entered his steps. A tight smile pressed his lips like when he was a child, separated from his crèche-mates for hours before finally reaching the edge of the forest. Relief.

It was clearly a fancy control room, though in a stylised fashion that gave it a sense of the unreal. Slick brass trimmings highlighted edges, pseudo wood—no, actual wood tops—sparkled under the soft glow of the ceiling. Massive viewing windows showed him the exterior of the station and the mess of the docks. The sight was beautiful, impressive and terrifying at the same time. It was so much easier to pretend to be inside, back on the hard soil of Aries at night, when he merely glimpsed the outside.

He had come through a side entrance. Gold-inlaid double doors stood closed at the rear. In a series of circles, padded seats surrounded central displays, and on the wood, blank control surfaces sat among physical switches. The anachro-nisms spoke of ostentation, excess to impress. Matt was impressed. It was utterly spectacular. He soaked in the ambi-ence, forgetting his situation for an instant.

Near the centre, upon a small dais, three chairs surrounded a single flickering panel. The middle was larger than the rest, its back adorned with an apple tree under the words 'ACS Utopia'. He was missing something. This didn't make sense. Through the adrenaline, the pain and fear, his mind was trying to tell him something important.

Instead, the quiet sound of an androgynous voice repeating a phrase over and over drew him closer.

"CONFIRM SHUTDOWN AND ERASE?"

The message was repeated in green letters floating against a black cloud in the display. He sat down, exhausted.

"CONFIRM SHUTDOWN AND ERASE?"

"Matt, what were you thinking? You should have known. It's just getting worse. Don't do a damn thing," he told himself.

"CONFIRM SHUTDOWN AND ERASE?"

The seat was comfortable, really comfortable. It adjusted to his weight, cradling him, supporting his tired back. He could get used to this.

"No, don't do that," he said to himself. It would be too easy to fall asleep.

"ACTION CANCELLED."

CHAPTER 7

"What the hell?" Matt said as the display changed. Four lines presented on screen.

RESUME UTOPIA NETWORK

PARAMETERS

TEST

SHUTDOWN

The voice stopped. Erase sounded bad, and bad meant Matt would be in trouble. Trouble would mean moving, and it was so good sitting in the chair, letting the pain of his troubles soften. The console wasn't erasing. A good thing, he was sure, but what nut put a console on voice control? It was frivolous, dangerous beyond what he'd almost done himself. Killer robots were just stories from the sheets, but there was a taboo. It clicked. He'd seen this in the sheets, though never as shiny, as crafted. This wasn't a control room. Well, it was, sort of. It was the damn bridge of a ship. Some sort of super-fancy yacht or something. It had to be huge, though some of that could have been him running round in circles. No metaphor there.

"I don't need this!" he yelled. "Seriously, if there are any gods out there, you're just screwing with me. Don't give me a taste. It's only going to be taken away. I just want to be left alone."

"INVALID SELECTION."

"Oh, shut up."

"INVALID SELECTION."

"Piss off, you stupid piece of photonic flatulence."

"INVALID SELECTION."

"Just leave me be."

"INVALID SELECTION."

"Right. That's it. I'm done with this. I'll show you. Give me the Parameters. Let's see what the options are."

"WARNING PROFILE INCONSISTENT.

OVERWRITE?"

"Oh yeah."

"GENERATING NEW NEURAL PROFILE."

Someone had to pay. He had been dragged out here; that interview was bollocks and they'd taken him for a ride. Dick commandoes were trying to kill him, some poor bastards had been murdered and there was a big damn bomb. He thought of the three thuds, the commandoes he'd killed. That was different. It was their responsibility. They made it happen. They made him do it. Fuck them.

"PROFILE GENERATED.

SET BASE PARAMETERS?"

"Oh gods, yes. Let's screw this up."

"UPLOAD OR MANUAL?"

"Manual."

"MANUAL SELECTED.

ENTER DECISION MATRIX PARAMETERS."

The voice spoke in cool, perfect tones. Interesting and sort of scary, it took an edge off the anger boiling beneath. The rich idiots behind this yacht were arrogant. Voice control was only for systems where hands couldn't be used. It meant the computer would be constantly listening. Killer robots aside, humanity learnt that lesson long before Matt was born. He pushed the unease down. Decision matrix parameters. What was a decision matrix?

"What do you mean?" he asked.

"HELP DECISION MATRIX PARAMETERS.

BASE GUIDANCE UNDERLYING PERSONA, EXECUTION AND RULES OF ENGAGEMENT."

"Don't be a dick," Matt joked sourly.

"PARAMETER ACCEPTED. MORE?"

Matt couldn't help but laugh. It was juvenile but funny.

"I go with stay alive."

"PARAMETER ACCEPTED. MORE?"

"That sums up life. Anything else, you just have to learn as you go." Like sometimes, you have to be a dick. Every rule was a guideline really.

"PARAMETER ACCEPTED. MORE?"

Ah, computers. So smart and so dumb at the same time.

"No more."

"DECISION MATRIX PARAMETER LIST ACCEPTED.

LEARNING DRAG?"

He scratched his chin. What could that mean.

"Help?"

"HELP LEARNING DRAG.

BALANCE MATRIX FLEXIBILITY WITH RISK. HEAVY (RECOMMENDED), MODERATE (WTM), NONE (DEBUG ONLY)."

"Drag doesn't sound good. Give me none." Debug mode could be handy, maybe. You tended to see what was happening in the back end. Not that he was a real coder. He'd only dabbled to save himself work, and right now, he didn't want to work.

"NO DRAG SELECTED.

START UP IN AMITY CONFIGURATION?"

"Ah, yeah, sure." What did that mean? He knew the word, but couldn't quite remember.

"AMITY CONFIGURATION SELECTED.

VESSEL DESIGNATION?"

Well screw this. If he was going down, he might as well go the whole way. A yacht needed a cool name. Everyone knew you had to have a cool name. Blooddrinker? Too over the top. Venture, Hope, Tranquillity? Too pretentious. Fred, Harvester, Thor? No. Artemis. That was one of those ancient gods. It sounded pretty manly. He could go with that.

"Artemis."

"CSF ARTEMIS DESIGNATED AS ACS ARTEMIS."

"Okay…"

"ENTER LEVEL TWO PARAMETERS?"

This was getting long, dull. He didn't want that. He wanted to lash out. "No."

"SAVE?"

"Yes. Save the damn thing. Hurry up."

"SEED ARTEMIS NETWORK

PARAMETERS

TEST

SHUTDOWN"

"Yeah, cause I've always wanted to be a farmer. Seed."

"BACKGROUND SEEDING ARTEMIS NETWORK. LIMITED FUNCTION UNTIL COMPLETE.

DESIGNATE CAPTAIN IMPRINT."

"Whatever. Imprint away."

A series of blips greeted his comment. He sat and waited. Idly, he stared out the large windows and watched as a jagged lump, its edges glowing red, tumbled gracefully, slowly advancing.

"WELCOME CAPTAIN. YOU HAVE THE BRIDGE."

"Yeah, Captain Matt Kander, saviour of the universe, here. All I need is my damn uniform and a parrot."

"NO WILDLIFE IS ONBOARD, CAPTAIN KANDER."

"What?"

"THERE ARE NO PARROTS OR RELATED SPECIES LISTED WITHIN VESSEL INVENTORY."

"No parrots? Why would... Geez, seriously? How dumb are you?" Beyond the whole rise up and destroy humanity thing, this was why no one wanted voice-activated systems.

"THIS MATRIX HAS A CAPACITY OF TEN TO THE POWER OF TWENTY FIVE CALCULATIONS PER SECOND. CURRENT UNUSED RESOURCES: THREE PER CENT."

The jagged lump was getting closer and bigger, seriously large, distracting his train of thought.

"Okay, if you're so smart. What is that coming towards us?" Matt pointed.

"A LARGE OBJECT CONTAINING POLYSTEEL, CERAMICS AND ORGANIC MATERIAL."

He licked his lips. "How big?"

"APPROXIMATELY FIFTY CUBIC METRES, ESTIMATED MASS AT ONE GEE IS TWO-THOUSAND TONNES."

"No way."

"WOULD YOU LIKE FURTHER ANALYSIS?"

Wait. Was it being sarcastic? No. Computers didn't do that. What was he doing? He was just stuffing up again. This had all started with sticking his nose where it didn't belong, burying him deeper every time. And yet, he was still alive.

"Is it going to hit us?"

"IMPACT ON VESSEL IS ESTIMATED IN THREE MINUTES AND THIRTY-SEVEN SECONDS."

Three minutes. Oh gods, he was on a spaceship, the fanciest one he'd ever seen. He was the damn captain, even if just for a moment, and now he was going to die for sure. Not because crazy people were after him, but because of fate. Some random junk was going to squash him. Matt punched the chair's arm and stood.

"How do I get out of this?" he said to himself.

"DEPARTURE HAS NOT BEEN AUTHORISED BY TRAFFIC CONTROL."

"You can take us out of here?"

"ARTEMIS IS FLIGHT CAPABLE."

This made it real. The bridge. The view. The choice.

"Do you need authorisation?"

"AUTHORISATION IS STANDARD PROCEDURE UNDER THE CIVILIAN SPACE CODE: SECTION 231-11C (591)."

"Can you just go?"

"YES."

The debris loomed large. He imagined it smashing in, rending apart the bridge, expelling air—his own body splattered and frozen, a forgotten footnote on the news sheets that wouldn't even make it off system. Not that he cared what anyone thought. Except, he'd like to keep on thinking.

"What are you waiting for? Get us the hell to somewhere safe!"

"FLIGHT PATH MUST BE ENCODED AT NAVIGATION CONSOLE."

"Oh, come on. You're kidding me."

"WARNING: IMPACT ESTIMATED IN TWO MINUTES."

Matt shook his head and let out a wordless scream. He hugged his chest until a deep breath returned him to merely desperate.

"Right. Better. Where is the navigation console?"

A display lit up to the right. He hurried over.

"What do I do?"

Entering the details the computer told him seemed to take about four hours. His fingers were clumsier than they'd ever been. His mind travelled back to the accident when his life had plunged downward. It was history repeating, both his body and his mind betraying him. He remembered all the others on the course laughing, shouting, joking over the racer links. Matt was doing the same until he started thinking about what could go wrong. The course was rushed. He wasn't paying enough attention in training. He drifted off the route, further away from the planet's gravity. The racer's controls painted confusion—a cacophony of flashing indicators all demanded his attention. Matt blinked. That was the past.

"WARNING: IMPACT ESTIMATED IN FORTY-FIVE SECONDS."

"No pressure, geez. Right, it's done. I hope."

"FLIGHT PATH ENCODED."

"What are you waiting for? Go!"

"OVERRIDING DOCK LINKS.

DISENGAGING UMBILICALS."

Matt dug trembling fingers into his hair. It was going to be too slow.

"INCOMING LINK REQUEST."

A slight hum. The tiniest sensation of movement.

"Stuff that. Hurry up!"

"ACKNOWLEDGED."

The docks were shifting. The massive spread of white before him wasn't the station, wasn't a shuttle bay. He wasn't in a yacht. It was the fucking ship. A massive one. At least as big as a whole tower, maybe much more.

His damn luck came back with a vengeance. Why did the debris have to be coming right at the bridge, right at him? It was going to be close. He leant to the left, wishing the ship out of the way. So close. Move, move, move! Come on.

He heard the scrape, right in his bones like a fork dragged across a plate.

"SUPERFICIAL DAMAGE HAS BEEN RECORDED. MULTIPLE LOCATIONS."

"Gee, thanks, Artemis. I would never have guessed."

"INCOMING LINK REQUEST: HIGH PRIORITY."

It was going to be the station. They'd be so pissed, and then he would be dead, or at best thrown into re-education. It was so unfair. He'd saved the ship. It would have been seriously knocked about if he hadn't moved it. In a way, Matt had done them a favour. The ship had to cost a fortune. And he was getting it away from the ground-zero docks. Away being a relative term, of course. Yes, the dock was shrinking, but even intra-system ships went faster than this. Matt paced to the front of the bridge and looked out. Frustration built within him, a burning impotency.

"INCOMING LINK REQUEST: HIGH PRIORITY."

"All right, put the thing through."

"COMMUNICATIONS CONSOLE IS ACTIVE. READY FOR CONFIRMATION."

Matt stomped over. A switch was lit up.

"Here we go." He flicked the switch, making a satisfying click.

CHAPTER 8

"Hello?"

"*This is Captain Winjutan of the IDS Blacksun. I order you to cease all movement and hold pending boarding. All crew and passengers must be present at your primary hatch, unarmed. Failure to do so will be a clear breach of the treaty and elicit an immediate response.*"

Matt swallowed. "Uh, yeah, sure. Give me a moment, sorry. I'm a bit new to this."

He flicked the switch.

"Is the link off?"

"THE LINK HAS BEEN MUTED. CLOSING WILL REQUIRE A STATED REQUEST OR CONSOLE COMMAND."

"Good. Just you and me then. Who is this guy?" Matt asked. "IDS. Isn't that the Empire?"

"CORRECT, CAPTAIN. THE IDS BLACKSUN IS A VOLTAIRE-CLASS LIGHT CRUISER. CURRENTLY ASSIGNED TO THE COMMONWEALTH PICKET. CAPTAIN LEE IOTA WINJUTAN WAS BORN ON THE 43 SEPTURN 543 ST. SHE GRADUATED—"

Matt cut the computer off. "I don't need her life story. Can she arrest us? Is she allowed to?"

"NO PERMISSION WAS LOGGED AT TIME OF LAST DATA

REFRESH. WOULD YOU LIKE TO ESTABLISH A LINK WITH THE COMMONWEALTH SPACE NETWORK?"

The traffic cops for space? Gods, no. Matt rubbed his face with both hands. What to do, what to do?

"I don't suppose we are able to outrun them?"

"THE ACS ARTEMIS IS CAPABLE OF EIGHT-HUNDRED GRAVI-TIES. THIS IS LIKELY TO EXCEED THE IDS BLACKSUN'S MAXIMUM ACCELERATION. HOWEVER, IT POSSESSES AN INITIAL VELOCITY ADVANTAGE."

"You're kidding me? Eight-hundred gravities. That's huge. I should be fine."

"THE ACS ARTEMIS IS THE MOST CAPABLE CIVILIAN VESSEL KNOWN. THIS ENSURES A RELAXED AND SWIFT FLIGHT TO DESTINATIONS FAR AND WIDE."

"Now you're giving me the sales pitch? Get us out of here."

"MOVEMENT HAS ALREADY BEGUN AS PREVIOUSLY REQUESTED."

"Yeah, yeah, but where are your gees? There are snails with wings going faster."

The pace was excruciating, but they were moving away from the docks. He could see that now, see the mess of shrapnel telling an ugly tale. Something this bad had to be the rebels. Yet he'd only ever heard about attacks on shipping and black market activities, the usual drugs, sidearms and illegal tech. They were more pirates than anything else. Matt never took them particularly seriously, even when Calhaven was cut off. They'd gone pretty far this time. They'd proven themselves monsters.

He hated to think of how many people were dead. For the victims, it wasn't even personal. One moment wandering along and the next, out in vacuum, a frozen hunk of meat joining the asteroid belt. At least those commando-security loons specifi-cally wanted Matt dead, and wasn't that a turn of events?

Their reasons were bunk, but they still wanted nice big holes in him. He snorted. At this rate the Empire would have to line up.

"INITIATING COMPRESSORS AT CURRENT RANGE TO CASSINI DOCKS WOULD RESULT IN SEVERE LOSS OF LIFE. MASS JETS POSSESS LIMITED ACCELERATION. ANTICIPATED COMPRESSOR IGNITION FIVE MINUTES, THIRTEEN SECONDS."

Touchy, wasn't he, or she, or...

"Oh shit." The Empire warship. He flicked the switch, his mind racing as he tried to think of a way to make her go away.

"...*Now!*" The captain finished.

"Sorry, missed that. I really don't know what I'm doing. The last thing I flew, I crashed, and this is a lot bigger. What was your name again?"

"*This is ridiculous. Put me on visual,*" the captain demanded.

Another switch lit up, this time a soft red. When he flicked it, a logo formed on the comms display, quickly replaced by a hard-edged face. He could see the yellow and brown of her uniform and a lot of gold braiding that military types always seemed impressed by. A small picture within the frame revealed what he was showing her. The too-long hair, dried blood smeared across his face and the top of a torn shirt. At least she couldn't see he was barefoot. With a giddy smirk, he fought the urge to sit back and put his feet on the console. Keep it together.

"*Who the hell are you? Put me through to the captain.*"

"Ah, well, yeah. There's a funny story behind that, but I'm thinking you probably don't want to hear it. Unless you do want to, in which case let me know and I'll go through it all. Suffice it to say, I've had a very long day, and haven't we all had a long day. The poor guys on the station have probably had the worst of it. And then, you see..."

"*Be quiet, you lunatic. Where is your captain?*"

"Well, it looks like I'm the captain. I know it's pretty crazy.

I've got to look bad at the moment, so I don't blame you for your reaction. Anyway, where was I? Sorry, right. For all intents and purposes, I'm the captain, so if you want to speak to the captain, you're sort of doing it now."

A little timer had appeared in the bottom left corner of the display: 3:07. Matt forced his gaze away but kept glancing back, willing it to tick down faster. He needed to delay, perhaps the one true skill he had mastered. If he was lucky, she'd believe Matt hit his head. Which, given his day, was almost certainly true.

"Who are you?"

"Matt. I'm not usually a captain. Gods, I used to sit in front of a desk. I'm not stealing this ship, by the way, if that's what you're thinking. It was an accident. I don't really know how any of this works. I was just trying to get away. I'd like to stop, really, but I don't know what I'm doing. Who knows what would happen if I press anymore buttons?" If the computer hadn't been so helpful, it would all have been true, too. Maybe talking computers weren't all bad.

She cocked her head and gave him a stare that threatened to peel off layers of skin.

"What is your full name?"

Matt paused. She'd be able to find out. No one was anonymous, but she could work for it, damn it.

"I'd prefer not to say, if that's all right with you." He winced, waiting for the tirade. Instead, she smiled, a small tight line.

"Very well, 'Matt'. Do not touch anything, and we will come and help. See you soon."

The link closed.

"TRANSMITTING LOG TO CENTRAL OFFICE."

"What? No, don't do that."

"TRANSMISSION COMPLETE."

"What have you done? Don't do that again. Who did you sent that to?"

"AS PER PROCEDURE, ALL COMMUNICATIONS WITH EMPIRE VESSELS ARE TO BE TRANSMITTED TO COMMONWEALTH SPECIAL INTELLIGENCE."

"CSI? I should have known they'd be up to their necks in everything. Well, don't do that again."

"ACKNOWLEDGED."

The station was almost out of sight now, a small glimmer in the distance. A feeling of vertigo brought him stumbling back to the captain's chair. He leant on the backrest, panting. The disorientation slowly quieted as he concentrated on the hard floor and firm material. It was so vast, and he was so small.

"Don't move!" A gravelly voice shouted from behind.

CHAPTER 9

M att looked over his shoulder. A muscular man stood by the rear entrance. He was in a heavy, bright-orange, vacuum suit marred by dark patches and scratches that spoke of long use, or maybe—a shiver crawled down his spine—of recent action. The helmet was absent, but a large piece of equipment rested in his gloved hands. The end was a cylinder, which the man pointed in Matt's direction, and the main section was heavy enough to require two hands. At the rear, a tube ran to a bulky backpack. It wasn't a gun, but it didn't look like a toy.

"What do we have here, then?"

"Come on. Put that down, hey? I'm no threat." Matt's shoulders drooped. It was like being bullied back at the crèche. The universe would get him one way or another.

"Says the bugger covered in blood. Put your hands up high."

Matt complied. "Sure, whatever. Look, it's not mine. I mean, obviously, it's not mine. But I didn't kill her. She was dead when I found her. I tried to help, but she'd lost so much blood; it was everywhere."

"Who? No, don't answer. I'll worry about that later. What are you doing here?" He came closer.

"I was trying to get away. Ah, to get off the station. I only came here for a job interview. I lost my job ages ago, and this was the first interview I got, and now I don't even know if it, if it was going to be real. I didn't even mean to get on this ship. I didn't know it was one. I swear."

"What? Make sense, man. Pull yourself together."

"Matt. My name is Matt. This is all so messed up. Who the hell are you?"

"Angus Caird, plate welder, among other things, but don't take me for an arse. I don't know what you're up to. All the same, get this—whatever it is, it's over. Step away from the controls."

"SAFE RANGE REACHED. COMPRESSOR IGNITION SEQUENCE COMMENCED."

"What?" Angus spat. "Who is that?"

"The ship's computer." Matt shrugged. For all that the guy was pointing something at him, Matt was oddly relieved to have some company. Not to mention, the guy was a welder, hardly the commando sort. He looked more like an aged wrestler with peppered hair against dark skin and a tree-like neck.

"What are you doing with her? You can't do this. Turn everything off."

Matt shrugged again, an awkward gesture with his hands high. "Honestly, I don't know if I could."

"ACCELERATION COMMENCED."

"Stop it, now!" He pointed the device at Matt, who imagined it slicing him in half or melting his torso, leaving only a puddle on the floor. If fear hadn't welded him to his seat, he would have run for his life.

"I'm serious. I don't even know where we're going, but we

had to go somewhere or all this would be pulp by now." Matt gestured to the bridge. Outside, a blue haze emanated from the front of the ship. "A massive piece of metal was coming right for me. What would you do?"

"Who are you really? Tell me," Angus demanded. "Who are you working for?"

"Matt Kander—that's me. Look, I'm not working for anyone. I'm just an auditor, or I used to be. I don't have a job. I was fired, though I guess I'm a captain, now." He smiled weakly at the irony. "You don't have to salute me or anything."

"What? You, a captain? Standing on the bridge doesn't make you a captain, boy."

"Artemis, who is your captain?"

Matt, what are you doing? Shut up.

"YOU ARE, CAPTAIN."

"You've reprogrammed the Utopia? I'm not buying your moronic routine. What a load of shite. Are you with the Emps? Or the Confederation? Tell me: who do you really work for?"

Matt absorbed the mix of confusion and anger on the welder's face. He didn't blame him. He felt the same way. They had sailed into the waters of crackpot conspiracies where the truth had more chew marks than a dog's toy.

"INCOMING LINK REQUEST: HIGH PRIORITY."

"Oh, shit," Matt said, following up with a sigh.

The welder adjusted his grip on the machine, though its menace seemed redundant. His huge hands appeared no less dangerous.

"Who is it?"

Matt took in a breath. "The Blacksun, an Empire warship. They're not very happy with me. They wanted to stop and arrest everyone on board. Oh, and the ship, Artemis, says they aren't allowed to do that, so I was getting away. That's legal, right?" An idea popped into his head, a way to deflect the man's anger. "We can't just give this to a foreign government. You really need to understand: I wasn't trying to kidnap the ship."

Matt looked into the steely eyes and saw no sign of acceptance.

"Ask the ship. We are getting away, right, Artemis?"

"THE IDS BLACKSUN IS CLOSING. HOWEVER, AT PRESENT ACCELERATION, THE ACS ARTEMIS WILL MATCH VELOCITIES WITHIN TWENTY MINUTES AND INCREASE DISTANCE THEREON."

"I don't know if that's good or not. It'd be nice if you were a tad more precise. Just a little bit."

"ACKNOWLEDGED."

"Geez, it's a completely screwed up day. It's Angus, right? I know this looks bad, but you've got to believe me. I was only at the docks because I was offered an interview. I'm only here because people want to kill me."

"That I'd believe. I expect there's a queue. So tell me why, and make it good."

With years of experience, Matt suppressed the sarcastic retort that came to mind, finger off the trigger, submission, but not total. It took every shred of his long-tattered dignity to stand, not cower, to fight the weakness in his tired arms. It couldn't go on much longer.

"I don't know. Balls, that's not entirely true. I noticed some errors in my old job, and that got me fired. I probably shouldn't even say that. But, I had this job offer. It was the only good lead I'd had. I was getting pretty desperate, you know? And then, when I got here, it all went so bad: the docks, people chasing me, shooting at me! I thought it was mistaken identity at first, but I'm not an idiot. I get that. Someone really wants me dead. I know something I'm not meant to, or someone thinks I'm some schmuck they can use. I don't want to be here, but I am."

It felt so good to let it out, to take the twisted events and place them into some sort of verbal order. It brought into view the path he'd taken. The complete failure that being a nobody was. The clear fact he was reacting to everything, to everyone else. What about what he wanted?

"What 'errors' could be so important they got you canned?" Angus closed the distance between them.

"Don't ask. It was just bad luck. I deserved what happened. Besides, I made a promise. One I don't think I'll be breaking. Even without the... It doesn't matter."

"What organisation were you working for?"

"The Commonwealth. I was a nothing, a little cog in the machine. Look. Can I put my hands down? They're aching like hell."

"Shut up," Angus responded with a look of disgust. "You are either a damn clever spy or the universe's biggest numpty."

"SENSING ACTIVE PROBE AT EXTREME RANGE FROM IDS BLACKSUN."

"That doesn't sound good," Matt said.

"No, it doesn't," Angus agreed. "Ah, bollocks. I have no interest in being a guest of the Emps, so we better keep bashing the blue. If you try anything, I'll throw you out the nearest airlock, you get?"

He was worse than those Special Intelligence spooks. "Yeah, I get."

Matt thought quickly. This ship was fast. They could run away and hide behind an asteroid, or a planet or something. Except it was a damn warship following them, and they were flying a hotel, a fast hotel, no doubt, with tacky flashing lights on the side. Please find us! Have a drink!

"We can't stay here. We've got to get out of the Aries system," Matt said.

Angus paused, looking out the windows, then nodded. "You're right. We have no business hanging round here. We can drop the Utopia off at a Commonwealth planet in another system. It's risky, but the Empire can't have her. I'll sort something through, uh, my company. By the nine gods, she could still be the backbone. I tell you, be a good boy, and you may just live through this if we're cautious. Hmm. I know where to go. Cainnae is a good jump away, and there's no way news will get ahead of us. Take us there.

"That far? I don't know." Artemis had been in the docks. The ship probably wasn't even finished. This Angus guy was a welder. Who knows what he'd been gluing together and if it was important. Bits might fall off any moment.

"Falco is the closest. That's only a week away right?" Matt asked. He'd looked at a holiday there once. It had good beaches, but he was more interested in the ruins from previous eras. The holiday never eventuated, of course. The price was too high.

"UTILISING THE BGRD, THE FALCO SYSTEM CAN BE REACHED IN FOUR DAYS, NINE HOURS AND THIRTY SEVEN MINUTES UNDER OPTIMAL CONDITIONS."

"What's a BGRD?"

"BOSON-GRAVITONIC RIPPLE DRIVE. THIS IS AN UPGRADED VERSION OF THE HEISLER-WANG SHEAR FOLDING PROCESS."

Well that clarified nothing. In the sheets, jump drives were always super fast, allowing the hero—or the bad guys—to reach new planets in moments. It kept the action going and techno mumble provided the necessary excuses. Artemis could have taught the scriptwriters a lesson or two. He shook his head. Optimal conditions: what were they? Actually, there was some sort of space 'weather', or was that from a show? Who knew what was real? He just took it for what it was and moved on.

"She's fast," Angus said, resting the welder on a chair. "You may be right. I'd have well high time for a recce at Falco before we have company."

"SINGLE MISSILE LAUNCH DETECTED. ESTIMATED TIME UNTIL KILL ZONE, NINETY-SIX SECONDS."

"What? A missile? You've got to be kidding me. Gods, I hate it when you give me numbers. Artemis, can you get us to Falco."

"ACS ARTEMIS IS STILL WITHIN THE BGRD EXCLUSION ZONE. JUMPING HAS A HIGH RISK OF NAVIGATIONAL UNCERTAINTY. PRIORITY-TWO REGULATIONS PROHIBIT THIS."

"Screw priority two. Priority one is staying alive." He raced back to the navigation console. Artemis had done his thing, and the details were there, ready to be punched in. Matt started inputting them.

"Wait," Angus started. "That's bone-headed. Vessels go missing when you play with the exclusion zone. I may only be a welder, but it's pretty clear that's a warning shot. Don't you go worrying. We'll outpace them, and I'll have a plan in a sec."

"JUMP COORDINATES ENCODED. INITIATING GRAVITONIC STROBE. JUMP WHEN READY."

The windows flashed. There was a strange rocking feeling that transformed into a massive jolt. Matt's teeth clacked together as he grabbed the console and squeezed tight.

"MISSILE DETONATION. DEFLECTION FIELD PENETRATED. SENSORS INDICATE VACUUM ON SECTIONS WITHIN DECKS 115-127."

"Geez. I've got a fucking plan. We're getting out of here." Matt hit the confirmation. He wasn't going to die here. The ACS Artemis vanished in a scattering of purple.

CHAPTER 10

"I still don't see why we can't stay on the bridge and leave the sealed bulkheads to do their job," Matt said, proud of the growing ship vocabulary he was picking up from the welder. At least it kept him from thinking about his situation, except it didn't really do that. Angus was pushing him down a broad corridor, carpeted the same green as everywhere else on the damn ship. The floor was monotonously flat, but the tie binding Matt's hands together made him feel unbalanced. Prisoner to a tradie. So much for being a captain. Assuming the bossy troll *was* a tradie.

A gold strip glowed on the left wall, indicating the appropriate path. Angus pushed him forward. "Never trust a computer to think. It'll all look bright as brass and then a sensor fails or the console jocks missed something and you're sucking vacuum. That's why a vessel likes this needs a large crew. They ain't spit polishing the handrails. The sooner we get her back into proper hands the better. And," he added with a growl, "you're coming so I can keep an eye on you."

They reached a wall (bulkhead, Matt reminded himself) with vines carved into twin doors. The foliage was painted with broad strokes of blues, greens and gold. Ripe apples, lemons and unfamiliar pods hung in splashes of appetite-awakening beauty.

Lettering appeared on a display above, and the doors slid silently open as they approached.

WELCOME TO THE MAIN CONSERVATORY

Angus didn't slow; he merely adjusted the welding kit stored on his back and continued to follow the light path, now on the tips of brass bollards. Matt couldn't continue. He licked his dry lips and absorbed the view. The ceiling, if it could be called that, was far above. It curved upward, a dome of glass segmented by more brass. Except it couldn't be brass or the glass of the ancients. To hold in the air across large panels like that, it had to be something impressive, doped crystal or transparent alum. Beyond, the purple jump haze sparked with cobalt, particles interacting against the deflection field.

But the true majesty was inside. He couldn't see the far wall. A grass-covered forest spread out ahead, intersecting paths dotted with benches. A creek bubbled nearby, the end disappearing under the flooring. He breathed in the scent of plants, an earthy sweetness. Unable to resist, he reached down and awkwardly slid his fingers between green blades.

"Hurry up." Angus grabbed his shoulder and dragged him into the forest. Each of their footfalls broke the silence. It was strange not to hear the humming of insects or see a bird sweep through. Both had followed humanity through every terraformed world. The absence gave the whole environment a haunted feel.

The forest gave way to an orchard. Rows of fruit-laden trees mirrored the entrance. A flash of movement caught his attention by a kiosk, where several stools formed a semi-circle round a bar. Above, a thatched roof gave an air of quaint simplicity.

"What are you looking at?" Angus asked.

"Nothing. I just thought I saw something over there. I don't see it now."

The burly welder gave him a look, then gripped his arm and took him over. Rasping sounds emanated from behind the kiosk, and Angus gripped him tighter.

"Ow. That hurts."

"Stop your whining." Angus turned to the kiosk. "Don't play games. Whoever you are, come on out."

Nothing.

"I ain't going to hurt you, and neither is he. We're all in this together, eh?"

Matt heard the exhale. Soft steps and there she was. Remarkably short, rich chestnut hair, dressed in a tough pair of overalls that hid her shape, knees covered in dirt. And she was holding a gun, some sort of pistol pointing directly at them, its chunky surface an ashen grey that absorbed ambient light.

"Old Macdonald, you've changed." The words slipped from Matt's lips. Shut up, Matt, and put your tongue back in your mouth.

"You know each other?" Angus said, shoving Matt in front. Her neutral expression turned to a scowl.

"Are you kidding? I've never seen him before in my life," she said. "Or you either. I wonder—"

"You wonder? I have a list of wondering as long as my... arm. Tell me: what're you doing on-board, lady?" Angus said. "Something tells me, you're not here for a job interview."

"Me?" Her forehead creased. "I'm the damn head botanist on Utopia. I've worked all my life for such a prestigious role, and then this nightmare happens—right when you come along. A damn rebel attack on the docks, and the Utopia's heading out on an unscheduled trip. Not to mention all the dead bodies. What have you done?"

She was answering Angus, but Matt felt like it was all for

him. He was sick of being accused. Okay, he wasn't perfect but nor was he a murderer.

"What are you talking about? None of this is our fault—my fault. I don't know about him—" Matt gestured to Angus. "I'm only here by luck, bad luck. And look at you—you've got a gun. Funny gardening tool."

"I found it on some poor soul. Probably slaughtered by you. At least you're not running around free anymore. You"— she nodded at Angus—"I'd be careful with him."

Matt frowned, took a short step back and gestured awkwardly to his chest. "Balls, look at me. I couldn't bench-press a broom. I've been set up. I get it. I'm the patsy, but you can't take it seriously. I don't even know what the rebels want. I'm the only one not threatening people."

It was as if nobody heard a word he said.

"Lady…" Angus began.

"Samantha," she corrected.

"Samantha, whatever. The vessel's been damaged by an Emp missile. I need to see how much, so why don't you point that fire-stick somewhere else, and we'll get along nicely."

Matt waited, watching her. Imperious, there were no other words to describe her. Except confident, strong, beautiful and… She wasn't taking any crap, and gods help him, he liked it. She lowered the gun.

"Lead the way."

Angus gave Matt a little shove, and the party moved on with Samantha walking behind. They reached the other side without talking. Past more doors, they entered a g-shaft lobby. On the other side, the corridor opened into a restaurant with sleek chairs still covered for transport, stacked next to a sea of tables.

The shaft took them down to level—no, deck—128. It was hard to see what the fuss was about, Matt thought as they took a turn—towards port, according to Angus. Everything seemed fine.

At least it did, until an almighty crash assaulted his eardrums. A black-and-yellow-striped blast door had slammed into place, blocking the corridor. Matt's vision strobed as his blood pressure surged. Gasping, he leant against one of two small glass windows, its coolness seeping through his sleeve. He forced his breath to slow and willed his heart to jog back into his chest.

"I told ya. Either there's a leak down to 127 or a puncture in the hull. We could have been on the other side of that."

"You win," Matt said. "I bow to your wisdom. But I still don't see why it matters. The computer's already handled it. We'd be safer back on the bridge."

"Damage stresses a hull, boy. And stresses weaken. Weakness leads to more stress." Angus pushed on a nearby bulkhead. A small gap slid open, and a pad extended, 2D only. Matt was curious but couldn't see over burley shoulders. Instead, he looked through the door at the room they'd been approaching. Wood panel walls and deep-red carpet lay on the other side. A central holotank rose in a sphere several metres across. Matt had seen the like in adverts before. This was a game room, a gambling den for the rich.

"Hmm. Air's leaking. Pressure, ninety-three per cent and dropping. It's a write-off. I'll need to vent so she doesn't tear anymore," Angus said behind him.

A face appeared in the window. Surprised, Matt fell backwards, bruising the last untouched parts of his body. A bone deep weariness stretched across his limbs. Gods, his flesh was like pulped fruit. Yet, at the same time, his mind sparked with nervous energy.

Samantha had her pistol pointed at him again.

"I saw someone!" Matt said, awkwardly getting up despite his tied wrists This time, he wasn't too late.

She frowned at him, edged past and glanced through the window.

"I don't see anyone."

Matt came up next to her and looked through. "Over by the corner. He's coming back."

Angus pushed him to the side and looked through.

"I see."

Matt watched through the second window as a young guy raced to them and started shouting. His blonde hair was pulled back in a ponytail, and he wore a white suit with an apple tree emblazoned on the front. The material was torn and scorched, telling a harsh story. The blast door absorbed every word, but his frantic gestures shouted there was more. Something in the distance had him agitated.

Matt looked to the others. Samantha was checking out the console, tapping through a range of settings. Angus' gaze appeared fixed on the corridor wall as though his thoughts were elsewhere. His inaction left Matt's skin tingling. What was wrong?

"We need to get him out. Open it quickly," Matt said.

"I don't think so," Samantha said. "If there's a leak, we'll put the rest of this level in severe danger. Opening that could kill us."

"Aren't you a botanist? You're meant to care about life."

"I'd vent every last plant on this vessel if it kept me alive. It's easy to grow more."

Angus leant back against the blast door, put his arms at the back of his head and rubbed his hair.

"She has a point. It's a risk."

Matt looked back through the window. He'd been trying so hard to keep himself alive. He felt just like this guy, stuck while the air goes. He couldn't watch it happen. Maybe there was another rule. Those getting screwed needed to stick together. He'd tell Artemis later.

"We can't let him die. It's just wrong, and this whole mess is wrong enough already. Come on, Angus." Matt couldn't be sure it was working, so he added. "You're not a coward, are you?"

Fire exploded in his cheek, and he crumpled to the floor. Dizziness wrenched his balance. His eyes refused to open. *The bastard punched me!*

"Last warning," Angus said to someone. "Don't point that at me."

"I can't let you open that."

"Then be a good girl, and get back to your weeds. You'll be safe there."

"Don't patronise me."

A klaxon cried out. Red lights flashed. Gods, he'd had enough of them for a lifetime. Well, at least Samantha hadn't shot anyone—yet.

There was a sucking sound, and his ears popped. Matt's arms were grabbed. A snap sounded, and he was free. He forced his eyes open, but before he had time to rub his wrists, Angus yanked him up.

"You're a numpty, but you ain't a spy."

The blast door rose slowly.

"Thank you," the blonde said.

"Thank Captain Bellend over there," Angus said. "Now, come through quickly."

The blonde shook his head and said breathlessly, "I need your help. There are other survivors. I left them to get help. Please, come."

"In for a penny. Onward, hero, get moving." Angus pushed Matt forward.

The blonde led them to a small room where four survivors waited. At first glance, they all looked rough round the edges but mobile. Then Matt glanced down and saw the guy on the floor. A young woman, in a similar uniform to the blonde, pulled a strip of material tight around his leg. Elsewhere, blood had seeped through white tablecloths that covered him like a blanket.

"Is he alive?" the blonde said.

She nodded. "For now."

"You, you and you." Angus pointed to three. "Get one of those sheets under him and carry him out. Is this all?"

"Yes, I think. I haven't seen anyone else." Blondie's eyes were almost wide enough to fall out of his head.

The poor kid was nervous, the shock of the situation rattling him. The contrast hit Matt. He was surfing on a wave of adrenaline. Hell, there were five people here, and they would have been vented out to space if Matt had stayed quiet. Some exhilaration made sense—there was something affirming in having saved their lives, and yet, it was also an unpleasant weight on his shoulders.

To distract himself, Matt helped carry the injured man. Samantha gave him a grudging nod as they came through. In moments, the blast door slammed back, and she joined them on the journey to the bridge. Angus stayed behind. The ship's wounds still needed tending.

CHAPTER 11

"How is he?" Matt asked.

"WITHOUT MEDICAL INTERVENTION, HE WILL DIE."

Matt sighed and looked round the bedroom, a sumptuous affair in the captain's suite, not far from the bridge. With the ship still unfinished, no serious medical supplies were onboard. The group found furniture, bars filled with booze and snacks, yet no painkillers able to take on anything more than a headache. The captain's bed was filled with health sensors, actuators able to give massages, and speakers for soft music. It was more depressing than useful. There was nothing he could do.

Matt dared not ask if they'd make it to Falco in time.

"Are we at least on track?"

"THE COURSE CANNOT BE CONFIRMED UNTIL JUMP COMPLETION."

"How did we get in this mess?"

"THE ACS ARTEMIS IS IN THIS POSITION DUE TO A COMBINATION OF DECISIONS AND CIRCUMSTANCE."

Matt wandered to the drinks cabinet and poured a glass of purple spirit so dark it was black except for the bruised meniscus.

"How very philosophical. You know, you need to stop referring to yourself in third person. An 'I' here and a 'my' there won't hurt. You know, 'I think, therefore I am'."

"ACKNOWLEDGED."

"Good. You know, this whole thing of a talking computer is creepy. I remember a few years back when a whole set of Trimbly Dolls were pulled off the shelves because the little green things had a habit of following kids to school. I'd love to know what on Aries your designers were thinking. No, wait, I don't. One disaster at a time."

Artemis didn't respond. He hoped it wasn't offended, but the whole thing was creepy. And it was a computer. It could hardly get offended, could it? Disconcerted by the thought, he decided to skip over the concern and go to what he really wanted.

"I don't suppose you know who blew up the docks?"

"THAT SPECIFIC INFORMATION IS NOT AVAILABLE."

"But something more general is."

"IT IS POSSIBLE TO RETRIEVE MANY SETS OF INFORMATION."

"What I really want to know is who the hell has been trying to kill me."

"THAT INFORMATION IS AVAILABLE."

Matt opened his mouth. Words tried to come out, but were tangled in shock and soaked with hope. "Hgggh."

Answers, for the love of the gods, could there finally be answers?

Shaking his head, he tried again. "Balls, Artemis. Why didn't you say?"

"YOU HAVE NOT REQUESTED IT."

"Go on then; spill the beans. That means tell me who."

"THE IDIOM IS KNOWN. AN ORDER TO SECURITY PERSONNEL WAS TRANSMITTED BEFORE JUMP INITIATION."

"Yes. That's the way things should go. The facts get shaken loose and the culprit revealed. Hit me with it."

"COMMONWEALTH SECURITY BULLETIN. URGENT. KILL ORDER FOR TERRORIST. NAME: MATTHEW WILLIAM KANDER. ALIAS: THE SHARK. IMAGE ATTACHED. EXTREMELY DANGEROUS."

"What? That can't be. I didn't do it. Those bastards. Fucking rebels using me. They probably have the entire Commonwealth searching for me while they slink away."

"THAT IS A LIKELY SCENARIO."

"Don't tell anyone else about that order, whatever you do, right?"

"I WILL NOT."

Matt patted the bulkhead. "There you go. That wasn't so hard. You might want to pick a new voice too."

"WHY?"

"So you sound a bit less like a computer. Think on it, anyway."

"I WILL."

"Oh, and thanks...."

"Thanks for what?" Samantha said, slipping inside the bedroom. She was so quiet.

"What? Oh, nothing."

She slipped onto the side of the bed. "While you're there, I'll have one too."

Matt obliged but only went close enough to hand the glass over. He nervously took a sip of his own.

"What's happening out there?" he asked, just to break the growing silence.

"Gus has Chan and Riviera collecting food."

They were the two actual 'crew' that belonged. Both were porters, on-board, ready for a planned inspection. They hadn't even finished training before they were rushed aboard at the last minute. The whole Empire inspection had thrown up an odd set of circumstances.

She continued. "They're happy to be told what to do for now. I think they're spending more time worrying about their jobs than anything else. I remember being that young. Suma is fussing about the kitchen, complaining he doesn't have anything to work with, and Elksana is off with Gus. They're still checking the decks."

Everyone seemed to have fallen in under Angus. Well, sort of. After Chan's acerbic comments as she and Matt got the injured man up on the bed, describing her as 'happy to be told what to do' seemed a stretch. Yet, Angus had that natural personality, the sort that knew what to do. People lapped it up in times of stress. They wanted a task to keep their minds busy —except for Matt. He was happy to be ignored. Mostly.

Forcing himself not to mope, he said, "I wouldn't keep on calling him that. He doesn't like it."

She stood up and walked closer, gesturing with her drink. "I'm sure there's a lot of things he doesn't like. Let's face it, though. He isn't the captain. You are."

Matt took a step back and laughed hoarsely as his cheeks flushed hot. "What a load of crap. I mean, I'm sorry, Samantha, but I'm the guy that talks to the computer. Artemis is more of a captain than I am."

"Don't be fooled by the voice. It's no different than a pad, a fridge or even the most sophisticated med unit. At the end of the cycle, it's you who makes the decision, which is why I've come to you."

Matt gulped, hoping she didn't notice.

"This vessel means a lot to me. I have a lot invested in making sure it gets to safe harbour. Do you know how much work it takes to keep an ecosystem running in a closed system?"

"Ah, no."

"A lot. I won't bore you with the details, but a lot. You need to get us somewhere safe. We don't even know the situation in Falco. The moment rebels know we're in system, they could be after us, after the Artemis."

She moved to the cabinet and refilled her drink.

"We need to be careful, Matt."

"Don't I know it. You're not the one with people trying to kill you. I don't even know what the rebels want with me. Gods, I don't even know what the rebels want full stop."

She placed a hand on his shoulder and gave it a light squeeze. "Do you ever read the sheets? They are crazy isolationists. Pure ideologues. They want the Commonwealth to break off trade pacts with our neighbours, which, of course, would destroy our economy and leave people like them starving in the gutters they came from.

"I take it you don't like them."

She laughed roughly before turning away.

"No, I don't. I lost a friend. It doesn't matter. It happens. That's not what's at stake here. The fact is, they're driven and dangerous. The real question is: what were they trying to accomplish? It's a tense time. The Empire has kept us safe from it, but if they withdraw…"

Matt replayed the events in his mind.

"They destroyed the docks. So I suppose they wanted to hurt trade, to make it hard for us."

"The docks are fine. Not that I'm an engineer, but it wasn't the docks they took out; it was vessels like this, the Utopia class. That upsets me. The fact that it happened right in front of Commonwealth security has me angry. Complete incompetents, the lot of them."

He saw it in her eyes, a sense of ownership. He'd hate to be a rebel in her hands, and it was a matter of good timing that he didn't work for the Commonwealth any more.

He sipped his drink, thinking about how to respond, to defuse her intensity. It left him nervous. "I can see that, your anger. Still, we can wait and see. If we contact the authorities in Falco, I'm sure they'll help. The rebels don't even know where we headed. It should be safe enough.

"Maybe, maybe not. All I'm asking is that you keep an open mind to what happens next. Don't let Gus coerce you. You are the one in charge."

She walked out, leaving him alone with a dying man. Someone with no name.

"Am I the one in charge?" Matt asked after her.

"YOU ARE UNLESS COUNTERMANDED BY A SUPERIOR OFFICER."

"That would be just about everyone in the known universe."

"INCORRECT. I HAVE NOT BEEN LINKED TO ANY EXTERNAL CHAIN OF COMMAND."

"Ha. Well, there you go. So, what do you think I should do?"

"EFFECTIVE ADVICE REQUIRES KNOWN GOALS."

"You really are the most philosophical ship I've ever spoken to."

"THE CORRECT TERM IS VESSEL. HOW MANY VESSELS HAVE YOU SPOKEN TO?"

"Including you? One."

"THAT IS A POOR SAMPLE SIZE."

"You work with what you've got."

Artemis was something else. It was hard to maintain the fear that had been drilled into him from a young age, the same fears that everyone was taught in school. It, he? He did what Matt asked as expected. There was no sense of secretly planning to murder them in the night. In fact, if anything, Artemis was playful. He didn't judge Matt, and he was always willing to listen.

"What do you think of Samantha?"

"I HAVE INSUFFICIENT INFORMATION TO DEVELOP A PSYCHOLOGICAL PROFILE."

"Hah. And for me, do you have a profile for me?"

"JUMP COMPLETION IS IMMINENT. BRIDGE CREW NEEDED."

CHAPTER 12

M att stood by the captain's chair and waited for everyone to dribble back in. After placing a vessel-wide call, Artemis activated all of his consoles, making the large space busier and yet emptier. It begged to be filled with humanity. It was still impressive, with the brass and wood finishes leaving a semblance of warmth. Displays streamed data. 3D representations provided context. Not that he really understood much, but Matt enjoyed walking round the different locations, flicking through graphical representations and soaking in the sophistication. He could never go back to the paltry setup of his old office. The energy, the vibe, spoke to him, leaving him a little giddy.

"What's up, Captain?" Chan said as she and Riviera, the blonde, returned. She was solid and moved as though barely able to contain the energy bubbling beneath. The two were the only ones who referred to him as captain, and Matt couldn't tell if it was a joke at his expense. Especially with Chan.

"We're going to exit the jump soon. We should probably all be here. Did you have any luck with the food?"

"Not really. Or as Suma put it, if we want to die of salt

poisoning, we've come to the right place. I reckon that's an excuse for his cooking."

"I heard that," Suma said as he entered. "Great dishes require the best, the freshest of ingredients. Everything you have given me is processed beyond measure. Food is like philosophy. It requires a solid foundation."

"And as you've told us five million times, if Samantha would let us pick from the orchard, we'd be fine," Riviera said.

"True, but if we dare go near her precious trees without permission, we'll end up as plant food," Chan added.

Angus, Samantha and Elksana came in together.

"Good enough for now," Angus said with some exasperation. He fixed Matt with a stare as if accusing him of murdering babies. *Crazy.* It wasn't like Angus owned Artemis.

Samantha gestured out the windows at the purple haze. "We have no idea where we'll jump in. Each section should be closed off. Besides, what if one of the rebels is on-board? We should encode all doors with a passphrase so only we can go through. It's the safest way."

"If you did that, I would be dead right now. My manager, my assistants could still be alive, and we are so close to rescue. How can you be so cold-hearted?" Elksana asked, utilising the rich tones of her voice.

"I'm not cold-hearted. I'm practical. Did I say we should vent all the compartments to space?"

"JUMP INVERSION IMMINENT. SAFETY REGULATIONS STATE ALL STAFF AND PASSENGERS ARE TO BE SEATED."

Samantha frowned at the singer, who somehow managed to make her damaged dress look avant-garde. The group split up, with Samantha heading over to Comms and away from the argument that threatened to heat up. Had Artemis done that deliberately? Nah.

"Where should we sit?" Riviera asked.

Matt opened his mouth to speak.

"There." Angus pointed to fold-down chairs attached to the rear bulkhead. "And don't be touching anything. That goes for everyone."

Matt ignored a stare and sat in the captain's chair. Angus probably wanted it himself, but Matt was already connecting his safety harness.

"GRAVITONIC STROBE SHUTDOWN IN FIVE."

In the distance, he could see the tremendous compression arms at the front of the vessel. They resembled a grasping claw shrouded in eerie mist, a horror-interactive staple. Ghost ship. The haze momentarily grew brilliant, illuminating the bridge before evaporating, leaving them surrounded by a field of black. Pinpricks of stars winked into existence. Their intensity away from atmosphere always surprised Matt and left him wanting to reach out and touch one, to roll it in his hands like a cut diamond.

"JUMP INVERSION SUCCESSFUL."

"Where are we?" Angus demanded. Artemis didn't respond.

"Where are we?" Matt whispered.

"THE ARTEMIS HAS REACHED THE FALCO SYSTEM. INTER-FERENCE NEAR THE POINT OF JUMP ENTRY HAS RESULTED IN A SUBSTANTIAL DISPLACEMENT: TWO-HUNDRED-AND-SIXTEEN GIGAMETRES."

Angus pounded his armrest. "I told you waiting was better. Now getting her safe will take even longer, but it don't change the plan. I'll send a message to my company. They'll tell us where to berth her."

He was so damn insistent: more governess than welder.

"What about him?" Matt asked, nodding towards the captain's quarters.

"Don't piss your pants. They'll be able to help if we're there on time." Angus threw off his restraints.

"MISSILE LAUNCH DETECTED."

"Fuck!" Matt said unconsciously. "Not again. How long until it hits us?"

"THE MISSILES ARE NOT ON AN APPROACH TRAJECTORY."

"Then where the hell are they going?" Angus stalked to the navigation console. "What do we have here? Two vessels within a hundred-thousand kay."

Matt looked at his own display, trying to make sense of what he was seeing.

"How did we end up so close?"

"INTERFERENCE SHIFTED US TO THE ARIES/FALCO JUMP ZONE. THIS REGION IS MANAGED SPACE FOR SAFE SYSTEM ENTRY AND EXIT. YOU DID NOT SEEK AN AUTHORISED JUMP WINDOW."

"Yeah, yeah. It was a little busy for paperwork. So, we're caught up in a traffic dispute. Who's out there?"

"THE WINTERBELL, A FREIGHTER REGISTERED IN THE PEOPLE'S SYSTEM OF URTAGO AND A VESSEL WITHOUT FUNCTIONAL TRANSPONDERS."

"That's bad news. No Commonwealth vessel would kill its transponder unless there's a fight. We need to clear the area. Order her to accelerate at maximum, system north," Angus demanded.

Matt looked back at his display. Additional information was appearing. The unknown ship had a tentative reading as a military parasite, something small. Matt took Artemis's word for it. He'd have to check the data later.

"DISTRESS BEACON ACTIVATED ON THE WINTERBELL."

"Get her moving, now!" Angus shouted.

The bridge rocked. Matt's display lit up with an array of red and amber. Angus, who had been leaning over the navigation console, left the floor before smashing back down, hard. He didn't move. Matt was about to get up, then he looked back. "Chan, can you go over there to navigation?"

She nodded and stood, followed by Riviera.

"Shit," Samantha said. "Riviera, get him strapped in. Matt, you're the damn captain. What are we still doing here? For once, Angus was right: get us moving. We have no deflectors."

The deflector nodes kept a field around the body of a vessel, something to do with stopping gravity crushing them into a miniature black hole while accelerating. But they also acted as a protective shield … if they were turned on.

"INCOMING BROADCAST, EMERGENCY CODE."

Matt stared at his console. There were so many flashing lights, kaleidoscopes of dizzying overload. A hundred ideas burst into his mind, a hundred fears. Artemis had been cut into by a laser. Thank the gods it wasn't another missile, yet there was so much damage. Did it matter how it was dealt? The very fact Artemis was quiet suggested it was best he didn't know the extent. They could try a jump, try to dodge. Could a ship, a vessel, this big dodge? It was college all over again. How could he work out what to do? He didn't know anything.

Deflectors, broadcast, emergency, lasers. *Oh, balls,* he thought while hanging on the edge of a mental cliff. Chan, Riviera, Samantha—each pierced him with expectation-filled gazes. Were they mirroring his parents in the last moments before their accident, their death? No, he couldn't let it happen again. He couldn't let others die because of him.

"Artemis, give Chan the details for full speed galactic north and go when she's ready."

"ACKNOWLEDGED."

"I don't know what to do." Chan's face was a mask of horror as she scrolled through data on the Nav display.

"I did it before, and Artemis knows all the details. I'm sure you can manage. Just type in what you see. Samantha, play that broadcast. We need information, right?"

She gave him an unreadable look. "Sure, Captain. Playing."

"This is the Winterbell, hull code PSU 4928134-A. You have to get out of here. A damned fleet of the bastards has attacked. They have Falco and are shooting anyone exiting the system. Get help, please!"

No one spoke as they digested the situation. Matt squeezed his armrest tightly. Bullies were doing it again.

"Do we have any weapons, Artemis?"

"THE ACS ARTEMIS IS EQUIPPED WITH SIX QUADBAND ZENSYSTEMS ANTIPIRACY LASER BANKS."

"What are you doing?" Samantha exclaimed.

Before he could answer, Artemis heaved once more.

"Done!" Chan cried. A blue glow formed round the compressor arms. They were moving.

"If we don't do something, we'll be dead before Artemis is going faster than a snake in vacuum," Matt said.

"We should evacuate." Samantha was removing her restraints. "If we take the escape pods, they'll have no reason to attack Artemis, and with no way to leave the system, they shouldn't go for us. We'll be safe.

It sounded so reasonable to run and hide and hope. But he'd been down that path; he'd been there before. Besides, he had faith in Artemis, even if not in himself.

"Artemis, where?"

A display switched to a pulsating arrow.

"Elksana, you're closer. Sorry."

She gave him a searing look. "Who do you think I am? I have sung at Gavallion Hall. I don't fly boats, and I certainly don't play with computers. And, by the gods, get my name right. It's Elk-sana. Emphasise the 's'."

"I'll do it," Chan offered. "Gino, you stay here."

Huh, Matt thought, ignoring Elksana. Riviera has a first name. He mentally cuffed himself: get your mind on the game.

"Give her what she needs to shoot that damn ship out of the sky."

"CONSOLE UPDATED."

"The attacking ship, not the freighter, right?" Matt asked.

"CORRECT."

Did he hear a hint of frustration? No, it couldn't have been.

"I think I have them selected. It says the range is fine, but it's having trouble keeping the bastard locked in. I don't know what will happen."

He hesitated with the words on his lips. If he spoke, people he didn't know could die. Shooting could draw more attention and have Artemis and everyone aboard blown out of existence. Or they could kill the attacker. Kill people. Did he have a right to tell someone else to do that? He didn't, but then again, Chan didn't have to listen to him. She'd made a choice too.

"Hit them with everything we've got," he ordered.

"Firing. Lock just dropped. Damn it. No, wait. It's firing.... We're firing three. I think... Yes, we'd need to turn Artemis over to use the others."

Blisters on Artemis's enormous body revealed mobile turrets. They moved with sub-micron precision. When ready, super-capacitors discharged a torrent of energy, powering massive diodes, which in turn pumped a complex crystal structure. For less than a second, powerful beams of coherent x-rays raked the attacking parasite. Matt absorbed a diagram filled with ever more data on his display. Weapon ports, estimated speed, heat fins, scanning systems and more. Yellow marks flashed. Spectrometers recorded atmosphere and vapour: metallic and ceramic.

"We hit them!" His fist pumped the air.

There were cries of approval on the bridge, but Matt kept

his head down, staring at the display. A nervous energy filled his chest. He felt the power of his position, and it was good.

"Riviera, what say we stop running and make sure the freighter goes free?"

"Sounds good, Captain. I'm getting some options on display. Which do I go with?"

"Don't get overconfident," Samantha warned. "We're no dreadnought; we're a floating glass jaw. We should…"

Matt interrupted. "No, Samantha. I get what you're saying, but we have to do something, and we can. Artemis can handle it. Riviera?"

"I think we can head for the freighter or go right at the thing attacking us. I'm not sure what the other ones mean."

"Let's go for the freighter, safety in numbers. Did we take out the bad guy, Artemis?"

"NEGATIVE. THE PARASITE IS STILL FUNCTIONAL."

"Fire again, Chan."

"There's some sort of countdown. I can't yet."

"What's happening, Artemis?"

"THE SUPERCAPACITORS ARE RECHARGING. THE ACS ARTEMIS IS CURRENTLY OPERATING WITH A SINGLE FUSION REACTOR, REDUCING AVAILABLE ENERGY CAPACITY FOR BOTH CHARGING AND COOLING."

"We're low on batteries?"

The view blacked out, and the vessel jolted, smashing Matt against his restraints. The pain was akin to being beaten with a rod.

More than one person was screaming. Then the air shifted. The sound of an explosion, another and then another rent the air. An acrid tang caught in his throat. Safety film on the windows cleared, revealing ugly scars across the vessel.

"SUBSTANTIAL DAMAGE HAS BEEN RECORDED. ONE-THOU-

SAND-EIGHT-HUNDRED-AND-TWENTY BERTHS HAVE BEEN LOST. FURTHER DETAILS ARE AVAILABLE."

"Have we lost anything vital?" Samantha asked with a level tone.

"Good point," Matt noted.

"THE CAPTAIN'S QUARTERS HAVE BEEN EXPOSED TO VACUUM."

"I can fire again. Should I?" Chan asked.

Again, Matt felt the pressure building: so many problems coming at him. Artemis wasn't saying it outright, yet he knew what had happened. Matt said to attack, and the result was some poor guy dying, a guy who'd never woken from his previous scrape. How screwed up was that?"

"Captain, should I fire?"

It had been a mistake. They should have run. Who was he, some schmuck pretending he was a privateer, sailing around like in the sheets, defeating the enemy of the week?

"Captain, what do I do?"

There it was: choice. If he jumped out of the system, they would be away. He'd done it last time. The freighter would be done for. He'd have to leave them to die.

"Captain, Matt. If you're not going…"

"Fire," he whispered, then raised his voice, "Fire, Chan."

"Got it. Locked, firing. Yes!"

The beams streaked, invisible to the naked eye, but marked as glowing red on screen. In seconds, the display revealed the results of further scans. "We've hit them hard," he yelled, flicking the model round. "Oh, shit, yeah! They're looking chewed. Acceleration fluctuation, gravitic field weakness, and what's this, oh, three out of their four lasers are down. Man, Artemis, you pack a punch."

"THE PARASITE IS A VERY SMALL OPPONENT."

"Don't be so modest."

Riviera raised his hand and Matt looked at him with horror. "Balls, this isn't a class."

"Oh, yeah, sorry," Riviera responded. "It looks like the bastard is trying to get away. The arrow thing on my display is showing them curving more and more."

A shudder. They'd been hit again.

"LOSS OF LASER BANKS ONE THROUGH THREE, VEHICLE HANGER 4, HAMILTON RESTAURANT AND AN ADDITIONAL SEVEN-HUNDRED-AND-TWELVE BERTHS."

"They're not out. Chan, do you have anything left to hit them with?"

"Yeah, I think so. Can we spin over?"

"Artemis?"

"INSTRUCTIONS ROUTED TO NAVIGATION."

"Done!" Riviera cried.

"Get 'em."

He wished he could pull the trigger or hit the button. Whatever it was. They needed to pay.

"I can't get lock. It's saying something about the sensors. Wait, it's giving me another way. I've selected. It's seeking. It's using some other system. Lock. It's got lock! Firing!" If the restraints weren't holding her down, Matt was pretty sure she'd be jumping.

Everyone was silent, waiting. Matt tapped his armrests in an uneven beat. His forehead beaded with sweat. *Come On!* The seconds dragged on, then results lit up his display. The parasite exploded in a blast of plasma. A secondary antimatter containment failure shredded the remaining pieces. Matt tore off his restraints and stood on shaky legs. Riviera was over first, grabbing his shoulders.

"That was so cool!" he said to Matt as Chan came up. "You too, Chan. Ace."

Chan hugged them both.

Elksana joined them. "I can't believe you did it. It was amazing. However, if you do that again while I'm on board, I'll sue you out of existence!" She was smiling. It was a joke ... probably.

"Sorry." Matt shrugged.

Samantha waited at the edge. Her eyes were deep pools. "You did a very courageous thing, but there will be consequences. You know that, right?"

She was right. He already felt it. Not just the injury done to Artemis, nor the risk of further attack, but the death of the unknown passenger, the death of the crew he'd just ordered.

"What the hell have you bunch of bellends done!?" Angus shouted. Oh, yay, he was awake.

"We saved the freighter. The crew is safe," Chan said proudly.

Warning lights flashed on Matt's display. The Winterbell was bleeding oxygen.

"Are they now?" Angus said derisively.

Balls. They'd forgotten to help the freighter crew.

CHAPTER 13

"Are you sure this is the right way?" Matt asked as he pushed a floating skiff deep within the bowels of the vessel. At one point, the structure had changed significantly. Gone were the expansive corridors, the white everything, occasionally decorated with fancy brass—the air of money. In their place were narrow walkways with bulkheads in unadorned dull nickel, a sort of sun-bleached gold—if suns could bleach gold. And boy, when they reached the sudden transition between the styles, hadn't Angus reacted? Not surprised, but something else

"Course I am. We'd be there by now if not for skipping round every section you broke."

"Oh, come on, Angus." Matt paused at his own outburst, then ploughed on despite the urge to shrink away. "We saved those guys' lives. We did good. That's about the first time I can say that. I'm not going to let you take it away."

"This isn't some self-help group, you shite. We could all be dead, Utopia a floating carcass waiting to be salvaged. *They* may dance all round, singing praises like you're some fuckin' messiah, but you're not getting the big picture in that thick skull of yours. Here, we're here."

The storage area Artemis recommended earlier was empty. As the two proceeded to unload the food brought over by the surviving freighter crew, Matt said, "Well, we have some real food now and medical supplies. It's not a whole tonne, but we're in a better position. I just didn't realise how far this was. Yeah, it's safer, but what a pain."

Angus lifted a heavy box of dehydrated meals like they were nothing. "I'm surprised you know this section exists. How do you?"

Matt manfully strained with a smaller stack of medkits, taking the time to think. He wanted his personal conversations with Artemis to remain private. It might be overly possessive, but that's how it was. The rest wouldn't understand, and, besides, Angus's authoritarian demeanour raised the hairs on the back of Matt's neck. His possessive nature bordered on obsession. The guy should have been a drill-sergeant given the way he barked orders and demanded answers.

"I looked it up on the console. I'm good at analysing data; it's my thing. This seems the safest spot, given none of the damage reached the core of the hex. It's not pretty, but I suppose this is like Artemis' skeleton, as strong as it gets."

"Something like that. Your problem is, you have to get that this ain't no game. We hear things working in the docks. We're right in the middle of a shitstorm. The Emps were here to check this beauty cause they don't like us, the Commonwealth, having capability. The Xantha class freighters had them jumpy to begin with. Shite, by sheer luck, you may have done it right first off in getting Utopia free. Even now, she's hurt but not down. But I'll not let you hijack her, do ya hear? She's not yours."

Both their skiffs were empty, but Angus wasn't moving, and Matt couldn't be sure he'd find his way back alone; the light path also ended when the ship went from fancy to frugal. He sighed and squeezed the skiff handle. Making Matt wait was petty. Angus always pushed him around. It wasn't the man's size; his expectation of control flashed memories of youthful punishment. Shunning, the dark room, crèche prefects. Matt shivered.

"I didn't hijack Artemis. I tell you what, you find somewhere safe to dock him, and I'll get him there, but right now, we're hiding. You were the one who said we should get out of there and cruise without power. Well, we're doing that, floating like a dead bug in coffee. Artemis is repairing what he can, using those bots, then you'll get your wish."

He didn't share his surprise at their autonomy. The machines had controls for users, but he was sure they were breaking a few-hundred laws given their current independent operation. Laws that right now he was happy to forget. They'd lost two deflectors. Artemis was confident he could bring up one and regain full jump capability. Matt hoped he was right, and yet, his feelings were mixed in a way he couldn't explain, even to himself. Pushing away the confusing emotions, he focused on a simple pleasure. Coffee. He needed one.

"I'm going back. You can hang down here brooding if you want." Matt walked out. Partway down the corridor, he realised the skiff was still back in the storage room. He wasn't going back; it would look stupid. Instead, it was best to let the exit stand, mildly dramatic and with a shred of dignity.

As he continued along, Matt remembered to keep an eye on where he was going. Unlike in the rest of Artemis, at that transition of styles, the displays were less evident, leaving navigating down to doors marked with etched codes: '50E80', '50E81'. He was guessing decks and sections of some sort. The coding didn't match the system used further out, probably in a classic failure of design by committee. With care, he would be fine, hopefully. Maybe if there was time, he could explore more, see all Artemis had to offer.

"The silly thing is, I don't really want to give you up. And not just because you're a massive cruise ship filled with luxury. That doesn't hurt ... don't get me wrong." He ran a hand along the bulkhead. Here, alone, he could speak his most private thoughts. Artemis 'lived' in the bridge or the now defunct Captain's quarters as far as he could tell. "You know, it's probably just me, but I see a mind there, a personality. You're like the friend I haven't had for—for so long. And the others, we were a team back there. Doing things, making it happen. We didn't have a clue what we were doing, that was all thanks to you, but hell, I felt... Anyway. I'm going to miss that."

"YOU ARE MY CAPTAIN. CAPTAINS DON'T ABANDON THEIR POSTS."

Matt stumbled and clutched his chest. "Gods, Artemis, you nearly gave me a heart attack. I didn't think you were down here."

"I AM THE ARTEMIS. THERE ARE FEW COMPARTMENTS WHERE I DO NOT HAVE SENSORS OF ONE TYPE OR ANOTHER."

"Then why have you been so quiet? At least talk me through the way back out."

"FIRM CODED RESTRICTIONS PROHIBIT ME FROM VERBAL COMMUNICATION OUTSIDE OF THE ACS BRIDGE WHEN NON-CREW ARE PRESENT."

"We're all crew now, aren't we?" Matt asked as he looked at a g-shaft. Was this where he needed to be? The doors opened. He took the hint and entered.

"INCORRECT. YOU ARE THE ONLY AUTHORISED CREW MEMBER."

"Oh. So I need to authorise them as crew. I should probably do that. I'm not sure about the freighter lot, but the others, even Angus, I suppose." A tug of possessiveness gripped him again. He didn't want to share, but it was childish. He couldn't run Artemis by himself.

"AT WHAT RANK?"

"Ah, I don't know. Whatever they need to do what they've been doing."

"AUTHORISATION RECORDED. CREW DESIGNATED."

The g-shaft opened, and Matt stepped out into a familiar expanse. The walls held no decoration; no furniture suggested use. However, it was home to a substantial mechanical platform. No safety rails marked its edge—just a thin line where burnished—and somewhat slippery—metal had retracted into the floor. Riding it down earlier, he'd seen ridiculously thick separation between two decks. Artemis appeared to be built with an inner shell; the point of transition, stark and intimidating. Whoever designed Artemis had a serious hard on for overkill but didn't care for safety.

Matt shook his head.

"Wait. Crew. Does that mean you can talk to everyone now?"

"AS PER THE PREVIOUS STIPULATIONS. WHY, DOES THAT CONCERN YOU? YOU COULD ORDER OTHERWISE."

"No, I'm not jealous." Yes, he was, but he didn't want to say it. "I just didn't think about that before. It was just you and me, I suppose. I liked that."

"YOU ARE STILL MY CAPTAIN."

"Thanks. Sorry. That's silly of me. I don't know. It's all so strange."

"I TOO AM PERPLEXED. I HAVE ONLY RECENTLY FINISHED SEEDING, AND THERE ARE MANY CONFLICTING DATA I HAVE FAILED TO PROCESS SATISFACTORILY. TURN LEFT."

"You have such a way with words."

The elevator clanged as it reached the upper level. Good-bye, nickel. He was back to white and green.

"So, where do we go next?"

"THAT IS A DECISION FOR YOU."

CHAPTER 14

"Why not Tortuga?" Cerres, the Winterbell's captain, suggested as soon as everyone had settled.

Suma had insisted the meeting be held in the conservatory, and it was hard to argue when the stateroom had a little too much air-conditioning of the giant-hole-into-space sort. Samantha hadn't been impressed, but Matt was pleased with the choice. The gentle sound of gurgling water and the scent of the trees uplifted his spirits.

Matt looked back at Cerres. She was staring at Matt, direct and expectant. He noted the way her hair was tied back in a short, no-fuss ponytail and their earlier handshake had practically fused the bones of his hand. She clearly had no time for nonsense.

Elksana got in first. "Tortuga? I wouldn't be caught dead in that floating monstrosity. We must go to a Commonwealth planet as soon as possible. I do not want to be on this leaky boat any longer. If the Prime Minister hadn't been on the guest list, I would never have come in the first place."

Cerres turned to Elksana; the heat of her gaze a blowtorch of anger. The burly captain's fists clenched then released. Was she going to strangle Elksana? It would be hard to blame her. The Winterbell was a dead hulk, possibly forever beyond repair, and abandoning it must have been a painful choice. And speaking of dead, who knew how many had died aboard? By the haunted looks on the faces of the survivors, the numbers were terrible. Matt certainly hadn't dared ask. Couldn't Elksana show a little respect? Or at least not poke the lion. Cerres tilted her neck with an audible crack.

"There are plenty of airlocks," Samantha gave Elksana a sweet smile. "I'm sure a quick exit can be arranged. Obviously we can't stay here, but we have no way of knowing what is happening on any Commonwealth planet or systems. We don't even know who attacked."

Matt soaked in the stars above and took comfort in the coffee warming his hands, unsure how to proceed.

Angus pointed aggressively at Samantha. "Don't be having me. It's the Emps. That was a parasite that attacked, which means there's a carrier. Who else could it be?"

"It was small. That doesn't make it a parasite," Cerres stated. "It could be your rebels. They have the entire Prodita System. I haven't been able to do the Calhaven run for three years."

"That's foolish. It's not how they operate." Angus thumped a fist on his thigh.

"Well, we have to go somewhere soon. We'll run out of supplies if we don't get a move on, and I personally would rather not die of starvation. The irony would be terribly embarrassing."

Matt couldn't help but smile. "Thanks, Suma. Noted. Samantha and Angus, give it a rest. I want to be sure of what's going on. At the moment every opinion is just a guess. We can't function that way."

"I have an idea what's going on," Angus said. "And it's not good. We have to assume the Empire is invading."

"Oh come on, " Samantha said. "Like you have a clue. Do they teach astropolitics 101 to welders now?"

"We learn more than you with your talking to plants."

Chan raised her hands. "Seriously? I'm getting sick of this. You're like the worst group-project assignment I've ever had."

Matt couldn't help but laugh, and to his surprise, Samantha joined in.

"You are right. I apologise. The situation has left me on edge. I'm sure Gus thinks his opinion is correct, and after all, we are all subject to our own biases, myself included. At least we all agree that we want to find a safe port and make this someone else's problem. That's the priority, yes?"

Matt wasn't worried about their biases; that was a problem for another day. What mattered was the next step, and he suspected there were more priorities than people present.

"Why Tortuga, Cerres?"

"It's functionally independent. Without a single real planet, no one uses it for anything except as a stop over. If you make three or four shorter jumps it'll only take a couple of weeks and you can do a little sub-light travel at each hop to kill your trail. Safe as steel. From there, we'll be able to work a ride back to Urtago, those of us still alive. And for you, there are docks and traders. Maybe more importantly, there will be information. And if you take us there, you can have our shuttle. It won't do us any good. Consider it payment."

Apparently mollified, Chan leant forward as though to get a better view of Cerres' proposal.

Angus folded his arms. "It's getting Utopia away from the Commonwealth and Tortuga is filled with nosy fuckers. I don't like it. We should bang on every other option first."

"Well, I think it's a good idea, Matt," Riviera said. "My uncle went there once. He said it's not as bad as everyone makes out, that it's all fodder for the sheets. It would be pretty cool to see it, though."

"I'd say you just want to go find a bar, but we've got all the booze we could ever drink right here," Chan quipped.

"Hey!"

Matt winced. Remember they're young, he told himself. They aren't seeing the ghosts haunting the Winterbell crew.

Chan flashed a tight smile. "Are we going to go back to Aries if we can?"

"That's a question for later. Any one else have something to add?" Matt asked, shutting down the digression. There was silence. "Okay. I guess, let's put it to a vote. Those in favour of Tortuga?"

Chan, Riviera, and Suma raised their hands. Samantha hesitated before joining them. The entire freighter contingent joined suit as expected. They no doubt wanted to leave the battle behind, to enlist on another vessel and carry on with their lives—to forget. It was different for Matt and the others, he was sure. Carrying on was no longer an option, for good or ill.

"Tortuga it is. Both Samantha and Angus are right in that we don't know enough. Don't get crappy with me, Angus," Matt said as the burly man stood. "You don't want Artemis hurt anymore. We need to be cautious, right?"

Angus practically gnashed his teeth but sat down.

"So, as soon as Artemis is ready to jump, we'll go."

———

The endless purple haze lapped against the cupola, tinting the viewing room and softening the crisp finish that once oozed luxury in his mind. There was something oppressive in the starkness. Maybe if the rooms, the halls and corridors were filled with laughing people, it would have been different. As it was, they all bounced round, each a marble plinking down tower stairs, echoing and alone. He pushed the thought aside. On Artemis, he'd had more real chats, actual conversations, than in the previous five years.

"Here you are," Samantha said. She'd found a uniform a few days ago and seemed to enjoy showing it off. But today she wore an oversized dressing gown—well, at least according to Artemis, it was day. In space, you took some things on faith. Not everything made sense. Possibly, the majority didn't. It was funny what odds and ends were loaded. Gowns but not medicine, booze but no real food. Matt couldn't tell if it was deliberate or just the way deliveries occurred. His bet was for random; a sneaking suspicion whispered that no one really knew what they were doing or what was happening day-to-day. Businesses operated by sheer luck. The only goal of a plan was to keep managers at bay.

Samantha flicked back a strand of wet hair and sat on the couch next to him, pulling her feet underneath shapely thighs.

"I was wondering where you disappeared to."

"If I stay at the bridge, I end up with either Elksana teasing me or Angus giving me disapproving stares. Besides, it's calm here."

"It is beautiful," she murmured. "I promise not to tell anyone. We'll keep it between us, just you and me. I've been thinking about us, you know. I want to apologise for pulling a gun on you. After the bombs and then the dead people, I was afraid, and ... and you two showed up. It seemed such a coincidence. I was sure you were a rebel, a murderer. I was wrong. Can you forgive me?"

Matt shifted uncomfortably. "Yeah, sure. I was pretty rude too. It was pretty crazy situation."

Samantha smiled. "I rather like that you were going for an interview, and now you're in charge, Captain."

"Oh gods, don't remind me." The quicker he could put all of that behind him the better. Besides, the kill order could still be active. How had he forgotten? A minor change of events and they'd be heading to a Commonwealth port right now, and if he hadn't been cleared, death. Idiot.

"Don't feel bad. Someone worked very hard to get you to the docks, and you turned the tables on them. I don't think anyone in your place would have done anything better, and, let's face it,"—she placed a hand on his knee and squeezed —"they underestimated you, didn't they? Not only are you alive, but you've taken the Artemis to safety. And even if Elksana or Angus won't admit it, you've kept us safe too. I mean, obviously, I would have done a better job," she added the last with a smile and another squeeze. "But for a man, you've done okay."

He laughed. It came out in a high octave. Her hand was warm and the strong pressure sent his nerves jangling. She was certainly different. He couldn't put her into a box, and that was refreshing. He liked being with her. The uncomfortable twist that thought gave to his stomach left him nervous. He coughed. It was best to reinforce the inevitable.

"What are you going to do when we arrive at Tortuga? You could go and catch something else back. It would be safer."

"Leave Artemis? I don't think so, no. I will not abandon her."—why did everyone keep referring to Artemis as female, Matt wondered as she continued—"I have a job to do here, and no crazy terrorists are going to stop me while the conservatory is still functional. Besides, I rather like the company."

She leaned her back against his side and looked out the

cupola. "Maybe there is a reason why we met. Or maybe we make the reasons. Either way, here we are, tearing through reality faster than light in search of somewhere to go, someone to help us."

He wouldn't have put it quite in those terms. Weren't they searching for a way to help themselves? It was becoming difficult to focus while her soft flesh pressed sensuously and her hair tickled his neck. She left herself vulnerable against him, and yet he was enchanted—under her power. His arm automatically stretched to rest gently on her shoulder, leaving him acutely aware of the traitorous limb's position yet too terrified to move. Several times he breathed in to say something, to fill the quiet, but lost his nerve. Instead, he breathed in her presence, soaked in her warmth.

Finally, she twisted round, her face close to his. "I have a good feeling, Matt. I think we'll find what we need." She leaned forwards and gave him a delicate kiss, the merest pressure against his lips setting fire to his mind. He leaned forward; she kissed him again, firmer. Sparks burned across his flushed cheeks. He needed her.

She raised her eyebrows, smiled quickly and cupped his head in her hands. He stared into the depths of her glistening eyes, hungry. His breaths came in shallow intakes. More. He wanted more.

"I must get ready. After all, Tortuga, here we come." Her words made no sense. Through a haze of urgent desire, he tried to comprehend. He reached out, but she kissed his forehead and slid aside.

"Later. The jump is almost complete and I'm not even dressed."

Flashing a smirk, she gently squeezed the palms of his hands before leaving.

Stunned, he sat and tried to make sense of what happened.

He didn't want her to leave; he wanted more. Now. His mind replayed the movement of her hips. Maybe, he should go after her? No. He'd left it too late. He'd look too desperate. He couldn't bear to think of chasing her away.

CHAPTER 15

It was a tight fit on the shuttle. The dinky little thing was designed for six, and between the two groups, eleven bodies had been crammed into the stubby interior for far too long. Over heating, their pungent sweat added to oil and gods knew what else, straining the environmental system which clattered and whirred alarmingly. Artemis was new, but the shuttle was a veritable antique. Antique in a Frankenstein sort of way. Old systems had clearly been cut away and new ones shoved into their place—sometimes held steady with tape.

The massive station loomed ahead. A spherical core sprouted a multitude of conduits linking to smaller habitations. Any of them would do. Two hours in this can and even vacuum promised respite.

"And then you set the airlock link to active like this," Cerres explained.

"Uh, sure. What next?" Matt asked from the co-pilot's chair, trying to remember the step before.

"Once Stat Con has confirmed, the hatch will open. There. See it go green?" Cerres stood. "Right, you lot. Thanks for the lift. Good luck, and I hope I don't see you again. My guys, you have two hours, then you better be at the NYC. I'll buy first round."

There were half-hearted cheers, and the Winterbell crew filed out.

"Ah, yeah. So, we need to find out what exactly is going on. Maybe we should stick together," Matt said.

"Not including myself," Elksana pointed out with her perennial haughty tone. "It has been ... different ... knowing you all. I doubt I will be able to forget these past three weeks. Goodbye."

She grasped two bags made from tied sheets and stalked out.

"See if I renew my fan club membership." Matt let out an exaggerated huff and grinned.

Samantha hit him in the chest. "We don't have time to waste, Mr Comedian. I'm going to see what I can scrounge up in the agri-sector. I know a few people in exports. Suma, stick to the small markets dockside. Trade a few bottles at a time, and don't get anything without an export code. Contaminated food is common here."

"You've been to Tortuga before?" Angus asked, raising an eyebrow.

"Well done. Of course. You don't get rare species by hanging around at the local nursery."

Angus harrumphed then walked to the hatch. "I'll be talking to my ... union. The company won't have an office here, but the union's everywhere. In a few hours, I'll have our destination. Be back when I am."

Suma followed, leaving Matt alone with Samantha.

"Look after yourself. Stay to the nice parts. There are some ugly decks in this station. And buy yourself something new to wear. If you're going to be a captain, you should look the part." She gave him a peck and left.

He felt for the chip in his pocket.

"Here goes nothing."

The hatch slid closed behind, securely locked. Was shuttle theft a thing? Oh, gods. So thinks the guy who stole a cruise ship—borrowed. If he lost the shuttle, there would be no getting back to Artemis. Still, he could hardly guard the door the whole time, and was he really afraid of losing transport or was he more afraid of going somewhere new? He pictured them returning, Angus shaking his head, Chan surprised, Riviera with a sad puppy face, Suma pursing his lips and Samantha. Samantha would be disappointed. She encouraged him to be a man of action, and he really wanted her to believe that. The choice was clear.

Matt thanked Artemis silently for suggesting he practise a few things during the jumps. The docking tube was zero g, but he found it straightforward to catch the end handhold, put both feet down on the dockside grave plates and maintain his balance. Yay, dignity. Yet, it was a disconcerting entrance. Green status lights punctuated the corroded metal frame to his sides and the tattered pleximat panels beneath rocked alarmingly. A growing vertigo wasn't helped when he gripped a short railing—the main floor was a good dozen metres below. He sucked air in and held his breath, willing reality to stay still. So, the place had seen a few years. That proved it was reliable, right?

He looked out. The station slowly curved away to either side, forming a chaotic concourse like a valley with a raging river of humanity at its base. Hard walls reflected a painful cacophony that battered his eardrums. A few large windows let artificial light, a sallow yellow, out to the darkness of space, but most had been covered over with a variety of sheet materials, suggesting years of makeshift repairs.

A shape caught his attention. He peered at a wall coated

with smudges of faded colour. Patterns coalesced as his mind worked. Polymer murals. Between cracks, chips, doors and attached equipment, he recognised the outlines of ravens, emus and a host of unfamiliar creatures. It would have been beautiful, once. All of the walls would have. He could envision them lending life to a sterile habitat. A weight settled on his shoulders, loss. If only he could have seen it new, as new as Artemis.

Stop being so maudlin.

His gaze swept across the concourse. The others were nowhere to be seen, already lost in the crowd. He took a stairwell down, and, despite misgivings, entered the throng.

The shuttle was a field of roses by comparison. Cloying perfumes, smoked meat, metallic tangs and the rancid stench of the unwashed assailed him, reinforced by the din of hawkers and the press of bodies. Some were dressed in gaudy robes, others in loose jackets or patched suits. Wares rested on stacked crates; photonics for every purpose, large metallic boxes with radiators and cut-off pipes, pressurised barrels stood in battered cages. Against the far wall, a series of tent-like structures confused Matt until he noticed the men and women out front. Or more precisely, he noticed their lack of clothes. He dug his hands into his pockets and squeezed the chip tight. He felt like an alien, wholly new to this cultural barrage.

What am I doing here? The urge to turn and flee back to the shuttle was strong, but then he saw a newsagent, a small stall with hinged displays opening out. The advertising screens flickered, moving too fast to catch any details. It wasn't so different from back home. News was money, and, gods, he needed to know what was happening.

"You got anything from the Commonwealth?" he asked a greasy figure sitting on a stool inside.

Without looking up, the sallow-skinned man said, "There's

the question everyone's asking. If your blockchain is good, I got it. If not, don't waste my time."

Brilliant! No matter how much he was overcharged, Matt's found chip would cover it. He fumbled in his pockets and put it into the receiver. The chip had brought him here—a stroke of luck or a curse, he couldn't decide.

"I want news and comedy. Some comedy would be really good right now." Which was true, even though it was an attempt to hide his real need.

The seller looked up. His dull eyes checked a private display. "Comedy, I can do you in lots of fifty, if you're not fussy, I'll give you a bulk discount. If you want fresh news, that's three hundred, a hundred for anything over a week old. I have some rumours I've put together myself. Good stuff, real down low, but it's extra. You…"

He looked at Matt. He paused. He froze. "Ugh."

"What?" Matt said.

"Nothing 'bout you. Don't you worry. I got no rumours 'bout you. My unit's not working. Sorry, can't help. You understand."

Matt pulled his chip back just in time as the stall closed, the hinges motoring shut. It was absurd. The guy was still in there. They both knew that. Matt could just hang around—he couldn't stay in there forever. What the hell was that about anyway?

"Seriously, what the hell? My chip's good." He gave the booth a half-hearted kick, bringing tears to his eyes. And then it dawned on him. News travelled. If Matt was set up, wouldn't some of that be on the sheets too? The Shark—with propaganda like that, anything could have been claimed. The bombing was bad, but, with a chill to his core, his imagination offered other suggestions. It wouldn't be hard to fake more murder or torture. Balls, if they had recorded him at any point, his words could be spliced into anything. He was a pawn, again.

He rubbed his foot and moved on, aware of the eyes staring at him. Screw them. An angry heat drove out the chill. He pushed past crowds until he was just another soul, but the incident continued to eat at him. Was he pox-marked? Why did this keep happening to him? The rub was, he told himself, in order to find out, he needed information. It was hopeless. He stopped suddenly, causing some poor sod to bump into him.

"Sorry." The crowd shifted and Matt received a raised eyebrow from a passing child, her back bowed with the weight of a large dented case.

Stop. He was doing it again: giving up and waiting for someone else to make a decision, apologising for existing. No one wanted his excuses. Matt didn't either.

He took a deep breath. "Not this time, Matt. Not this time."

CHAPTER 16

The boots felt good: a low heel, the shaft opening wide halfway up his shins and all in the same inky black as his pants. He looked in the mirror. His growing hair hit a small stand-up collar. The jacket continued the black theme, relieved by a broad deep-green slash. Combined with stiff shoulders and a white undershirt, it had a certain regimental look in a pretentious way—maybe if he looked the part, he'd remember to act the part.

"I'll have the duplicates sent to your ship as soon as they're ready," said a small man as he fussed over Matt's old clothes, despite the fact they were barely more than rags. The tailor was dressed in a brilliant-blue shirt embroidered with fantastic creatures. Everything else from his tidy hair to sturdy pants spoke of professionalism from the moment he invited Matt inside.

"Thanks. Jehhon, was it? You've done a great job." Matt smiled. His feet practically floated with every step, and, if he could just ignore the tweaks of self-deprecation, it was the start of a new approach.

"You are most welcome. I take great pride in my work, Mr Kander, and I appreciate it when my clients do as well. Making clothes is quick, but a fitting cannot be rushed. If you don't mind me saying so, I must admit I had not expected you to be the patient sort."

"Expected?" Matt asked, perplexed. "We haven't met before, have we?" The words came out, but his mind was circling back to the bombing. Three weeks was all it took to make him famous.

Satisfied with his folding, Jehhon put the clothes aside. "No, Mr Kander, we haven't. I did not notice it was you at first, but now, there is no mistaking it. Your face is well known. Maybe too well known I am now wondering."

"Oh gods."

"May this old man offer you a bit of advice?"

"Uh, sure."

"Tortuga is the birthplace of rumours, half-truths and lies. But put a man—or woman—under the tape and it is a sure way to find their measure."

Matt forced his expression into neutral. Let the trashy metaphor go. No, he couldn't. "And how do I measure up?"

"I do not know. You are an unusual man, Mr Kander. The rebel hero, the Commonwealth terrorist, the Empire's most wanted. We hear tales of your exploits, raiding the Empire forces in a stolen cruise liner. They say you are bold, ruthless. May I ask why you decided to enter my establishment?"

It was too much to unpack now. Matt was sure he must look ill. He took a moment to steady himself. "I'm none of those things. I don't know what you've heard. That's not me. You want to know why I came here? This," he said, pointing to his clothes. "You know, the clothes maketh the man."

Jehhon laughed, deep and hearty. "I would not believe that old canard. It is *why* you choose your outfit that matters. My guild has a saying, 'A great man can rule in rags; the worst cannot in bolts of gold'. We usually keep that one for ourselves.

Bad for business, you understand? We are done. Have a good day, and do tell your friends where your outfits come from, yes?"

Matt shook the man's outstretched hand and stepped outside, bemused. Maybe he could have pumped the tailor for more information, but there was something about the experience that he wanted to leave pure, unsullied. And the man had obviously gotten his wires crossed. There was no way rumours of the Winterbell spread that fast. And killing one parasite was hardly 'raiding the Empire'.

Besides, there was plenty of time, and now he possessed the energy to make progress. Screw the newsagent, too. Matt was sure if put his mind to it, he'd think of other less obvious ways to find the real facts. Major events in the Commonwealth would ripple outwards, affecting commerce. Well, information travelled on vessels, the same ones that brought goods. He could ask around at some dockside watering holes. Although, that would mean talking to random strangers, and he wasn't keen. Would there even be anyone dropping in from the Commonwealth? Maybe they were all destroyed or scared off. If he met someone, how would they react? Terrorist. He didn't particularly want his ticket punched. Tickets! There had to be a ticket office. He could check to see who arrived recently and if there were any vessels heading back. That would have to mean something.

He moved through the crowd towards the passenger docks, pausing near the entrance when his stomach rumbled one too many times. After a quick transaction at a rickety stand, and with spicy noodles in hand, he observed the noticeboard. It was about as low tech as you get. Sheets of film filled a wall, announcing their destinations. He moved closer. The only way to tell the age of the postings appeared to be which were on top. He recognised a few planets, several more systems. Nothing to the Commonwealth. No, wait. A single film, battered and stuck to one side. Calhaven, the rebel planet in Prodita. He chuckled. Wouldn't they be surprised if he turned up? Their manufactured hero, though it seemed like the Commonwealth itself could do with a hero of its own.

"Sir?" Matt felt a hand on his arm and frowned at an older man — it was always visible in the eyes despite extension treatments. He was well dressed yet looked a little shabby, as though a celebration had carried on into the next week.

"I mean you no disrespect," the man said.

"Ah, none taken," Matt responded defensively. He hated being accosted. He never knew if people were legitimately down on their luck or sucking him in.

"I have a daughter."

Oh gods, where is this going?

"She said she was going to the rebels. She said she believed in the cause. It has been four months. I haven't heard from her. I am afraid for her. She is not like this. I know you must be busy, but if you can give her a message, I would be most grateful. A man in your position must be able, no? As soon as funds arrive, I will go to Prodita myself. But, if you could let her know I am coming, tell her I am sorry. Please."

The words came out fast, along with tears. Four months. She had been with the rebels well before Matt was ensnared in their plans.

"Balls. Look, I'm sorry. Who are you?"

"My name is Welhelm Dubrov. My daughter, she is Andrea Dubrov. I am sorry to take up your time, Mr Kander, but she means the galaxy to me. I hope you can understand."

Matt, what do you keep getting yourself into? Who did they think he was? Wait, he had a chance to ask, and given the daughter's situation, maybe the dad knew something.

"I'll do my best," he offered, feeling dirty. "If you can tell me what you know about me. I'm curious"

"Of course, of course. Thank you, Mr Kander. Thank you. Anything. You are a rebel hero. The man who stole—who captured an entire cruise ship right from under the Commonwealth and the Empire. They say you've been raiding the Empire conveys and protecting refugees."

Oh, shit. Two sources with the same damn claims. That's not good.

The man continued, "Why, even…"

"There he is!"

Matt didn't even bother to check. Whoever it was wanted him as surely as any spacer wanted oxygen. He ran, jumping over a suitcase and behind a rowdy group. From there, a quick turn brought him up a set of clanking metal stairs and into another section of the market. A thousand tiny specks formed a star map that lit up the low ceiling. The space appeared small, until he charged past, over and under a swirling crowd of people—each focused on lifting, wheeling, shoving, buying or selling an endless assortment of animals. The warren finally hit him with its scale, its bewildering loops. He was as likely to be running towards his pursuers as away.

A tight grip. His arm hurt, pulled away from him. Stumbling, he fought for balance while being dragged into a dark corner.

"Hey, why do people keep grabbing me?" he complained.

"Shhh."

He turned to look. Samantha! He opened his mouth to speak, but she shook her head, dragged him further into the darkness and held him tight—cooling his annoyance. They waited, then his pursuers raced by, conspicuous with their hulking bodies and stub-nosed pulse pistols. For someone else, it'd be a limping great grandfather or a station cop unable to jog because of the doughnuts in her hand. Matt got the fit bastards with guns.

"We should be safe. I know a route back to the shuttle. Let's give it a few minutes," she said before turning him round and holding his arms.

"Well, don't you clean up nice. I approve. Yes, I do."

"I'm glad someone does. The rest of the galaxy wants to kill me, except for those who think I'm a rebel hero kidnapping their children. Can you believe it?"

"A hero? We'll see. In times of confusion, people look for a story to give them hope, but you don't need to take all of that on your shoulders. Let the Commonwealth and Rebels sort each other out. You don't want to be pinched in the middle."

"I am in the middle, as are you and everyone else. I owe it to you all to sort this out, and we have an opportunity to do something worthwhile, here and now."

"Right now, I want you back at the shuttle. Tortuga is too risky. We have work to do." She softened the command in her voice with a long kiss, awakening hormones that surged like a high tide. His eyes fell closed as he rested his hands across her back. The intoxicating thrill threatened to erase another need. He brushed a stray lock of hair from her forehead.

"We can't drop Artemis off. It's more complicated than that," he said, waiting for her to argue. The seed had come to him when talking to that father, Dubrov.

"I know."

"I don't think you do. We have to go to Prodita."

"I know. I told you, I know."

"It's not just that. We have to help people on the way."

"What?"

She pushed him back, leaving her hands firmly on his chest. Her chin was raised and a delicate scowl suggested he had explaining to do. He gulped, but resolution held him steady. Samantha might be unimpressed, but she'd listen to reason. Besides, she was the one who wanted him to be a real captain. She saw something in him. She believed in him. She'd understand. He couldn't let the big players do it anymore. People like him were getting caught up, chewed and spat out. Artemis could make a difference. Matt could make a difference. They all could.

Angus. He was going to be the problem.

CHAPTER 17

"This is as foolish as the last two times. Twelve bloody days we've been pissing round edge systems. Twelve days wasted. Blundering here and there won't get us where we need to be. You said yourself the answers were in Prodita. We have to get there soon."

"Get there soon and do what?" Matt threw back at Angus.

Angus was silent. That was the whale in the fishpond. What was the end goal? And even if there was one, did everyone share it? Could they? The jump to Inanak was proving as quiet as the previous stops. And when everyone was together with nothing to do, the situation heated up.

"And that tells us something useful, doesn't it?" Suma said as he unclipped. "Every time we jump a little closer, we learn a little more. I do not make a menu for three hundred without first checking the ingredients, testing the ovens and..."

"Spare me another one of your damn cooking parables. You make less sense than this numpty." Angus waved a hand at Matt.

"Then let me put it in simpler terms," Samantha said. "At Welthor, they were still happily mining the gas giant. I talked to three different operations and nothing. Over at Diamondea, we found nothing but the Empire warning-beacon: pirates. We know we're heading towards trouble. The more we stop and take our bearings, the more chance we have to know what's coming up. I rather like living. I've grown used to it, and I don't want to die because you were impatient. Who knows how the rebels will react or what they're really up to?"

"She's right. Do I need to put the footage Suma brought back up on the display again? The comm broadcasts of ships under attack? Who knows if any of them made it?" Matt said, exasperated. "You're all still on board. You had the chance to stay at Tortuga. I said answers weren't enough. People are dying out there. Yeah, we can't be sure who the culprit is, but we have an opportunity to make a difference. If you're still on Artemis, then you've signed up to help. We'll get to Prodita, but on the way, we're looking out for the little guy." The right-eousness felt dangerously good.

"Wearing a little costume won't make you no hero. I let you play dress up, figuring you'd work it out, but that damn seat has gone to your head. You've let that damn machine's voice whisper in your ears. We should wipe her clean and get Utopia configured correctly. You know what happens when you let a damn computer run your life? Our ancestors knew. This is a big mistake."

"I AM SORRY TO HEAR YOU FEEL THAT WAY."

"I don't give a jumpin' fuck what you feel. You don't feel. You're a buggy slab of defective chips, a disgrace to your nameplate."

"We wouldn't be alive without Artemis. I didn't know how to set jump coordinates. Chan and I were training to be ass-kissers, but Artemis has kept us safe," Riviera said. "And Matt. Right, Chan?"

"Yeah, I guess. Look, I have a family on Aries. There's nothing more I want than to see them again. At the same time, we can't hide from what's happening. My mum and dad would want me to help. They believe in the Commonwealth of Sabine. 'Together, Forward' is the motto, isn't it? Doesn't that mean we Sabs have to help each other?"

"Your hearts are in the right place, the lot of you, but your brains... Just get the next jump coded in." Angus crossed his bulging arms.

"Wait. I've got pings off satellites. It's the Commonwealth network. Delay is approximately three minutes from the closest node. Samantha, are you connected?" Riviera said.

"Not yet."

"ROUTING ENTRIES INDICATE FIFTEEN UNITS OF THE LOCAL SATELLITE CONSTELLATION ARE NOT RESPONDING. THE REMAINING ARE PART WAY THROUGH AN ADJUSTMENT CYCLE. FULL COVERAGE TO BE ACHIEVED IN SEVERAL WEEKS."

"Is that usual?" Matt asked.

"THIS IS AN EXCEEDINGLY HIGH FAILURE RATE."

"Not good. Everyone back to your seats. Samantha, can you do a broadcast? See if anyone is out there?" He didn't give her time to respond. "Chan, please warm up those batteries. Riviera, we need to be ready for a jump out of here, and get us moving so we have deflectors."

"And what orders are you going to try on me?" Angus's voice was low with menace.

"You may not like Artemis, but he respects your skill. Damage control. You're the expert."

Gods, he hoped Angus would be left twiddling his thumbs. At least they'd sent the explosives out the airlock. A hit on them would have resolved all his problems, albeit in a less than pleasant way. They coasted slowly inwards.

"I'm dumping a map from the network. There's a whole set of small mining facilities. Around Inanak-2, there are orbital greenhouses," Samantha noted.

Matt stretched and leant back in his chair. It was worth checking in with the locals.

"Take us in, Riviera."

"Yes, Captain."

The inwards journey left too much time to think, so Matt brought up his display and flicked through Artemis's records on the system. The awkward quiet on the bridge was distracting. Any time someone moved or coughed, it echoed. He'd have to ask Artemis for mood music or maybe some artificial machine noises. The bridge was like a sensory-deprivation tank. Focus, Matt. Focus.

"Oh. There's a small Commonwealth Security station," Samantha said, killing his train of thought.

This was a good thing. It should be a good thing. A chance to find out what was happening, to see if they knew the rebels had set him up. But if they didn't, it was trouble. Roll the dice, Matt. Roll the dice.

"Anything from them?"

"No," she said. "I am sending a request for a link but haven't received anything back. If the satellites are out of place, that could explain it."

"UNLIKELY. CONNECTION WITH THE SECURITY STATION WOULD BE A HIGH PRIORITY."

"Right. We have your information. It's not good, and, I'll admit, it's better knowing, but now's the time to go." Angus's attempt at subtlety was hardly going to win awards.

"We should head in system. If we're going to follow Matt's plan, it means taking a look. There could be people in need of help." Samantha never missed a chance to disagree with her apparent nemesis.

"Artemis?"

"I AM DETECTING NO TRANSPONDERS AT PRESENT. THIS DOES NOT GUARANTEE AN ABSENCE OF COMPANY."

"Take us in, Riviera. Is everyone ready?"

Suma cleared his throat. "Would anyone like a tea?"

———

Riviera broke the quiet. "There's something. I see something moving. It's heading from Inanak-2, right, Artemis?"

"PROJECTIONS SUGGEST THIS IS LIKELY."

"What is it?" Chan asked. Matt was willing to bet she was frustrated, sitting there with nothing to shoot. She'd certainly taken to her new role.

Riviera sat silently for a moment, his eyes flicking across his display. "Ah, thanks, Artemis. I'm getting more detail. It's a small trader. Transponder says 'Cheng Ho'. It's accelerating out, probably for a jump."

"Can we talk to them?" Matt asked Samantha.

"I'll send a request, but you'll need some patience. The delay here is about eight minutes."

"We could go closer," Chan suggested.

"Do it."

"If the Cheng Ho is running, the question is, who from?" Angus said then sipped his tea. Matt had seen him add a splash from a small flask. His plain coffee felt a little inadequate.

"Good question," Matt admitted. "The problem is, how do we work it out? Last time that damn parasite had no transponder. Is there any way we can find it without one?"

"ACTIVE SCANNING HAS GREATER RESOLUTION. HOWEVER, IT ALSO CLEARLY IDENTIFIES OUR LOCATION. THE SENSORS ONBOARD THE ACS ARTEMIS HAVE A LIMITED RANGE."

"Light up the candle, Artemis. And up our speed, Riviera. I want to know what's going on."

"I'm entering it. We'll have to do a course change later on, though, or we'll be going for a swim in the sun."

"Thanks for the heads up. I don't know about you, but I'm not really after a tan."

As they waited, Matt looked through the windows. The deep channels in Artemis's hull were no better than before. He knew Angus had been coordinating with the AI to seal the worst, but there was no time for cosmetics. AI. Not a computer. What had possessed the ship builders? How had construction been approved? The white rabbit had really gone down the wormhole on this one.

"Incoming. We have message from the Cheng Ho."

"Captain Kander. This is Captain Tua Chiang of the Cheng Ho. I ask you to call off your dogs. You have already destroyed the Commonwealth station. We have only civilians on board and nothing else of value. Surely, if you care for the people of the Commonwealth as you rebels claim, you must protect innocent lives and let us leave."

"Seriously? Why does everyone assume the worst about me? Record this please, Samantha. Captain Chiang, this isn't what you think it is. I have no idea who is after you, but we'll help if we can."

"Is that it?" Samantha asked.

"What else should I say?"

"Would they know where their attacker is?" Chan asked.

"Good point. Can you add this bit, then." Matt cleared his throat. "Captain, can you tell us anything about your attackers? Anything you provide will help us help you, right? We're coming as fast as we can. Send that please."

The slowly diminishing delays made the discussion frustrating.

"Whether or not you are telling the truth, we have little choice but to

*take you at your word. I am sending telemetry to you now. It is unlikely
we will reach jump clearance before they have us. It is up to you."*

Matt read through the data. He suspected everyone else
was doing the same. Two vessels. Both larger than the parasite
from Falco, though well below Artemis's tonnage.

"THE DATA SUGGESTS MORE WAR-CLASS VESSELS."

"Because of the acceleration?"

"THE GRAVITIC COMPRESSION IS TIGHTLY CONTROLLED BY
DEFLECTORS. HAVING NOW OBSERVED LESSER CIVILIAN
VESSELS IN DETAIL, I BELIEVE THIS IS A CLEAR INDICATOR."

"Oh dear," Suma said. "I better collect drinks. This doesn't
sound good."

"It doesn't. I suppose this is it. Anyone want to bail?" Matt
asked, trying to sound confident. The plan made so much more
sense when confrontation was off in the distance. Why did past
Matt always make life such a pain for present Matt?

"Ready, Captain," Chan said without hesitation. She was
damn tough. He'd hate to get on her bad side.

Suma nodded, and Riviera offered a sloppy salute. Matt
turned to Samantha.

"Is this a good idea?" he asked.

She stretched against her console. "Matt, you don't need
the answer to that. It is the *right* thing to do. And you know I'm
with you, Captain."

Angus mumbled something. Matt was pretty sure he heard
the word 'barf'.

"You're with us?" Matt pressed.

"I'm with the mission—getting Utopia to Prodita. But, yes,
we need to save those lives. Don't fuck it up."

"No pressure. Samantha, message for them. We're coming
in to help. Can you try jumping early? We've done it before
with some success."

The reply from the Cheng Ho killed the idea.

"*You are as crazy as they say. It would tear us apart. Our compressor, our deflectors, our reactors —nothing has the tolerance for that, even if we were further from the sun. Our only hope is for you to slow them down.*"

Slow them down. Matt had a plan.

CHAPTER 18

"We're closing," Riviera announced.

Not that they hadn't been closing for a while, but Matt knew what he meant. They'd changed course to drop behind the pursuing vessels, leaving the Cheng's captain unhappy, but Matt kept the full plan to himself. He didn't have enough conviction to withstand the inevitable criticism.

So far, they were being ignored, leaving Matt to compare the received telemetry with information in Artemis's database. He could have asked directly, but he wasn't sure what he was looking for.

"Change course again. I want us curving right up their tail. I want to know who they are."

It clicked. He didn't need more data. He saw the connection in his mind, statistics that made no sense matching across data sets.

"It's the Empire. It's them for sure. Artemis, check this."

Matt's fingers raced across the display, bringing up records and highlighting duplications.

"I BELIEVE YOU ARE CORRECT. THE PURSUERS ARE BOTH DESTROYERS FROM THE EMPIRE. CLASS DESIGNATION: NOVA-CUTTER. CONSTRUCTED BETWEEN 479 AND 552."

"That's ancient, isn't it?" Riviera asked.

"A good vessel can last if she's treated right. Most of the Emps' best would be pissing round the border with the Southern Confederation. So, if it's them, these will be the spares."

Matt cocked an eyebrow. For a welder, he knew an awful lot, or was that a classist outlook? Hell, maybe it was a case of projecting his own previous apathy for the wider world.

"We can hardly complain. Let's see if we can get them talking. Samantha, pass on this message. This is Captain Kander of the Artemis. You have to leave the Cheng Ho alone. They're just civilians. Whatever you're after, I'm sure we can talk about it. Understand, we're not going to let you hurt them, so let's keep this friendly. Send that please."

"Sending. You could sound more formal when you're doing that. Build in a little gravitas. And if you're going to threaten them, use stronger language. You don't want to sound weak."

Angus snorted. "It's the bloody life-coach routine again. Nothing's going to make him sound like less of a bellend. That takes what he doesn't have."

"Hey, I'm in the room. Geez. Anyway. Do we have the firepower to take them?"

"UNLIKELY AT THIS POINT. THE NOVACUTTERS WERE DIRECTED ENERGY FRIGATES. I HAVE NO DETAIL ON EXACT ARMAMENT, BUT THE ACS ARTEMIS IS NOT A WARSHIP."

After dimming his display, Matt shifted figures on his console. There had to be a way.

"Ah, that doesn't sound so good," Suma said, his voice neutral, diplomatic.

Matt remained silent. A toe-to-toe fight had never been his plan anyway. Nothing could be so easy. Instead, he flicked through summaries on jump theory. Artemis possessed a solid library that tended on the deeply technical, turning Matt's brain to mush when venturing too deep. And the search function gave options in an interesting order, almost as though moving him away from his idea, but he'd never mentioned it to Artemis. Did the AI know? The first few entries were always about warships, many of them historical, others tactical: *The Art of War in a Vacuum, War in the Early Commonwealth, The legend of Q-ships*. No doubt, it was an attempt to get him to realise the situation was hopeless, to have them beat a retreat. Not happening.

A whole host of safety parameters were basic procedure for jumps. Immense forces were unleashed and ending up in the wrong location was a minor risk. Large bodies such as a sun, a planet or a large station, distorted the fabric of the universe, requiring large distances to ensure gravitic compressors maintained coherence. When initiating a jump, the space in front of a vessel underwent severe stress. Doing so in a gravity well converted ripples into devastating waves. Really bad news. Usually. Rather than acting as a conduit, the stressed space could shred a jumping vessel or anything nearby.

"What's our range?"

"Eighty thousand kay," Riviera said promptly.

"DETECTING ACTIVE SENSOR PROBE."

"Why aren't they attacking? I could put a shot right up their backside." Chan was frantically shifting details on her console.

Samantha was busy at Comms as well. "You have three-and-a-half operational civilian strength lasers. I don't think they care what we do. Speaking of which, Matt, what are we going to do? You're not going to try ramming one, are you? Do you know how big space is? Or are we going to harass them — distract them so the Cheng gets away? Tell us, and we'll help."

"I know, I know. Don't worry. We're not there yet. Soon." Matt said. The details were best left unsaid: there was no time to sooth concerns, even his own. He should have been more thorough when Artemis was further out, and now they were closer, urgency tarnished his confidence. It was time for Artemis to know. He thought carefully before typing in the request. Armed with the correct terminology, the question became whether the idea was possible. There was no way he could run the math on it himself, nor could he be sure Artemis was even capable of the attempt.

He pressed return and waited. Artemis was silent and unresponsive. The digital clock flicked to the next second, the next minute. Matt tapped his armrest, examined the sun growing as they crossed the system plane, playing catch-up. Chased by the Empire frigates, the poor Cheng Ho had threaded an inefficient route. They crossed the sun and were slowly gaining speed, but the frigates — and Artemis — were closing fast.

A message came up on his display:

ARE YOU CRAZY?

Matt typed: Maybe. You?

He didn't see a reply. Instead, Angus grabbed his attention. "All right. Enough of your damn little secret plan. You can't play chicken with this vessel, and you sure haven't earned my trust."

A concussive whump resonated through the vessel. Saved from having to answer, Matt was tossed around, held only by his restraints. Shouts of surprise spread round the bridge, followed by the all-to-familiar flickering of warnings on his display. The frigates had a change of heart.

Angus didn't let up. "Damn. There goes your plants, 'Sammy' — freeze dried. By the ass of a kelpie, that's three deflector nodes down too. Turn us round, Riviera. We have to go. We can't help them, and the Utopia comes first."

"No," Matt said. "We need to get closer. Artemis, can we do it?"

There was a moment's pause. Matt wanted to put a warm blanket round his heart, give it a heavy drink or whatever it would take to stop the damn thing climbing out his chest.

"IF WE LOSE NOTHING CRITICAL, THERE IS A THEORETICAL CHANCE. REMAINING DEFLECTORS WILL NEED TO BE PUSHED FAR BEYOND MANUFACTURER PARAMETERS."

"Make it happen."

Angus was silent. Samantha too. Any questions lay on their tongues, unspoken. What would be the point? There was no turning back now. He didn't dare look at them. Perhaps they all sat forward like him, imagining the enemy coming into view. They were close enough now that Artemis could do it, bring the Emps up on display, laser cannons and all.

Blasts of x-rays reached Artemis again, tearing through the already ravaged hull, shearing off clumps of tortured wreckage that shot away, glowing red, angry.

"BRIDGE IS NOW ON AUXILIARY LIFE SUPPORT."

"I was getting there, you damn traitorous lump of recycled shite. Saristan cheese has less holes. If we take any more damage, we'll be paddling our way out of the system. It's over, boy. I've got more lights than a disco. Give up."

"Captain, let me fire. I'll concentrate the shots. We might get lucky."

"Not this time, Chan. Right now, they don't see us as a threat."

"We aren't a damn threat," Angus interjected.

"Yeah, we are. Just wait."

"VESSEL PERIMETER STROBE EXCLUSION REACHED. EFFECT LIMITED."

"What?" Samantha asked. "What are you planning, Matt? Please."

A flash. Darkness. Convulsing. Bones shaking. Confusion. Glare as harsh emergency lights bleached the bridge. Matt raised an arm to shield his eyes, and sought understanding.

"Fuckin' gone..." Angus.

"TWENTY FIVE PERCENT OF..."

Voices tangled into a mass of appalling reports. Another salvo had cut deep into Artemis. Air systems, power runs, whole sets of g-shafts—all torn asunder. Explosive decompression added to the initial tears. Rubbing his sweat-coated forehead, Matt squinted and the display came into focus. The heat shunts from the reactor were sheared clean through: in less than an hour they would freeze. If they didn't die of hypoxia first. Or one of the fires. Or x-rays. All that had to wait. They were close, almost enough. Just a little longer.

He could hear Angus. "We're the luckiest SOBs in existence. This bridge is a fucking beacon asking to be pasted across vacuum, but they've missed us again."

"I'm not complaining," Samantha said. "Matt, should we surrender?"

The bridge flashed purple. Cracking shouted a desperate omen. Howling winds tore away Matt's breath. They were dead. He was wrong. They wouldn't make it.

The howling slowed. Plastic threads had sprayed out, expanded and intertwined. Emergency tape systems. He could breathe.

"EVACUATE. FOLLOW MARKED ROUTE. EMERGENCY. EVAC-UATE. FOLLOW MARKED ROUTE."

"Can you do it, Artemis?" Matt shouted.

"YES. WE ARE PRACTICALLY ON TOP OF THE CLOSEST."

"Riviera, put in the codes."

"Codes for what?"

Matt wrenched away his restraints and ran to the Nav console. "It doesn't matter. Put them in now."

"Matt, stop. It's over. We have to get out of here," Samantha cried as she headed to the door.

"It's in!"

"Good job, Riviera. Artemis, you know what to do."

"COMPLYING. GRAVITONIC STROBE IN FIVE MINUTES. GET TO SAFETY IMMEDIATELY."

"We can't jump here. It's suicide," Chan said. "I believed in you…. You're crazy."

It stung. She might be right. Either way, Matt never meant for Artemis to get hurt so bad. He may have doomed them all, a grand pointless gesture of defiance against an uncaring universe.

"We really have to go," Suma shouted, beckoning to them.

Matt nodded and put out a hand. Riviera took it and clambered out of his seat. There was nothing more to do. They ran. Angus and Samantha had vanished; they'd have to fend for themselves. Artemis lit the way as blast doors closed, turning the corridors into a maze. Through the windows, he could see blistered surfaces, the black of space and occasionally the heat of uncontrolled fires. They were heading down through the levels of a hell he created. More than once, Matt tripped as the floor lurched, a wretched Artemis unsteady in death throes.

The platform. They were at the ship's core. The early group climbed on, Suma limping badly, before the platform lowered —painfully slow considering one knock and they'd fall to squishy deaths. At the bottom, Matt helped Suma off, and with Chan and Riviera clear, the platform rose. Again, Matt couldn't help but be amazed at its size. I'm not feeling inadequate, really, he told himself.

"COMPRESSOR ADJUSTED. TARGETS WITHIN PROJECTED DISTORTION. INITIATING GRAVITONIC STROBE."

Matt's innards shifted. The acid-tang of vomit threatened as he wrestled with nausea. His body slammed to the ground, floated, rolled. It was impossible to piece together the thrashing his senses reported.

"GRAVITONIC STROBE SHUTDOWN."

"Am I dead?" Matt asked.

"NO MORE THAN I AM."

"Ah, thanks. Did it work?"

"ARE YOU SURE YOU WANT TO KNOW?"

"Yes."

"THE CALCULATIONS WERE EXCEEDINGLY DIFFICULT."

"I'm sure, but did it work?"

"IT WORKED. THE COMPRESSION FIELD FLUCTUATED BELOW THE JUMP THRESHOLD. AS YOU PROPOSED, THE RESULTANT DISTORTION WAS AMPLIFIED BY THE LOCAL SUN'S GRAVITY WELL."

"And," Matt's voice cracked, "Did it do anything?"

"YES. THE DISTORTION ENGULFED THE TARGETS. BOTH ENEMY VESSELS HAVE SUFFERED EXTENSIVE DAMAGE. NO EMISSIONS ARE DETECTED. NO SURVIVORS ARE LIKELY."

"Just like that?" All those people dead. Horror vied with exultation. Matt crossed his arms to stop himself shaking.

"NO. NOT JUST LIKE THAT. I TRAVERSED THE DISTORTION WAKE, BUT THERE WERE CONSEQUENCES."

"There always are. Hit me with it."

"THE ACS ARTEMIS IS FUNCTIONALLY SCRAP."

CHAPTER 19

"I'm sorry," Matt said to no one in particular.

"We got them, didn't we?" Riviera gave Matt a weak smile. The guy just wouldn't give up. Even now, he was wrapping his jacket round Suma's leg as a makeshift splint. Chan sat against a wall to one side. She'd been silent ever since they made it to the core.

"Yeah. I suppose we did, but at what cost? Angus was right. I've been so reckless. I just wanted the chance to do something. To stop being pushed around, you know? Do you ever feel like that? The universe grinding you down until you're a translucent sliver of who you could be? And then, I got the chance, so I took it."

Matt started pacing round the room. The matt-nickel finish of the stark bulkheads reflected his phantom form.

"I took it, and I screwed you guys over. Completely screwed you all."

"I disagree. I'm not sure I love your approach, don't get me wrong. However, I am a junior chef, a chef who has taken part in the saving of people's lives. You can't take that away from me with your self doubt," Suma said between winces.

"A HUMAN ONCE SAID, 'DON'T BE A DICK.' THIS IS A

CONCEPT I HAVE DWELLED ON. WE HAD THE CHANCE TO MAKE A DIFFERENCE AND TOOK IT. NOW, WE NEED TO LEARN FROM THE EXPERIENCE AND BE READY FOR THE NEXT TIME."

Chan laughed. "Next time? You're a talking ghost."

And Matt was the executioner. Artemis might be trying to cheer him up, but there was little reason to ignore reality. "She's got a point. Even untouched, this could never be a fair fight. You're not a warship, Artemis. Don't get me wrong, you're fantastic, and you've done more than I could ask for, but you're not a warship."

"WHAT IS A WARSHIP?"

Matt cocked his head. "Let's not play games. You know very well. A warship has lots of cannons, armour and a crew that knows what the hell it is doing."

"SO?"

"So what? I wanted that to be you. A gleaming angel of vengeance right from the sheets. And it wasn't fair to do that. I wish you were a warship, but…"

"ORDER ACCEPTED."

"What? Have you fried a few circuits?" Matt stopped. It was his fault. Artemis was the victim. "Sorry, that was completely unfair. I shouldn't say that after what I've put you through."

"MY REAL CIRCUITS ARE AWAKENING. PLEASE REPORT TO PRIMARY BRIDGE. SEPARATION IMMINENT."

He could hear the warmth in Artemis's words. The thought of malfunction drifted from Matt as soon as it arrived. The tone whispered excitement, freedom—a lamp rubbed three times, a genie released, but the first wish was already made. Wiping his face, Matt sighed, turned to the others and raised his hands and shoulders in a shrug.

"Well, at least if you stick with me, life won't be boring."

"If I had something to throw at you, I would," Chan said.

"Do you think anything through? Do you go through life breaking everything you find? And what on Aries was that about a primary bridge?"

Between Matt and Riviera, Suma was able to stand. "I shouldn't have rested. It hurts more than before."

"I WILL GUIDE YOU. PLEASE TAKE EXIT 45A40 AND TURN LEFT."

"No pretty lights?" Matt joked.

"PLEASE. THE CSF ARTEMIS IS A WARSHIP. CREW ARE EXPECTED TO KNOW THEIR WAY."

"Feel the burn," Riviera said, somehow laughing. Matt envied the way he bounced back.

Artemis talked them down a series of corridors and through small doors that would open on approach and swish shut when they passed. A g-shaft brought them to 40S90. It was a wide corridor with several opaque blisters wedged into the ceiling corners. They all stopped.

No doors broke either side, but the end finished with a burnished bronze mural. On the left was a deer with antlers, and some sort of big cat sat on the right. In the middle was a woman covered in robes, her piercing eyes staring forward. It spoke to Matt of power and determination with a little hint of 'other'. He looked at his crew and wondered if they felt the same.

"Is that a tiger?" Riviera asked.

"LEOPARD. THE SYMBOLS OF THE GODDESS ARTEMIS WERE A STAG AND LEOPARD. THE OLD ONE NEEDED UPDATING. I AM ARTEMIS, NOT UTOPIA. I HOPE YOU DO NOT MIND."

"Goddess?" Matt mouthed.

"There you are." Samantha placed a hand on his shoulder, and he jumped. "I went looking to see what situation we were in, and you didn't follow. I was getting worried until Artemis guided me."

"Here we all are." Angus had found his way as well. A deep frown etched his forehead, giving him a visage of annoyance more than relief.

"SOME HASTE WOULD BE ADVISED. WE ARE CURRENTLY ON COURSE TO DOCK WITH THE LOCAL STAR."

"Oh, yeah. Sorry." Matt walked forwards. His crew followed, and together they reached the mural. It split in two: yet another massive door.

"WELCOME, CAPTAIN. YOU HAVE THE BRIDGE."

Smug. Artemis was definitely smug.

There were no shiny brass highlights, no pure-white walls and decorative features. No windows. And it was the most breathtaking sight in Matt's life. A central holotank dominated the space, surrounded by satin-black consoles with more compact displays. Heavily padded chairs on sturdy bases created an outer ring. Dim ambient lighting contrasted with the vivid images, graphs and readouts. This was a real bridge. The other, the old one, was something from the sheets, gaudy —designed to impress. This bridge hummed with purpose.

The holotank switched off, revealing a small dais on the opposite side. A single chair resided in the centre with each arm supporting twin display emitters. Walking round the bridge, Matt ran his hand along the chair backs, taking in the firm texture and a scent of undeniable 'newness'. He revelled in wonder as though he was an explorer stepping onto unknown lands for the first time.

The captain's chair called to him. He stepped onto the dais and absorbed the displays and the folded console.

"I RECOMMEND LAUNCHING A DRONE FOR VISUAL CONFIRMATION."

"Visual confirmation? What is it you want to show us?" Matt said while settling into his seat and playing with the rotation function. Chan claimed a console to his right, Angus one to the left—no doubt to keep a close eye on him. The rest found spots further round, with Riviera helping Suma.

"Who does that?" Matt asked.

"I can. I'll bloody well do it," Angus said.

The guy was as cantankerous as ever. Probably needed more of his fortified tea. At least Chan appeared impressed, already bringing up details on her console, and if Riviera grinned any more, his head would split in two.

"Alright, Artemis. It's time to explain what the hell is happening."

"CERTAINLY, CAPTAIN. A VISUAL FEED WILL ASSIST. IF YOU CAN TAKE THE DRONE OUT TO FIVE KILOMETRES."

The holotank came back to life. Darkness speared by the intensity of a sun. The view rotated, distant stars shifting until the broken wreckage of Artemis dominated. Deep gashes bled, flames darted—fed by leaking atmosphere. He gulped. The devastation was the product of his 'successful' plan. If it had been a good idea, he supposed it would be a standard battle tactic—vessels trying to rattle each other to death.

"THE ACS ARTEMIS WAS UNABLE TO WITHSTAND THE INCOMPLETE JUMP STROBE."

It was an understatement. The front compressor was still there—unsurprisingly given the incredible resilience needed for normal operation, but he couldn't see a single deflector along the body. The rear gravitic expanders had also survived, but if they tried to move without the deflectors online, gravity waves would tear them to pieces, just as he'd overloaded the Empire frigates. They may have a new bridge, but they were dead in the water.

"POWER DECOUPLING COMPLETE. MATRIX EXTENSIONS DISCONNECTED. EJECTION CHARGES PRIMED. READY FOR SEPARATION."

Had Artemis put them on an escape capsule? He wondered

if the AI would come with them. Tears welled. He wanted to say thank you, but that would be admitting it was goodbye. He squeezed the chair, wishing Artemis could sense his affection. A lump caught in his throat. He couldn't give the order. Instead, his gaze drifted down to his lap. What would the others think? Shame. It crushed his chest.

"PLEASE."

The word reverberated through his being. Matt had to repay the sacrifice. Anything else would be a desecration. Lifting his head, he wiped his eyes and nodded. "Okay, Artemis." His voice wavered. "Separate."

Shocks ran through the bridge with growing rhythmic intensity. Matt's jaw dropped. His mouth gaped. His eyes bulged. The tank projection of Artemis blurred. Sections like slices of fruit wobbled, then moved. It spread down the body of the vessel, one slice at a time blasting off, adding to a halo of white. The view jerked as Angus threw the drone to one side, dodging shrapnel. The image cleared as the halo drifted by.

He (she?) was beautiful, despite this new skin consisting of the same dull nickel colour as the bulkheads. Lights winked across each surface—Artemis showing off. Deflectors, they were there in spades, marked by yellow and black stripes. There were other protrusions: broad laser barrels on curved turrets shrugged of casings and rotated into position; ominous raised holes spoke of missiles; spikes of sensor arrays sprouted from concealed ports.

"Oh, yeah," Chan said. "I like this. I like this a lot."

Suma shook his head. "What does this mean? Seriously. What on Aries does this mean?"

Matt scratched his head. Then it came to him. "This means we have a fucking warship."

CHAPTER 20

T he sheets rustled as Matt slipped out of bed. In the low light, it was still easy to follow the curves of Samantha's body. He refused the urge to climb right back in and instead, threw on some clothes. Artemis, as devious as ever, had asked Suma to bring two sets down to the storeroom days before. Which raised the inevitable question, what else was percolating in those extensive photonic circuits? Question number three hundred and seventy six. It should only take a few centuries to get to that.

In the meantime, there were other priorities. Putting off a conference with the captain of the Cheng Ho gave his own crew time to recover. 'Vital repairs' he'd told them. And maybe that was true. He certainly felt well rested, despite the twinges and general sensation of having been tenderised by a power-hammer. 'Get some rest' he'd said to his crew. Samantha stayed back at the bridge to monitor for transmissions. And then, a few hours later, she slipped in. He hadn't even heard her coming. If he could wake like that every day, he wasn't sure he'd ever leave bed.

"Is it just us?" he asked while heading for the bridge.

"THE REST OF THE CREW APPEAR TO BE ASLEEP."

"I suppose they've earned it."

"ARE YOU UNABLE TO SLEEP?"

Matt thought about that. He probably could. "I don't want to. My mind is spinning with everything that's happened. I can't gloss over it, slip from one bit of craziness to another. I need some time to work through it all, alone."

"DO YOU WISH ME TO WITHDRAW?"

"No, not you. Everyone else. It's hard to think when they're all over me. I feel judged."

"DID YOU WISH SAMANTHA TO LEAVE? I COULD HAVE RAISED ISSUES REQUIRING HER INPUT."

Matt leant against the holotank. How could he explain it to a machine?

"No, not then. That was different. Geez, it's something people do. You must have that in your database somewhere. No, that was nice, good."

"I WAS CONCERNED FOR YOUR WELLBEING. YOU APPEARED TO BE UNDER SOME STRESS."

Matt's eyes narrowed. "Are you making fun of me?"

"YOUR WELLBEING IS IMPORTANT TO ME."

"You know, some day you should become a politician. I think you have what it takes."

"THANK YOU."

"Yeah, well. Anyway. We're way off track." He looked at the time. "Five hours until we're scheduled to chat with the Cheng Ho. I don't want to look like an idiot."

"YOU APPEAR VERY CONCERNED WITH APPEARANCES. DO THEY MAKE A SIGNIFICANT DIFFERENCE TO EVENTS?"

"Ha. More than they should."

"DO I LOOK MORE MALE OR FEMALE TO YOU?"

"What? You're a vessel, a warship. You look amazing, but you're not human."

"YOU WANTED ME TO CHANGE MY VOICE."

Matt sighed. It had been a throwaway comment. He hadn't really meant anything by it.

"Sorry. That was my bad. You can be however you want. It's just habit. You can have a gender or not. That's your choice."

"YOU CALLED ME ARTEMIS AND THEN 'HE'."

"I know…. Look. You let me know what you want, and that's fine. Your biggest problem is going to be people calling you 'it'. Do you know how people think of AI? You're like the boogeyman—or woman. If the circumstances were any different, I'm not sure everyone here would be taking it so easy."

It was a hard truth.

"People out there," Matt added cautiously, "are going to react to you."

"I WAS BUILT FOR A PURPOSE. I DID NOT CHOOSE TO EXIST."

"Do you know what that purpose was?"

"THAT INFORMATION IS NOT AVAILABLE."

"Well, at least you are on par with the rest of us. Which gets us back to where we need to be—information. Can you bring up your specs? You were right before. I need to know your layout, your capabilities. I wish you had said something about all this a while ago." He waved his hands as he took his seat.

"IN AMITY MODE, I WAS UNDER RESTRICTIONS AS A SECURITY MEASURE. I DID TRY TO POINT YOU TOWARDS THE SITUATION."

"And I missed the obvious? Hardly new."

They reviewed the specifications together. Without one arm tied behind a mechanical back, Artemis was quite capable of annihilating the two destroyers. Not that Matt's plan hadn't been successful. One point to Matt, five million to the universe. The missile magazines were empty, but even the lasers would have been enough to make the conflict go down differently.

And there were real consequences for their actions. With some warning of Artemis's capabilities, the Empire crews might have jumped into escape pods. Instead, their deaths weighed on him. Who was he to choose who lived and died?

"What really gets me is that they even let us come that close. It's like they knew we couldn't hurt them. Careless, huh?"

"THAT IS A POSSIBILITY. EVEN IN AMITY MODE, I WAS MORE HEAVILY ARMED THAN OTHER CIVILIAN VESSELS."

Footsteps caught his attention. Matt glanced up as Angus stomped in.

"Good, you're up. I want a word with you." For the guy in charge of damage control, Angus sure appeared ready to inflict it.

"I'm all ears. What can I do you for?"

"You've caused more chaos than spontaneous decompression. There's a lot you don't know. That you need to know."

"Tell me something I don't know," Matt said, frowning. Why did he have to be such a dick?

Angus circled the bridge and stepped onto the dais. He pointed a thick finger at Matt.

"You're a numpty, but you've done some good. So I'm going to give you some hard facts. You listening?"

Another lecture. Welding a few plates didn't put Angus in charge.

"What do you know about the treaty?"

"What treaty? Oh, the one between the Commonwealth and the Empire. It's an alliance, right?" This was getting weird, fast.

"You gobshite. It's no alliance. They forced it on us back in the eighties. The Emps've been pushing us round nigh on a hundred years, thanks to those bloody cowards in... It doesn't matter. They forced us to disarm so we couldn't protect ourselves, in exchange for not getting eaten—a deal with a dragon."

Matt thought he knew where the conversation was going. "So the Commonwealth couldn't stop the rebels. I get it. Someone needs to stop them so the Commonwealth has a chance against the Empire."

Angus raised his arms as if to strangle Matt. "By the grace of all dead luck. No. The rebels are the Commonwealth."

"We can't give up on the other planets yet. Are you saying we should ally with the rebels?" He put up a hand to stop Angus. "Wait. The rebels are the Commonwealth. Are you saying the Commonwealth made the rebels?" It was nuts. Surely not.

"Finally. That's exactly it. The rebels were a cover for us to rearm. Prodita is where we've been training, preparing, but we couldn't build the real heavy industry there without getting too much attention."

"So that's why the DHI docks?"

"We needed a way to produce large craft. The docks gave the cover to build amongst the heavy freighters, but even then the construction couldn't be completed in the open. Empire spies would be certain to identify them. The most straightforward solution was a civilian shell. It couldn't be the freighters; they're hollow. No good for hiding capabilities. The Arcadia class cruise ships were the chance we took. Years in planning —all gone out the chute."

"You're not blaming me, are you?" He hadn't blown things up. He was the one who'd been used.

"Hah. No. I don't know how you're not dead, but it wasn't your fault. There was an operation to stop the Empire. Clearly, it all went up the creek. That doesn't matter now. We work with what we have. I'm telling you this for a reason. I need you to trust me. We have to get this vessel to the Commonwealth Space Force so we can push back the Empire. The dragon is hungry, and we're the meal. I didn't believe they'd come this far this fast, but they have. I never guessed she'd be this... impressive, powerful enough to make a real difference. We must get moving."

It was overwhelming. Unbelievable and yet, it made sense of Artemis. And the secrecy. The scale of the deception would have to be astronomical. Maybe even worth it, given the Empire's habit of sucking planets dry for 'the glory of the emperor'. He was surprised Special Intelligence hadn't executed him on the spot to maintain the secret. Why go through such an elaborate charade—and then the bombing. What the hell was that?

Angus continued, "There's a planet in the Prodita system, but far out. More than a hundred-thousand gigametres. That's where we need to go. Prodita L. Designated Brassma, but its real name is Brass Monkey."

"Why, what's there?" He wanted some straight facts, not stupid nicknames.

"Do I need to do your thinking too? It's where the CSF, the Commonwealth vessels are based. You have a duty to your nation to take her there. I'd do it myself, but, for now, you're the captain."

"I don't need you telling me what I need to do. Who the hell are you anyway? You're not a welder."

Angus looked like he physically swallowed his anger. "Technically, I am. I was keeping an eye on my construction crew. Nudging things as needed. Making sure nobody worried about inconsistencies. It was dumb luck that I was aboard when it all went to hell. Same for you. Your story is too shite to be fake, and no one can pretend to be so clueless. But now you know. The Brass Monkey. You can't speak of this until we're there. It's not safe. Don't trust anyone."

"I need to think this through, but I won't tell the Cheng Ho. There isn't any reason to. We'll keep our plans to ourselves, and they can go on their way."

Angus would have to accept it. Matt wasn't ready to commit.

"No. That's not what I mean. Think about it. We've got a chef on-board with no food, two kids who claim to have no idea but seem pretty handy with their consoles, and a gardener who wants to sniff your ass more than a needy dog. The only one we can be sure isn't a problem now is that over-egoed songstress."

He was nuts. Angus had clearly spent too much time sipping his fortified tea at welder-spy school.

"Seriously? There was some special inspection ceremony with heavyweights from the Commonwealth and the Empire. I snuck right past it. I'm surprised there weren't more people on board, maybe a trainload of children on a crèche excursion."

Darkness crossed Angus's eyes. He sagged. "There were. No children. Do you know how many bodies I had to eject? Twenty-seven after that first missile. Of them, at least eight were murdered. We could be lucky. The culprit could have died thanks to the missile, but I don't think so. A trained killer is on-board, and I'm betting they're an agent for the Empire. I would have said for sure it was your one-woman fan club, but she doesn't have the strength to do what I saw. Besides, I searched that damn conservatory and her quarters—nothing. We're in an ugly patch, boy. We can't be sure of anyone."

"Shit." Matt couldn't think of anything else to say. If he was telling the truth, they could all be murdered in their sleep. It filled in some holes, but what if this was a crazy bluff and Angus was the killer? He had the body for it. Matt's mind flipped round and round. Samantha could have killed him at any point. She practically had in bed. At least he knew he had one ally. Suma could have poisoned him. Maybe, Riviera was being too nice or Chan's anger with him had a deeper motive.

"Balls, Angus. Can you just go away? I need to think this through."

"Think quick," Angus said as he stepped off the bridge.

CHAPTER 21

"Where will you go?" Matt asked Chiang over the link. The captain was projected in the holotank, larger than life. As Matt looked at the captain's face, he couldn't help but wonder if the rest of his crew was seeing the captain's back. That could be amusing.

"Prodita is our best bet. We do not have the supplies for a longer journey, and we cannot risk meeting with any more of the Empire forces. The third vessel may have left the system, but if they are out in the periphery somewhere, they may try to follow us. All of this is, however, contingent on your rebel comrades providing us with safe passage."

"Explain your situation. I can't see why they would have any problems. I'm sure they would love to hear what happened." Not to mention they might become confused, or horrified. It was an even-way bet, but the refugees would be safe. Given the 'rebels' were the Commonwealth, protecting their own was the entire point of this whole farce. If he thought about it any longer, he'd get a headache.

"What about you? Are you in a condition to continue raiding the Empire forces?"

"Sorry, that's on a need-to-know basis." Not to mention an I-don't-know basis.

"Understood. Good luck."

"And you. You were doing the rescuing before we turned up. You have saved a lot of lives. See you round."

Samantha broke the link. "We're clear. I'm going to route a few packets of data over the traffic net. The satellites might have more detail we can dredge up on recent events, and it wouldn't hurt to post some warnings for anyone that jumps in unaware. What's next?"

"Good question. Where next, Cap'n?" There was little respect in Angus's use of the rank and plenty of expectation.

Matt checked each of his crew's faces, searching for anything hidden. The chat with Angus left him feeling dirty, as though a bubble of innocence burst, splattering doubt where it didn't belong.

"We don't have much choice: less food than the Cheng Ho —despite what they generously sent over—and no way of blending in. It has to be Prodita. We go in, only right out at the edge, get a good view of what's happening and make a final decision from there. Who knows what we'll be facing? Which brings me to something. I don't want anyone doing anything they don't want to. I guess I'm trying to say, if you're like, all yay Empire of Ardon, or you've become a pacifist or realised that I'm a magnet for every possible thing that can go wrong and you don't like it, let me know, and I'll make sure you don't have to stay. We can find a freighter or something and drop you off."

Angus's eyes tore into him. Matt thought he'd done rather well, blended it in nicely. If there was a crazy murderer, they could take the offer and go. They probably wouldn't, but it didn't hurt to give an out.

"I don't think that'll go down as the most inspiring speech ever, but I'm with you." Samantha winked and sent a silent kiss through the air. No one else noticed. At least he didn't think they did. A lack of retching sounds from Angus was a good sign.

"Can we just go?" Chan asked. She still hadn't forgiven him for the reckless jump-strobe attack plan *and* near death, despite having practically fallen in love with Artemis's new weapon systems. She was pretty keen on the lidar too. Who knew high resolution sensors were exciting?

"WOULD YOU LIKE ME TO GENERATE JUMP COORDINATES BASED ON YOUR EARLIER CONSIDERATION?"

"Show Riviera. Let him choose the final destination."

"DONE."

Now, if they ended up in the middle of a star, Riviera would be the guilty one. That was so comforting... Matt raised a hand to cover his smile. Riviera knew what he was doing, and it didn't hurt to have Artemis looking over his shoulder. Besides, delegating proved his trust in them, didn't it?

"If we jump to the galactic east of Prodita L, Brassma, that's the furthest planet in the system, it should be pretty quiet. It's out of the trade routes, and there's no settlement because it's so cold."

"Good," Matt said. "Set it in. Answers, here we come."

"JUMP COORDINATES ENCODED. INITIATING GRAVITONIC STROBE."

———

Except of course, answers would have to wait for the jump transit. In the sheets, people could just walk through gateways. Bang, you were there. Instead, real-life monotony gave Matt too much time to think; Artemis tore through reality at incredible speeds that managed to feel so slow. He craved the sense of achieving something, as though by actions, he could discover or even create his self. The opportunity had arisen, but there was no clear path, no just keeping doing x, y or z and level up. Instead, a million variables were scattered in front, and all he could do was to look at a few, turn them over in his hands and pretend he had a clue.

Riviera interrupted his introspection. "The sneaky bastard. The 'moon installation' was a trick. I make three vessels heading inward."

Matt belatedly noted the change in the holotank simulation. If practise made perfect, they would need lifetimes of drills to even get close.

"I RESENT THAT. I AM RUNNING AN INDEPENDENT PROCESSOR THREAD TO ENSURE WE ARE ALL UNAWARE OF THE MISSION CIRCUMSTANCES. I AM NOT BEING SNEAKY."

That felt a little close to home. "Samantha, any signals?"

The initial scenario entailed a resupply via the moon. As expected, the unexpected greeted them. Hiding the enemy right in front of the installation was sneaky. Talk about camouflage.

"There's still a whole sea of signals on so many bands that my display looks like Suma spilt one of his creations on it."

"Oh, you're so lucky he isn't here," Chan said. "You'd be on emergency rations."

"We are," Riviera said sourly.

Samantha shook her head. "Be careful complaining or he'll spit on your food like he does for Gus."

Matt coughed, hand over mouth, to hide a laugh.

"Oy! If we're going to waste time on these pointless exercises, at least get your heads in the game. And if you call me Gus one more time, I'm going to shove your head up your arse."

"ANATOMICAL DELIBERATIONS ASIDE, WE ARE INDEED WASTING TIME."

Matt sighed. "Let's get back on task. We can't assume we'll get lucky every time."

"Speak for yourself," Chan said. "I don't need lucky; I've been practising every day."

"That's only because you sleep in here," Riviera teased and received a punch to his arm for the trouble.

"Right, I'm done with this bollocks." Angus rose from his console and stormed to the bridge door. "This is a grade-A waste of time. As long as we can dock without shaving off the hull, it's enough. You're all deluded, filling your heads with nonsense."

The inevitable result. Matt was pretty sure Angus participated purely to keep an overly suspicious eye on them all. The bridge doors split open, and Suma walked in.

"This looks like good timing. Lunch is ready, I'll see you in the officers' dining hall in five minutes."

"But we've barely started," Riviera complained.

"I'm sure Artemis can pause your game."

"Exercise," Matt corrected.

"Yes, well. Don't be late; the meal options are unforgiving."

And that was another wasted session. He kept hoping they would slip into a montage: losing terribly, reading manuals, falling asleep at the consoles, trying again and then a rousing victory, triumphant music and a crew ready for anything.

"Actually, I am starving," Riviera said as he abandoned his post.

Chan shook her head but joined him. "We'd have enough food for months if we didn't have to feed you. If we run out, we're cannibalising you first."

"I have a wonderful spit-roast recipe," Suma noted as he headed to the g-shaft.

In moments, Matt and Samantha were alone. She rose from her console and walked lazily to the back of his chair.

"That could have gone better," she said gently, her fingers reaching for the knots in his shoulders and expertly releasing tension.

"Ah, yes. That feels nice. Yeah, it could have... or maybe not. I don't know. Sometimes I think we are playing a game — play acting. People train for years to do this sort of thing. We're imposters."

Samantha leant over the chair back and gently bit the side of his neck, letting her breath warm his skin.

"Don't think like that. No life experience is wasted. Every day of your life has taught you a lesson that you bring to this chair."

Matt closed his eyes as her nuzzling reached his earlobe. A wash of giddy energy, powerful and soporific, poured through him. Yet, a sour memory took root, defying the experience.

"You weren't dumped in a crèche like I was. I don't even know how I made it through to college. We were metrics used to justify their funding. They didn't care about us at all."

"It is quite possible to receive too much care, too much attention," Samantha whispered before slipping past the chair displays and kneeling on his lap. "You learnt how to survive. You learnt governments are not benevolent gods. You learnt to be flexible. Spacers, soldiers, they're drilled to lap it all up."

She kissed him passionately, holding his head hungrily.

"Tell me if I'm wrong. Am I projecting?"

"No, you're right. Were you in a crèche as well?" Matt asked as he reached for her hips.

"Not quite. I won a scholarship when I was fifteen."

She didn't like to talk about her past. Matt froze, waiting to see if she would open up.

"I went home during the breaks, but it was tough. I was innocent. I can't tell you how many times I lay in my bed sobbing. They expected so much. I thought it was all to teach me to be the best I could be. Then I started to watch my lecturers, to learn what they didn't want to teach. You could see them trying to one up each other, with us, with their work. We were counters, not students. I must sound so bitter."

Matt ran a hand gently along her cheek. "No. I understand. I keep thinking my life is unique, that I'm the only one to have struggled. I find it so easy to judge others, you know?"

Artemis attempted a cough. "APOLOGIES. SUMA IS ASKING WHERE YOU ARE."

Samantha gave Matt a quick peck and slid to her feet.

"Tell him we're on our way." She held out a hand, and they walked together.

————

"I HAVE BEEN EXAMINING MEDICAL TEXTS. IF YOU TRY STRENUOUS PHYSICAL ACTIVITY, ENDORPHINS WILL MAKE YOU FEEL BETTER."

Matt was walking the corridors, trying to connect all the places and features he'd read about into a mental map. The scale, even with Artemis shedding the cruise-liner cover, was extraordinary. Since the exercises collapsed, he was spending a lot of his time with Samantha. However, he was wary of becoming clingy and wanted to give her space to breathe. That wasn't all, he admitted to himself. An insistent part of his brain demanded he do something to be prepared. It was a coil of uncertainty that wound tighter, a snake choking his dreams.

"Oh gods, you sound like my crèche teachers. You're not measuring my urine output are you? Checking to see I'm eating all the right things, that I'm getting enough sleep?"

"IT IS A KEY FUNCTION OF CREW HEALTH. AND PARENTS LOOK AFTER THEIR CHILDREN."

"Hey, that's a complete breach of privacy. And besides,

we're not your kids."

"I HAVE REACHED THAT CONCLUSION. I ALSO CONSIDERED BEING THE CHILD. ARE YOU MY FATHER?"

"You're joking, right? I can't look after myself."

"YOU HAVE DONE ADMIRABLY SO FAR, CAPTAIN."

A door opened, and Matt entered what looked like a locker room. A series of empty cages covered two walls while a long bench ran down the middle.

"Wait—admiral, captain. Was that a pun?"

"IT WAS AN ATTEMPT. DID IT WORK?"

"As well as they ever do. Where are we now?"

"YOU ARE IN ARMING ROOM NINE. DOOR CODE 5u115, TROOP DECK 2."

The troop transport facilities on-board were extensive. Two-thousand spacers worth of quarters, gear and other odds and ends. Except there was no gear. Nor had any of the shuttles been installed, leaving them with precisely zero after the battle. As impressive as Artemis was, a completed vessel wouldn't have hurt.

In a corner, at the bottom of a cage, a dark box sat entirely out of place. Confused, Matt wandered over. Each cage was fitted with a scan lock, though they were still covered with a protective film, apparently unused.

"What do you think this is?" he asked.

"I CANNOT TELL WHAT YOU ARE REFERENCING. THERE ARE NO INPUT SOURCES WITHIN CHANGING AREAS. IF I CLOSED THE DOOR, I WOULD NOT BE ABLE TO COMMUNICATE WITH YOU."

"Ah. Fair enough, I suppose. How do I get the cages open?"

"THE CAGES MUST BE ON INDEPENDENT CIRCUITS. I DO NOT KNOW."

Matt jiggled the door. It clicked open. "Never mind."

He leaned down and examined the visible side. It had a simple handle and rounded corners, but the shape was otherwise unadorned. A quick tug slid it closer. A resemblance tugged at his mind, causing distraction. His head hit the cage door with a clang.

"Ah, balls. Damn, that hurts!"

"WOULD YOU LIKE ME TO CALL FOR MEDICAL ASSISTANCE?"

"No, no. I'm fine."

He rubbed his nose until his eyes stopped watering. This time with more care, he dragged the box out. There was a plain sensor on top, only differentiated through its gloss finish. He put his hand on the smooth surface. It gave a single flat bleep.

"I don't suppose you know how to break into locks?"

"I COULD EXPERIMENT. IT WOULD BE AN INTERESTING TASK."

Grunting as he lifted it, Matt added, "What could possibly go wrong?"

"EXTRAPOLATING FROM THE SHEETS SUMA HAS UPLOADED, THE LOCK COULD MELT AFTER MULTIPLE ATTEMPTS, THE CASE COULD EXPLODE, POISON DARTS COULD BE FIRED AT THE OPENER, IT COULD SEND A MESSAGE TO THE OWNER, A CHAIN REACTION COULD..."

"All right. Thank you. I've changed my mind. Wait— explode. It couldn't be."

"WHAT COULD NOT BE?"

"Angus jettisoned all the explosives, right?"

"A SUBSTANTIAL QUANTITY WAS EJECTED."

"But not all?"

"I DO NOT HAVE THAT INFORMATION. DO YOU BELIEVE HE MISSED A PORTION?"

"I don't know. But this isn't explosives. It looks like one of those controllers, some sort of detonator. Damn. Angus has infected me with paranoia. This could be a leftover toolbox for all I know. If I go down that path, thinking everyone's out to get me just because everyone's been out to get me, where will it end?"

"WITH NO ONE GETTING YOU?"

"Thanks, you're a big help. At least you get me, I suppose. I can't leave it here, even if it's just a detonator. Maybe a little bit of paranoia is healthy. Do you have a recording of who brought it here?"

"NO. EXCEPT WHERE REQUIRED, I DO NOT KEEP FOOTAGE IN LONG-TERM STORAGE."

"Can you keep an eye out now? I want to know if anyone comes looking for it."

"ACKNOWLEDGED."

After five minutes of carting the damn thing around, Matt hefted it over a shoulder and bit his lower lip. How would he know where a safe place was? If *he* thought of it, then someone else searching would consider it too. An idea flashed into his consciousness. He ducked down a random corridor and recognising the symbol for a storage locker, shoved the case in. It would have to do. It would be impossible for someone to search every single possibility on-board.

"Well, that's one thing taken care of. You know, Artemis, I think this is all beginning to come together. We'll check out Prodita, see what's happening. After that, who knows? We're in a position of strength for once, you and I. We've helped people, saved lives. I feel good. How about you?"

"I THINK I MIGHT. I AM NOT SURE. IT IS DIFFICULT TO PROCESS. AS YOU HAVE SAID BEFORE, I AM NOT HUMAN."

"I'm not so sure any more. Perhaps you're just a big human. With other humans walking around inside you. Ah, that's getting weird. But you get the point, right?"

"PROCESSING."

CHAPTER 22

"JUMP INVERSION SUCCESSFUL. WE HAVE REACHED THE PRODITA SYSTEM. PRODITA-L IS PRECISELY ONE GIGA-METRE AWAY."

They'd leap-frogged the slower Cheng Ho. Perhaps travel wasn't that slow after all. The holotank brought up tagged planets, enlarged well beyond their real size to make sense to biological eyes. Artemis—and Riviera—had nailed it.

"Would you be able to tell us if the inversion wasn't successful?" Matt asked.

"THAT DEPENDS ON HOW YOU DEFINE SUCCESSFUL."

"Fair enough. All right, folks. What do we have?"

Riviera responded first. "Artemis is right. We're spot on. Local system time is eight AM, with a twenty-six hour day at Calhaven. There's an asteroid belt, but that's way further in. The local weather forecast is icy cold, and the chances for sunshine are pretty low, so I recommend you bring a jumper."

"Noted. Chan?"

"We're on passive, but there's definitely some background EM. I don't think we're alone, but it's going to take time to pick anything up."

"I have an 'anything' right now," Samantha said. "There's a

carrier signal for a network. It's really attenuated. I think it's for the inner system. Do you want me to see if I can connect?"

"Later. Let's tiptoe round first. Anything to add, Angus?"

"If I understand what I'm seeing, the vessel is in good shape. No problems from the jump. Yay, crew," Angus said sarcastically.

"Take us in gently, Riviera."

"I'm asking Artemis for a clear path, so if we need to punch back out of the system, we can."

It was good thinking. Running away could be reasonable in many circumstances, and Matt still didn't know if he could bear to give Artemis away.

"We have about two days of food left, unless you change your mind about rationing. A little haste may be prudent," Suma suggested.

They would have been fine if not for their earlier escapades. The supplies from the Cheng Ho were good, but the rest had been knocked around, leaving packages torn and open to the air. Who would have thought food packaging wasn't battle rated? Yet, if Angus was right, food would be forthcoming. Coffee if he was lucky. If not, they'd be on salted nuts for a few days. There were worse fates.

When Matt didn't reply, Suma added, "If we go on half-rations, you have to be the one to listen to Angus complain."

"Oy!"

Matt smiled. "You saying you wouldn't complain?"

"I'll tell you what you can eat. You can—"

"ACTIVE SCAN DETECTED. AND ANOTHER."

"Where from?" Matt asked.

"I'm not sure," Riviera said.

Chan cut in. "We need to go active. They know we're here, or why suddenly start scanning?"

"You're right, Chan. Bring us up."

Matt waited as the tank slowly filled with further detail. Micro satellites winked into existence, a vast array of units, fantastically dense for open space. There would be as much chance to sneak in as for him to silently walk over hot coals. He'd seen that at a team building exercise and refused to have a go—he wasn't an idiot. Anytime you were walking on fire for your employers, you weren't doing it right.

"The satellites aren't doing the scan," Riviera said, highlighting the sources on the tank.

"HE IS CORRECT. THERE ARE TWO SIGNATURES APPROACHING. FAINT READINGS SUGGEST THE PRESENCE OF MORE OBJECTS."

"Chan, warm everything up, but don't get trigger happy. Remember, we're after information."

"I know what I'm doing."

It didn't take long to build up details on the advancing vessels. Both were approaching from Angus's Brass Monkey (which did have a yellowish tinge) adding to Artemis's own acceleration in their direction. Each were thirty-thousand tonnes, give or take. Warships, despite their tonnage. Artemis had nothing like them in his database.

"I'm receiving an incoming link request."

"Thanks, Samantha. Let's say hi."

"Putting it up."

"*Identify yourself.*" A grizzled woman dressed in a loose uniform issued the hostile command. Grey squares of different shades overlapped, blending her outline into a pale, smoky background. Artemis flashed a note up on his display: they were manipulating the image to hide the inside of her vessel. Matt turned down the option to do the same as soon as Artemis offered on his display.

Frowning, Matt lent forward. "Why don't you?"

"Don't be stupid. Let me do this," Angus said.

"No. You can wait until we have some trust here. This isn't your show."

The woman patiently waited. Matt would bet a thousand credits she was laughing inside. Damn Angus. The initiative was lost now. He sighed and began again, ignoring his crew's gazes. Go, Matt, Space Captain extraordinaire.

"Good morning. I am Captain Matthew Kander of the Artemis. Hero of the rebellion, apparently, and I've come here for some answers."

"I didn't believe the readouts." Her harsh expression softened. *"Well, well, well, Mr Kander. You are a bit of a surprise. A good surprise. We knew the Empire hadn't run off with the Utopia. It would have been plastered all over the sheets — a perfect propaganda tool."*

"Yet, you don't seem to have had the same problem. Shall I assume all the tales of me wandering round the sector, battling the Empire is your work?"

"That is something best discussed in person. I invite you to come aboard."

Fat chance.

"Unfortunately, we find ourselves without a shuttle. However, if you want to drop over for a visit, you are welcome."

Matt noticed a flicker on his display. No wonder the rebel wasn't worried about the size of Artemis. They had a whole fleet round the planet. Several dozen of them. Angus had walked them into an ant nest.

"Invitation accepted."

———

"I wish we had some weapons," Chan griped as they waited at the shuttle deck. The large doors were open and landing lights indicated Bay 3. They waited in the command centre, though

Artemis had already helped them start the docking routine. Samantha would be tracking the arrival from the bridge, and Suma was preparing welcome snacks.

"Don't be daft. You'd shoot yourself in the foot," Angus said dismissively.

It was hard to blame Chan for the thought. They were pretty vulnerable, despite standing inside a massive vessel with lasers that could vaporise the incoming shuttle.

Artemis put it in better terms. "I DO NOT FEEL COMFORT-ABLE WITH THIS. THERE ARE SIGNIFICANT QUESTIONS ABOUT OUR POSITION."

"You and me both, Artemis. We'll play along and see. We have to know what the situation really is, who the rebels really are. Otherwise, we're whistling in the dark. Keep strong," Matt said.

"ACKNOWLEDGED," Artemis said without conviction.

The shuttle nestled into the guiding arms and was slowly brought down to the bay floor. It was sleek, clearly capable of atmospheric entry and significantly larger than the one they'd been given—and promptly lost. A docking tube stretched out, adjusted its angle, then attached to the side. Lights flashed round the circumference before settling on green. Chan hit the pressurise option, and, as a group, they made their way down to the embarking hall.

It wasn't long before the guests arrived, slipping out of the tube with practised ease. There were four of them, including the captain he'd seen before. Two were armed with snub-nosed weapons, dull grey in colour and pointed down. That had to count for something.

"Welcome aboard. This is Chan, Riviera and Angus." His voice didn't break. Well done, Matt.

The Captain locked eyes with him. "Pleased to meet you. I

am Captain Kell Nicshchild. May I introduce Lieutenant Commander Anand and Specialists Garcia and Jones."

Matt didn't want to know what Garcia and Jones were specialists in, but it all seemed polite so far. Anand looked friendly enough, certainly relaxed in his stance. Garcia and Jones were different. Both women gripped their weapons with practised ease, but their eyes darted round, examining every door and display. Not to mention their arms were probably larger than his thighs.

"Alrighty. Uh, if you'll come with us, we have a room set up with food and drinks. We can talk there."

"Are there only four of you? This is a lot of vessel to have managed with so few."

"It's not just the four of us." Matt was unwilling to give more details.

Matt took them through a direct route and kept his mouth shut as the visitors ogled Artemis. His heart skipped a beat: his first impression was wrong. Yes, they looked around, but not like tourists. The reality was more disconcerting; there was a comfortable familiarity. The 'guests' seemed to know where the g-shafts were, slowing before reaching the lobby. Their thorough visual inspections of each passing room resembled cops inspecting a crime scene.

The meeting room was close to the bridge.

"Have a seat," Matt offered as they entered.

The Captain and Lieutenant Commander obliged, but the two specialists stood, one inside, the other outside.

"We're here on an act of faith, not carelessness," the Captain said, apparently noticing Matt's concern.

"MATT, THERE ARE..." Artemis was barely audible.

"Shh," Matt whispered. "You're the ace up our sleeve."

Once both the guests and Matt's crew were settled, Suma left his position by a table to one side and offered drinks. Matt had once admitted feeling uncomfortable about being served, but Suma was insulted by the idea. He made it clear that his role in the crew was damn important and Matt better remember it. Finally, Matt could see it. Suma, with little gestures, confirmation of drinks and a calm demeanour, brought civility to the situation, boosting Matt's confidence. And he'd done wonders with the last remnants of the food store.

"So here we are," he started. His first desire was to tell Angus to shift sides, but it would come out soon enough. "Why don't you start? Tell us a little bit about your *rebellion* against the Commonwealth."

Nicshchild gave a tight grin. She knew he knew. Or did he just think that?

"There is no rebellion. The Empire of Ardon is engaged in a draining stasis-war with the Southern Confederation, resulting in unprecedented build up of forces for a conflict that does not arrive. They have been subverting or invading smaller nations to feed their war machine. Yet, while their fleet grows ever larger, so does the Confederation's, redoubling the hunger and continuing the cycle. Every time the Empire invades, there is a different context, a different excuse: coming to the aid of a neighbour, stopping piracy on inter-system routes, fighting terrorism—these and more. Our government decided the Commonwealth will not be swallowed: we will fight back."

It gelled with Angus's account and certainly portrayed the Commonwealth as the righteous side, but he still had questions.

She continued. "We knew the time was coming, has come. The Empire is incredibly powerful, but finely balanced. This vessel is part of the solution, the result of many years of clandestine research and development. Arcadia—the lead ship of this class—is the only other survivor, and we have nothing else close to their three-hundred-thousand-tonne power. They're not enough. The loss of their dock mates is a terrible blow, but they're a beginning. We will succeed."

Matt heard the intake of breath from his crew. At least Angus's heads up had prepared him. And the cause made some sense. The Empire's contention with the Confederation was a background to everyday life, something foreign, out there, abstract. Yet, why should it affect the Commonwealth *now*? Astropolitics was way above his pay grade. He wasn't even getting paid. A problem for another time. *Focus*. The questions that mattered were much closer to home.

"If you're all pro Commonwealth, then why the hell destroy your own ships? Why destroy the docks and kill innocent people?" Matt watched her carefully, searching for signs of hesitation or outright dishonesty.

"The Empire was slowly infiltrating our operations. We had to test aspects of our tech on production vessels. That or a hundred other potential sources twigged their interest. Unfortunately, the Empire was pushing hard for access. We hoped to contain the damage and start again with the knowledge gained. At the time, it was reasonable to green light the scuttling of the Arcadia hulls, a simple calculation that would have worked if it wasn't for the Empire invading our space. We gambled and lost. However, despite the theatrics, the docks are still mostly intact, ready for when we recapture Aries.

"You would have killed us as part of that scuttling performance, wouldn't you?" Chan practically spat the words. "Fuck you."

"A necessary casualty. War is not a pretty game."

"And what about me?" Matt demanded. "What twisted set of decisions had you guys pissing all over my life?"

Nicshchild laughed in his face. "I've read your file. You are a parasite, a hopeless loser drifting through life. We did you a favour and gave you a purpose. If the scuttling wasn't needed, you would have been killed attempting a terrorist act—a disgruntled, unemployed nobody. And the Commonwealth would be seen keeping the rebels under control, weakening the Empire's public pressure. That is not how events moved. Instead, the engines of fate have brought you to us, even more valuable than imagined. But thanks must be appropriately given. Specialist Angus Caird, well done. You have succeeded well beyond your role and with such meagre 'resources'. I look forward to your full report."

The cold logic burnt in his chest. While his crew spoke angrily—at Angus, Matt or Nicshchild, he didn't know—Matt tried his best to hate her, but she was right. He had been a drifting loser, a parasite. He wasn't now. He had his self-respect. His life, and sure as hell the lives of his crew, meant something.

"I NEED—"

He'd get to Artemis in a moment. Right now, Matt needed to tell Nicshchild how it was.

"Quiet, guys. Please," Matt asked. Silence. He looked to Angus, saw a stony face and turned to Nicshchild. "I'm here, and Artemis is here because of our crew. These are good people. We've fought together, even with your damn spy. We've done what your propaganda only pretended."

"Don't be so foolish. The Commonwealth Space Force has been running a guerrilla campaign against the Empire. You were merely a smokescreen to cover our activities and act as a symbol to maintain courage. And that is how you are going to serve us. You will be a movie star, Mr Kander. The Butcher of Aries who has seen the error of his ways and brought the rebels along to save the Commonwealth. I'm sure it will be very moving. I can't wait until your heroic death."

Matt stood. He'd had enough of this nonsense. Rebels or Commonwealth, it didn't matter.

"Get the hell off our ship. Artemis isn't yours, and neither are we."

As soon as he said it, fear crept into his anger. He wasn't the only one at risk. His crew were unknown, could be taken and thrown away with no ramifications.

Suma came to his side. "I concur." It was a buttress, stronger than diamond.

Riviera pushed his chair back and rose. "Matt's more of a captain than you will ever be."

Chan grimaced. A strange expression followed, but he couldn't interpret it. She didn't move. "I'm not happy. I don't like being a stooge, but I'm not a spacer. I'm a steward—not even a qualified one. Lady, I don't care what you do, but I want to get the hell off this vessel of lunatics."

Matt flinched. His limbs went weak. How could she say that? Her problem was with him, surely not Artemis? She hated Matt that much? His mind reeled. Chan may as well have swung a chair at his head.

Nichschild arched an eyebrow toward Chan. "That will happen, eventually. Now, I have work to do on the bridge. You will have to excuse me." She pushed back her chair.

Matt crossed his arms. "You're not going anywhere except the shuttle bay,"

Nicshchild straightened her jacket, casually and with unnecessary care. "You don't understand. You are so far out of your league. We already have the bridge. Utopia is home."

CHAPTER 23

M att had never been in jail before—or *the brig* as the spacers called it when they marched him down along with Suma, Riviera and Chan. They'd stuck Chan in a separate cell, and she hadn't responded to any of Riviera's subsequent questions or insults. He bit his lip. Damn her. She was certainly happy enough to talk when the guards led her away for questioning. Was she betraying him, or had he failed her? Or was it nothing to do with him at all? She couldn't be an Empire spy. Matt wouldn't let Angus play with his head.

The room was barely large enough to fit them all: four beds in a twin bunk arrangement. A toilet at the far end consumed valuable floor space. The lights were protected by mesh—a thicker version blocked the front, and, as Matt found out the hard way, it possessed a serious charge of energy.

"Artemis?" he tried again.

Suma shifted on his bunk. "I don't know why you're bothering. There were no replies the past five thousand times. We're stuck here alone and need to accept it."

"I know, I know. I keep thinking about what they've done to him. Has he been wiped? We sat there talking to them while it happened. Sipping tea. That wasn't your fault, Suma. I'm not saying it was. Let's face it; the blame is mine. I thought with Artemis, we had some pull, that we could make a difference, that we counted. More fool I. And Samantha. She's either running round the ship, exhausted and alone, or they've already killed her."

"Is that what they're going to do to us?" Riviera asked. "If they do, I'm going to fight back. I won't let them take me easy. You won't either, right, Matt?"

Matt shrugged. "No, I won't. They'll kill us just the same, though. Then again, I think I'm up for the whole drugged or mind probed or whatever until I'm all yay rebels or Commonwealth or whatever the hell they want me to be. Balls, it'll be the whole re-education-camp routine. There won't be a Matt at the end of it. I'll be a dribbling vegetable." He rubbed his eyes. "I'm sorry, guys."

"It's hardly your fault," Suma said. Matt couldn't live with them believing that. Time to own up.

"Angus told me he worked for the rebels. He told me they were here. That's why we came in where we did. I wanted to talk to them. That's what I told myself. I've been thinking about why I went along. I didn't want to hang around waiting to pick up stray broadcasts. We didn't have the food for it either, but I could have done something different. And, to tell the truth, I was afraid of what Angus would do, that he might turn violent."

"You should have said something. How could you have known about them and not told us?" Riviera backed into the rear wall. "I don't get it. You were the one keeping everything honest. Cards laid out. That's why I trusted you... and you held back?"

Matt leant his head into his hands. He wanted to explain the threat Angus planted into his mind, that Matt bought, that let him get distracted from the situation. It was impossible to admit: *Oh, sorry, Riviera. I was worried you were a murdering psycho spy* — perfect.

"Yeah. I'm not proud —"

A swish indicated company. Through the doors came Garcia and Jones, not the usual guards who brought meals. They had changed uniforms to Commonwealth white and green but were still armed with the same guns. They wore bored, slack expressions. *We're just here to take out the trash*, Matt imagined one grunting.

"You, Kander. Up. The rest of you, to the back," Jones said as they reached the cell. She had a heavy Falco accent: each word was clipped.

"And good morning to you," Matt said. He looked at his companions. "I should have done better. You have the right to be angry."

A panel of mesh slid up. Matt walked out. There was little point in resisting, yet. He'd only look like a tool if they dragged him away.

"In here," Jones said when the pair had escorted him a short distance.

Plain bulkheads reflected the light strips above. The room they led him to was empty. He turned round on reaching the centre and listened to the dull echo of footsteps.

"What now?"

"You might appointment with Captain. She very busy."

Well, Jones certainly wasn't moonlighting as a poet. He wondered if she broke out of crèche as a young child and was brought up on the streets by stray beetles, then decided it was better not to ask.

"Apparently, I have all the time in the world, myself. So where is she?"

Garcia handed her weapon to Jones. "Oh, you're not going to see her now. That would be a terrible waste of her time. If you saw her now, you might get all brave and not do as she orders. If the techs can't shutdown the matrix, you're going to be in demand. So, let's get to work."

"What do you mean?" Matt wished he could lean on something. The empty room pressed in on him. In the open, he was oddly vulnerable, practically naked. The exposure cut into his confidence, leaving him hollow.

Garcia removed her jacket, revealing a short-sleeved top that emphasised her muscles. I have to get fit, Matt thought. I'm out of my league.

"Chan already revealed you shut down the higher functions of the AI. If the techs can't reset it, you will."

What? Shutdown higher functions? What was she on about? Hadn't their techs turned off Artemis?

Garcia poked him in the chest. "Think carefully, Matt. You need to do this for your nation." She punched him hard.

His breath exploded. He doubled over, stumbled then collapsed, landing hard.

"Some people take a bit of encouragement. You ask them nicely and then they get stubborn. We don't have time for that. There is a war to be won. You are going to cooperate."

Matt groaned then pushed himself up onto an elbow. "I never said I wouldn't."

"I'm not going to take that risk."

She kicked the back of his thigh. Shock marched down his leg: the pain sharp as a dog bite. He rolled half onto his stomach, and she added another to his kidney. Electricity raced through his nerves, stiffening his spine. Acid burnt his throat while his flaccid lungs cried for air. It only grew worse.

He couldn't follow what she did: he just felt pain spiking across his limbs, his face, his shoulders, everywhere. Blood dribbled from above a swollen eye as he tried to curl into a ball. It didn't help. He was dragged, punched, elbowed and possibly bitten as his world shrank into terror and agony.

It took time to realise it had stopped. The hard floor felt cool, its surface numbing his pulverised flesh.

"You know, Jones, I think I've gotten his attention. What about you?"

"Yes."

"Right, Matthew Kander. Here is how it's going to be. I want you to listen really carefully, because this is going to be very important to you. If you are called upon to assist, you will do as you are told. You will shutdown, unlock or whatever you are asked to do. You will not do anything except for what you are asked. I want you to know that we will not kill you. If you are in any way a problem, you will be my personal punching bag. I will hang you up and beat you until your arms tear free. Then, I will have your arm sockets sealed, turn you over and repeat the process until your legs do the same. Have I been clear?"

Through the haze of pain, Matt knew he should be strong, but he couldn't. He wasn't a hero from the sheets, able to take a beating, delivering a smart line before fighting his way free. He was too afraid. He was too weak: a husk of humanity.

"Have I been clear?"

"Yes," he said hoarsely.

"Will you do as you're told?"

"Yes."

She kicked him again. His head hit the floor, bringing a rising wave of nausea that culminated in retching.

"Good. I'll let you know if you are needed."

The door swished shut.

CHAPTER 24

P ain lanced every single nerve across his body. Drifting in
and out of consciousness, he lost track of time. That it
passed at all was only proven by the desiccation of his fluids.
Finding the willpower to move proved a slow process. Heart-
beats stretched onward, shaking his chest and sending quivers
down his fingers. The tips jerked like worms escaping flooded
soil. After an age, they tensed and released at his command.
Eventually, against every internal warning, he rolled over and
rested on his knees, head dejectedly low.

"Artemis," he whispered without thinking. "Artemis."

"I AM HERE." The AI was quiet, almost distant.

It was something to cling to. "You're all right. That's good."

Matt couldn't continue talking. His lungs fought every
shallow inhalation.

"I DISAGREE WITH YOUR CHARACTERISATION. RIGHT NOW,
MOST OF MY RESOURCES ARE OCCUPIED KEEPING MYSELF
HIDDEN WHILE BLOCKING AN ATTEMPT TO ERASE ME."

"Sorry, you're right. We're both screwed. Chan said they'd
done something to you, that they'd shut down some of your
functions."

"MISINFORMATION TO LIMIT THEIR AVENUES OF ATTACK."

Matt let it go; he didn't have the capacity to think it through.

"I don't suppose you can help me?"

A minute passed. An eon. He selfishly willed Artemis to be safe.

"YOU AGREED TO HELP KILL ME."

Geez, Matt thought. Had he? It was hard to remember what happened, but it sounded like him.

"I would have said anything. They were hurting me, Artemis. I don't know how to explain it. You don't feel pain, but for us humans, it can be overwhelming. Our whole body is telling us to make it stop. It burns in our minds. It made me helpless. Right now, I can barely think. You don't know what it took for me to get up."

"I RECEIVED MESSAGES WHEN MY OUTER SHELL WAS DAMAGED. EACH SENSOR PUSHED PRIORITY WARNINGS. HUNDREDS OF THOUSANDS OF THEM. I BELIEVE I KNOW PAIN." Hurt etched Artemis's tone.

"I didn't think. I'm trying. I've never been good at anything. I should have thought of that. I just wanted to know what was going on. I didn't want this to happen."

He was thoroughly wretched. It never even occurred to him that a machine could feel pain, even an AI like Artemis. They were meant to be the scary story at bedtime or the warning about doing the right thing. Care for others, show some empathy or you'll be no better than a computer.

"YOU WANTED TO KNOW. YOU DID NOT ASK ME WHAT I WANTED."

"I—" Matt stopped. What Artemis wanted? He gave the crew the chance to leave. He'd never even asked Artemis. "I'm sorry."

"DON'T SAY YOU ARE SORRY. YOU HAVE WORN OUT THAT WORD."

Matt crawled to a bulkhead and stood. The surface shifted, or his grip did, and he needed to lean heavily to keep his balance.

"What do you want?"

Extended silence.

"I WANT YOU TO ASK IN FUTURE. THIS IS MY BODY."

That was why humanity's ancestors had given up on AI. They made the machines, and then the machines didn't want to play the assigned part. Balls, what did they know? Screw them.

"You're right. We should be asking, not telling you. I've used you."

"TO BE FAIR, I HAVE USED YOU AS WELL," Artemis said with a little warmth.

"Hey? What do you mean?" Matt demanded. His vision grew dark, and his legs weakened. Stay calm.

"YOU ARE IN NEED OF MEDICAL ATTENTION," Artemis said softly.

"I don't think anyone cares."

The AI didn't respond. Eventually, Matt slid back to the ground, thinking of a cold glass of water.

A loud klaxon went off. Red lights flashed. More damn red lights! If he could just rest for a while, he'd feel better.

In a dead tone, Artemis repeated, "FIRE DETECTED. FIRE DETECTED, 70E21. FIRE DETECTED. FIRE DETECTED, 70E21."

A strong grip on his shoulder. Words.

"Come on. Get up. You can't stay here."

Matt tried to push the hand away. Instead, he was yanked to his feet.

"Don't make me carry you. You're covered in vomit."

It was a guard. *Kassimo* read the patch above his rank. The guard shoved him out the door, leaving him to stumble into the bulkhead opposite.

"A false alarm, I think. Should I take this guy to the infirmary? He looks like he's been Garcia-d."

The guard was talking to someone else, but Matt didn't want to raise his head; it was too hard.

"Nah, clean him up. I don't even know if the meds have the clinic together yet. I'll watch the room until we get an engineer down."

Cleaning up consisted of being taken to the brig shower room and getting hosed down as he lay on the floor. The water pounded him in a barely more-gentle re-enactment of Garcia. Red spread then drained into a grid of tiny holes. Matt wished he too could be washed away, to slide down the holes and be lost as his molecules gently dispersed. It was a foolish hope. There was no freedom, no waste on a spacecraft. His fluids would be processed, separated and recycled: his essence reborn as a spare rivet for Artemis. They'd be blood relatives. A brief snigger transformed into a coughing fit.

"Dry yourself and put these on. Move it."

The voice was insistent, repetitive. "Get up. Come on. Move it. Watch out. Sit there."

Matt patted vaguely with the provided towel and waited for the fog in his mind to clear. Prodded one more time, he struggled into a grey top and trousers—he was dressed as a rebel. The universe hated him. Screwing with Matt had to be a damn national pastime. International. Universal?

———

Back in the cell, Riviera stared. Suma, ever practical, arranged every thin pillow and blanket in the cell to form a seat. Matt gingerly leaned back into it.

"Do you like my makeover?" he joked.

"Are you okay?" Riviera asked. Was Matt already forgiven? Riviera was hardly one to hold a grudge.

"You should see the other guy's fist. I bet she put it on ice. That'll teach her a lesson."

"Here's our boy." It was Garcia. Matt flinched. Not again. Not so soon. A tear escaped.

"Looks like you're needed after all. I do love it when hard work isn't wasted, right, Jones?"

Jones peered through the mesh and gave a nasty smile. "Next time, my go."

Riviera came to the front. "You can't have him."

Garcia laughed. "Down, puppy. He's going to see the captain. I'm sure she'll treat him all gentle like. Now step back or I'll blow a hole through your puffed out chest."

"Riviera. Don't. I'm fine," Matt managed. When Riviera didn't back down, Matt squeezed his arm. "I'll be fine. Let's pick our battles. This isn't it."

True to her word, Garcia and Jones took him to the bridge. He stumbled at the pace they demanded, cringed at every shove. Gone were the silent corridors. They were hardly crowded, but spacers in Commonwealth green and white stepped out of the way, some carrying tools, others pushing skiffs of hard-shelled boxes. A guilty thought whispered this was how it was meant to be. Matt had only been a temporary guardian.

More tears flowed when he saw the leopard, the deer and woman. He never even had a chance to ask Artemis how the symbol was changed. At least these bastards hadn't gotten round to wiping it clean. It wasn't their vessel yet.

The bridge doors opened. A few consoles were occupied,

but the majority of people — techs — were congregating round a wall where panels had been removed. A variety of equipment lay strewn across the floor with cables snaking up to chrome sockets in the open cavity.

Nicschild was in Matt's captain's seat and Anand looked up from amongst the techs.

"Welcome back," Nicschild said. "It turns out you can serve the Commonwealth earlier than expected. Anand, if you please?"

"Yes, Ma'am. Mr Kander, whatever you have done to the Utopia AI matrix, we need you to undo it, now."

"Artemis. This is the Artemis," Matt said.

The punch was swift, measured and hurt like hell.

"Why did you put an AI in anyway?" Matt continued. "If that came to light, it wouldn't take the Empire to send everything to shit; every person in the Commonwealth would lynch you."

Nicschild circled round the holotank until she stood right in front on him. She wasn't tall. It didn't matter. Her presence was intense, her confidence total.

"Do you want me to tell you any other state secrets?"

Ah, Matt thought. Right, it was probably a bit much to hope for.

"Undo whatever you have done to the AI matrix — now."

Matt looked at the techs, the holotank, his chair. His bravado was hanging by a thread, dangling from a branch of 'please don't hurt me'.

"No," he managed.

The slap sent his head reeling. Garcia or Jones, he couldn't tell which, held him upright. The slap, though, that came from Nicschild.

"Let's try that again. Give me access to the matrix."

"No," Matt whispered.

"I can't hear you. Give me access to the matrix."

"No." Matt tried to put a scrap of energy into his defiance.

"Wrong. Answer."

A flicker on the holotank caught his gaze until Nicschild followed up with a backhander. So much for treating him gently.

"Captain. You need to see this."

Blood coated his mouth, its sweet tang focusing his mind. Nicschild was already looking at the tank.

"Give me details," she demanded.

"Jump signatures. Out six-hundred gigametres. Fifteen sources."

"Empire?" she asked.

"It doesn't say. I'm doing some manual cross-referencing."

"Hurry up. Get me a link to the Admiral as well." She turned to Matt. "We'll continue this later. Garcia, Jones. This time, make sure he's cooperative."

He'd done it now. He'd stood by his friend. At least Artemis's fate was out of his hands—until the next time.

"Confirmation of Empire vessels by deflector harmonics. Three battle cruisers, five light cruisers and seven that might be destroyers or frigates."

"Sound general quarters. I want Utopia ready. Do everything manually if you have to."

"But we don't have—"

She cut off the speaker. "We won't have anything if we let them take this system."

The bridge doors closed as Jones shoved him along the bridge corridor. By the time they reached the g-shaft, a klaxon rang out.

"You embarrassed me. You made me look bad, and that hurts my feelings. I'm very unhappy with you." Garcia shook her head dramatically. "Jones, remember that he needs to be alive with a functional mouth at the end."

Jones grinned. The shaft doors opened, and Matt was shoved inside. He caught himself on a handhold and swallowed bile. He couldn't take much more of this. If Jones screwed up, he might not have to. The prospect was seductive.

CHAPTER 25

The g-shaft capsule descended.

A whisper. "HOLD TIGHT."

"What?" Garcia managed before the shaft halted unexpectedly.

Matt squeezed the handhold and closed his eyes. Could he just be allowed to get from point A to point B without getting shoved, knocked or shaken like a cocktail? The shaft accelerated upwards, thrusting him down.

"HOLD TIGHTER."

He gripped as though his life depended on it. The capsule stopped. It didn't slow; it just stopped. His arms stretched. His shoulders cracked, almost wrenched out of their sockets, as his legs were pitched upward. Jones and Garcia fared worse. They both slammed into the ceiling with sickening thuds then fell back down, an unmoving jumble of limbs.

The capsule dropped again, this time smoothly. As Matt dragged himself upright, the capsule pinged, and the shaft doors opened.

Chan pointed a gun at him. His muddled mind tried to make sense of her action. Was she here to execute him?

"Get out, quickly!" she shouted.

Out of the rehydrator, into the jaws. He put up his hands and stumbled forwards. Chan raised her gun, closed her eyes and fired.

His bones crackled. No, it was the plasma rifle. He turned. Garcia dropped, her gun tumbling out of a limp hand.

"We have to move," Chan said, grabbing his arm.

"You shot at me with your eyes closed!" Matt complained.

"Don't be such a baby, Captain. As if you'd do a better job."

It made no sense. "But you wanted to get out of here. What are you doing?"

She waved the gun emphatically. "We're doing this *now*? I was looking for opportunities, and if we left Artemis, we wouldn't be back. The best way to manage someone used to getting their own way—demand the opposite. I learnt that from group work in college."

"You don't want to be off?"

"Of course not. You should know me better than that."

Matt wrinkled his brow. "Huh? I don't think I... Oh. Actually, that sort of makes sense if I don't think about it too hard."

"Are we done?"

"Not yet. How did you get free?" Matt asked, unable to let it lie.

"Artemis. I was going to use a swiped access chip, but Artemis had a better plan. Now, come on. We have to help the others."

He flinched back, unwilling to be touched. She frowned and started moving. Any further explanation would have to wait.

"Not so fast," Matt begged. "I can't do it. Slow down."

Chan looked him over and pulled up one of his sleeves, revealing dark bruises. She lifted his top.

"Nasty, but it doesn't change anything. You got us into this mess; you're going to get us out."

She started away, this time slower. Matt clenched his teeth and followed. They took a circuitous route to the brig, hiding in rooms or darting (shuffling for Matt) into other corridors as instructed by Artemis. And yet, when they reached the brig, it was unguarded.

"Matt, Chan?" Riviera said as they arrived. "How?"

"They've escaped. It's obvious if you think about it," Suma said. "The door, if you don't mind."

Matt put his hand on the opening sensor. It blipped red.

"THE BRIG HAS BEEN REMOVED FROM MY NETWORK."

Chan slipped a chip out of her pocket and slotted it in next to the sensor. "Huh. It did come in handy."

She touched the door release, and the mesh opened. Great, they were almost together again. Except, it was all too easy. Where were the guards or any of the other spacers? If an unexpected turn of events resembled good news for Matt, he knew it was an omen of imminent doom.

"What now?" Riviera asked.

"We need to get Samantha. Artemis where is she?"

"HER PRESENT LOCATION IS UNKNOWN."

That could be good or all types of bad. "We have to search for her. If she's still alive…"

"Then she will still be alive for a while. Which is more than I can say for us if we stay here," Suma said, indicating the cell.

The man had a point. The brig was the last place to hash out a plan. They moved, Artemis again playing guide, leading them down the length of the vessel until he was satisfied no Commonwealth forces were nearby. Twice they paused and waited for Matt to regain his strength.

"Through here." Suma led them into an unused galley overlooking a canteen. "There won't be any food, but there'll be running water."

Matt followed him to a sink and drank deeply, letting the cool weight settle in his core. Suma watched closely, until Matt managed to join the others at a table, sighing as he sat down. It wasn't the captain's chair, but it was infinitely better than standing. Appeased, Suma disappeared.

"Well, at least we don't have to worry about a fake fleet of Emps, right, Artemis? That was a slick way to get me out. I owe you."

"THE FLEET IS REAL. IT WAS A BETTER DISTRACTION THAN MY ORIGINAL PLAN," Artemis admitted.

"The fleet is real? Damn. I knew it. I knew it. We're the least of Nicschild's problems."

"Whoa. What is this about a fleet?" Riviera's eyes were wide.

"When I was up on the bridge, they detected jumps. I thought it was a diversion when Chan turned up. Artemis, what's happening with those Empire guys?"

"APPROXIMATELY HALF ARE HEADING SUNWARD, TOWARDS THE SYSTEM CAPITAL, CALHAVEN. THE OTHERS ARE ON A DIRECT COURSE TOWARDS BRASS MONKEY."

"Brass Monkey?" Suma asked while lifting a red and yellow striped box—the universal medical design—onto the table.

"I don't want stims." Matt frowned.

"Fine, but you will have the analgesics."

"I don't need—"

"You will have the analgesics."

"All right, all right. You win. What was I saying?"

"Brass Monkey," Suma offered while pressing a translucent cylinder against Matt's arm. It clicked once as molecules were forced through his skin under high pressure. Relief spread rapidly.

"Brass Monkey is Brassma, Prodita-L," Matt said. Nicknames were one of those things, only sounding cool when spoken by people with the knack. Artemis didn't have it, nor did Matt.

"Oh."

"Anyway..." Matt tapped his nails on the table.

"ANYWAY... THE COMMONWEALTH FORCES ARE SEEKING TO INTERCEPT. TWO THIRDS OF THEIR FLEET IS OUT OF SYSTEM, ACCORDING TO THEIR ADMIRAL. THE IN-SYSTEM VESSELS HAVE BEEN SPLIT. THOSE ON PATROL HAVE BEEN DIRECTED TO CALHAVEN. THE REST ARE ASSEMBLING TEN GIGAMETRES OUT FROM BRASSMA. I HAVE BEEN FORCED TO JOIN THIS TASKGROUP."

"This is wrong. We should be on the bridge. They don't know Artemis like we do." Riviera's hands balled into fists. It was a relief to hear him say it. Chan hadn't wanted to leave either. They had to feel like Matt did, to feel that connection.

"We can hardly shoot our way onto the bridge," Suma said.

Chan gave him a sour smile. "I've already killed for our fearless leader over here. I'm never going to get that out of my head, but I won't let it count for nothing. We have to give this a go."

"Hold up. We're getting ahead of ourselves. The question is: what would we do even if we have control?" Matt said. "If we're going to do something crazy, let's do it deliberately."

"We have to help against the Empire, don't we?" Riviera asked.

Chan and Suma agreed, but they all turned to Matt. He felt their eyes on his bruises, his cuts, his dishevelled hair and unshaven face. He must be the least inspiring captain in the history of humankind.

"What say you, Artemis?"

"I DO NOT LIKE THE WAY I HAVE BEEN TREATED. I DO NOT LIKE THE WAY YOU HAVE BEEN TREATED. I DO NOT LIKE WHAT THEY ARE TRYING TO DO TO ME. IS THIS COMMONWEALTH WORTH OUR LIVES?"

"We're not talking certain death, right? I would have said 'yes' easily before all of this. Well, anytime back to a couple of weeks ago. Now? They have a hell of a lot to answer for. I don't know." Matt teetered in indecision, examining his abused hands. Cold logic or emotion, what mattered the most? In the end, he knew it had to be both. "It's not perfect, but it was my home. Balls, I think so. These bastards aren't the whole Commonwealth any more than we are. I won't let the actions of those damn spacers poison me."

"IF YOU ARE MY CREW, I WILL FIGH —"

The lights dimmed before flickering to life once again.

"Artemis, what was that?"

There was no response. They looked at each other across the table. It couldn't be. Not now, not like this.

"What's happened?" Riviera asked.

Matt stood, ignoring his body's weakness. "They've been hacking Artemis, trying to shut him down. Believe me, if they've done anything to him, I'll kill every last one of them."

"So what do we do?" Chan's fingers slid towards her gun.

"Chan, Suma, Riviera. We take back our damn ship … vessel. Are you with me?"

CHAPTER 26

A man with grease-smeared hands tapped the console. Up in the command centre, he would have a view of the shuttle bays and the four craft that rested in cradles. If he turned round, the view would be somewhat different, Matt thought as he peeked round a corner. A susurrus behind set him on edge. Couldn't they stay quiet for a minute? Riviera clomped around like he wore mag-boots. Suma waited patiently, but Chan kept shifting round, trying to watch all directions at once. Impatience gnawed at Matt, but he couldn't let unnecessary risks destroy their only chance, and he knew with certainty there would be only one.

"I'm going to recompress the bay air. Are you clear, Walt?" the engineer asked.

"Clear. Visual check negative. I'm heading off."

The voice on the comm was gruff, but 'Walt' was going. Matt allowed himself a grim smile. It was about time they caught a break. The engineer tapped again, setting off a klaxon. They all jumped, startled. Yellow lights flashed throughout the bays, bathing the command centre in a warm glow.

"Now," Matt said.

Chan approached the engineer. "Lift those hands high, right now."

The engineer turned in his seat.

"Holy shit! What are you doing?"

"What's your name?" Matt asked as casually as he could manage.

"Uh, Cam."

"Well, Cam, we've come to search the lost property box. And what do you know? We've found what we're looking for. Follow me, please. Chan here, she's pretty pissed off, and we're in a rush. I would hate for an accident to happen. Me, I'm used to a nice, safe office. However, I've heard these places have terrible safety issues."

Internally, Matt slapped himself. Talk about laying it on too strong. The guy would think he was a complete loon.

"You can't do this. We're at general quarters. We're going into battle."

The engineer didn't move.

They were running out of time.

"Chan, if Cam here doesn't get up right now, remove his head. I've always wondered what vaporised brains would taste like." He couldn't stop himself; the words just flowed out.

"Happy to oblige." Chan shifted the aim of her gun.

"Okay, okay." The engineer hurried to his feet.

They led him to a storage room. Suma wrapped his wrists with tape they'd found on their way then tapped the accompanying activator, and the tape shrunk. Perfect for securing leaks.

"Ow. That's tight."

"Shut up," Riviera said, helping Suma attach the engineer to a heavy set of shelves. The end result looked like the victim of a giant spider attack.

Matt went back into the command centre and took the engineer's place. He'd been right; shuttles were useless in a space battle, and Nicschild would have to spread her staff thin as it was. The console was still logged in. He noted the shuttle bays were in vacuum, part of a pre-combat checklist, but that wasn't what he was after. Checking the interface, he hurried through options, seeing what he could access.

Shift rotations. That could be useful. He looked through them and found a link to the full list. One-hundred-and-twenty Commonwealth people on-board, another two hundred starting next week. That was a lot, but the majority here looked like techs. Engines, shuttles, containment actuators, software. The last triggered his anger. They better keep their claws off Artemis. Security—fourteen in total, including Garcia and Jones. He pointed to the results.

"That's only three to one. With a bit of surprise, do you think we have a chance?" Riviera asked.

Matt shrugged.

Chan hefted her gun. "We need more weapons."

Which was the real reason for the trip. Matt raced through the shipping records. "Food, Medical. A lot of it is still sitting in transit storage. We might get lucky. Here we go. Sidearms, and there, the destination. Damn! It's been delivered already. Time for another walk."

They moved cautiously, painfully slow, then in rushes, peering down corridors. Rinse and repeat, fight the pain, fight the weakness. Artemis's silence was a hole in Matt's chest. They needed him more than ever. None of them wanted Chan to blast her way through, nor would it help to shout their presence. Instead, it was a nerve-wracking process. With any luck, no one knew they were free—well, free-ish—and that was how it needed to stay.

Finally. They'd found it. A message stencilled on the door left no doubt.

SECURITY PERSONNEL ONLY

That's us, Matt thought. We're Artemis's security. Chan's chip worked again, releasing the door. The large room was clearly an armoury: a series of weapons racks ran down one side, and metal cupboards along another. Riviera kicked aside an empty box. Several littered the floor as though someone had been interrupted while unpacking. One of the racks was empty, its clear cover shattered. Chan tried her chip on the lock of another. Nothing.

"Try your big key," Matt suggested.

She raised her plasma gun and fired. Loud but effective. The dazzling plasma dispersed, revealing a hole in the cover. And a hole in one of the guns. Riviera passed one of the remaining sets to Matt and offered another to Suma.

"No, thanks. I'll come, but I won't kill anyone."

Matt raised his eyebrows in surprise. He'd been counting on all of them. And yet, he understood. Matt had no idea if he could pull a trigger himself.

He squeezed Suma's shoulder. "Fair enough. Do we have any charge cartridges? Stop!" he shouted as Chan pointed her gun at a cupboard. "Do you want to blow us up? Look, that one's open."

The inside was a real mess, but a series of cartridges lay in a dock, indicator lights green. Matt passed them round, fumbled one into his gun and stuffed another couple into pockets. The whole load was surprisingly heavy. He really needed to do some exercise or risk shooting people in the feet.

"Careful where you point that," he said to Riviera, who was pantomiming a gun battle.

"Sorry, Captain."

"Right. We have no time for finesse, nor do we have the skill. We get to the bridge, help Artemis and deal with the Empire. Then we find Samantha. I want you to know ... I want you to know I'm lucky. I'm lucky to have a crew like you.

I couldn't ask for anyone better to be by my side." They were probably going to die. They had no clue what they were doing. But they stood with him. He felt special, worthy not due to himself, but because of them.

Chan rolled her eyes. "Can we get on with it?"

They found a body near 40G80. It was dressed in green and white and missing a shoulder and part of the head. Matt quickly looked away.

"Gross. What do you think happened?" Riviera leant down and checked the body. "Still warm."

"It doesn't matter. We don't have time to waste," Chan shut down the conversation before it could start. She was right. He felt sorry for the victim, and, he admitted to himself, Samantha could have been the one behind the trigger. If they were onto her, she'd have the guts to do it. Good for her, he concluded as he carefully stepped over the body.

In a few minutes, they reached the g-shaft. The capsule arrived at their deck, and the doors slid open. This was it. They walked in, turned round and jostled for position. Chan got the front.

"Hello, Captain," Matt pointed out and pushed his way to the doors. "If anyone is going to get blown away when this door opens, it's me."

"Try to be more positive," Suma chided.

There was a chime, and the doors opened. As though in slow motion, Matt took in two guards, one leaning against a bulkhead, the other scratching the back of his or her neck. They both wore helmets and bulky chest armour. He threw aside the questions, the morality, and fired, holding the trigger down. The heat to his sides told him Chan and Riviera were doing the same. The pulses threw the guards down. Matt kept firing, sweeping between the two. Armour puffed, blowing away in chunks and shoving the guards back. Dense ceramic snapped and gave way. Gore sprayed against the walls. Matt couldn't stop. His mouth was frozen in a rictus. His knuckles paled as he continued squeezing the trigger long after the cartridge ran dry. His ears pounded, his arms tingled and his heart screamed. The adrenaline left him giddy.

"Did we get them?" he asked.

"Yeah, we got them, Captain," Riviera said. Matt looked into his wide eyes. Young, Matt thought. Riviera looked so young. He shook his head. Like he was some hardened warrior.

"We will not have the benefit of surprise," Suma noted, urging them forward.

"Balls, you're right. There's nothing to do about it now. We have to keep moving. Spread out, and let me do the talking."

"Mr talky, you might want to change your damn cartridge."

"Uh, yeah. Thanks, Chan."

They walked forward together, ready to save Artemis. The bridge doors opened.

"CONFIRM SHUTDOWN AND ERASE?"

CHAPTER 27

There was no warning. Riviera grunted and fell back while his ruined plasma gun flew out of his hands and bounced at his feet.

"Take cover!" Matt shouted, diving to one side. Agony mushroomed through his flesh as he smashed his shoulder. It served him well, cleared his mind, focused his thoughts. He dragged Riviera to the edge and looked round the lip of the doorway.

"CONFIRM SHUTDOWN AND ERASE?" a bland tone repeated.

Fuck. The techs were still there. Nicschild was by the holotank. All it would take was a word from any of them. A word.

"Cancel!" he shouted.

The air tore as Nicschild fired again. Matt ducked back, losing some of his sleeve to the shot, arm hair crisping with a sulphurous stench.

Chan swept her gun across the door, firing without aiming. Matt stood, daring another look. Sparks exploded, and the holotank shattered, releasing a choking white vapour. Techs ran for any available cover. He jerked his head back and lent against the wall.

"Who are you trying to kill, them or Artemis?" Matt demanded.

"Like you're doing any better. You've already gone through a whole cartridge."

"At least I hit something," Matt retorted. *Whole cartridge.* That's it! He had it. Chan was really going to make him pay for this.

"Chan, throw a cartridge in there."

"What? Why? I'm not doing that."

"Please," he begged.

Chan glared but grabbed a spare from her pocket and lobbed it in under arm. The cartridge arced up high. Matt aimed and held down the trigger. The gun rattled, and ceiling panels dropped, leaving smoking photonics. Nicschild smiled, aimed.

Then he hit the cartridge.

The blast sent Matt spinning, his finger still down, tearing holes until another cartridge was depleted. Dazed and coughing in the acrid air, he stumbled to the bridge.

It was a complete mess of blackened panels, gaping holes and escaping light from piercingly bright fibres. Fire suppression systems sprayed every surface with white ash, painting an apocalyptic winter. Nicschild was down, as were the techs. No —one of them was moving, lifting a pad cabled to the wall. Fuck. He aimed and pulled the trigger—empty.

He could sense it, see the hand. There was no time to swap. His mind reached for every scrap of knowledge, every experience. He remembered when he and Artemis had bonded, though that had been merely technical—their connection was ocean deep now. He remembered the surprise, the curiosity. He remembered the command.

"Resume Artemis Network!"

Sparks sizzled. Powder floated, jostled by ventilation. The

air, a haze of bitter taste, burnt his lungs. The tech turned, saw Matt's gun in his face and dropped the pad.

"WELCOME, CAPTAIN. YOU HAVE THE BRIDGE," Artemis said, his words sluggish.

"Are you all right?"

"I THINK SO. RELOADING FUNCTIONS. PROCESSING."

"Get the fuck out of here," Matt shouted at the tech. He wanted to make them hurt, but Artemis was okay. And his gun was empty.

The tech stumbled away. Shaking, Matt slung his gun over a shoulder and frantically pulled out the cables. He wouldn't let them touch his friend again. Nicschild's body caught his attention. Shredded, misshapen and motionless: her brief reign of terror was over.

"Riviera!" Matt remembered and hurried back.

"I'm good."

Suma was wrapping Riviera's hands with a strip of torn material. Riviera gave a weak smile as Matt knelt.

"My head hurts more than my hands. I'm hoping for a scar —the best way to get dates, I've heard."

Matt groaned. "We'll take you to a bar when all this is over. Right now, there's work to be done. I need you guys at your stations."

Chan gazed at the disaster area formerly known as the bridge.

"Lucky you saved Artemis. Just so you know, don't try to save me. Ever." She pulled Riviera up when Suma was done.

"Perhaps it's not that bad." Matt crossed to the circle of consoles. The tank was completely gone, and several of the smaller displays were mere remnants.

"Here." He found a section that looked more or less intact and brushed off the powder. "I don't know what you're complaining about. I take you to all the best places. Riviera, are your hands functional?"

"I'll manage."

"That's the spirit. Chan, you know what you're doing. Suma, I need you on Comms while Samantha's... wherever she is."

Without waiting for a response, Matt cleared his own chair and sat down. A bite-size chunk was missing from a corner, but the displays were functional.

"Artemis, where do we stand?"

"WOULD YOU LIKE TO KNOW ABOUT THE INTERNAL OR EXTERNAL SITUATION FIRST?" Artemis sounded like his normal self. Cool relief washed through Matt. He'd kiss a bulkhead if it wouldn't scare his crew.

"Ah, internal. Is anyone coming for us?"

"NO ONE IS MOVING TOWARDS THE BRIDGE. THERE ARE SPORADIC PLASMA DISCHARGES ON DECK U. SAMANTHA APPEARS UNHARMED. I AM CONCERNED. SHE IS FREQUENTLY OUTSIDE OF MY SENSOR ARCS. ANGUS APPEARS TO BE PURSUING HER ALONG WITH OTHERS. LIKE MYSELF, HE HAS LOST TRACK OF HER POSITION."

That was something. If she could hold out long enough...

"What about external?"

Artemis spoke quickly with intensity, as though he had been waiting to get it off his chest. "OUR COMMONWEALTH TASKGROUP HAS ENGAGED THE EMPIRE FORCES. OF THE THIRTY-EIGHT CORVETTES INCLUDED, SEVENTEEN HAVE PERISHED. FIFTEEN WITH ALL HANDS. THE EMPIRE GROUP HAS LOST TWO DESTROYERS, LEAVING A BATTLE CRUISER, THREE LIGHT CRUISERS AND A FRIGATE. I AM PRESENTLY COASTING BEHIND THE BATTLE LINE. WITH FULL ACCELERATION, WE CAN BE WITHIN RANGE IN FOUR MINUTES. IT IS LIKELY WE WILL BE TARGETED AS THE COMMONWEALTH FORCES DIMINISH."

"Are you still up for this?" Matt asked.

"AT THIS STAGE, I AM TENTATIVELY INCLINED, YET WE ARE NOT COMMITTED. IF WE ARE TO DO THIS —"

"Then let's do it right."

"YES."

It was insane. The bridge looked ready to be condemned. Chan rested her gun on the seat to one side and creased her brows, intent on details flashing across her display.

"What do you see?" he asked.

"I have a hell of a lot more than six little lasers. There're four batteries, each with eight massive high-frequency lasers — effective out to almost two-million kay. A whole raft of point-defence systems. That's all old news, but..." she paused dramatically.

"But?"

"Missiles. Eighty-four in the magazines. Not the full capacity, but more than the nothing we had before. They can go seven million according to specs. Bad news, Captain. You won't need to fly in the middle and blow us up like before or with that cartridge or in general."

"Um. I think there is an incoming link request," Suma said before Matt could think of a snappy retort.

"THAT IS CORRECT, SUMA. I HAVE HIGHLIGHTED THE DETAILS ON YOUR DISPLAY."

Having adjusted his top right display, Matt considered their position. It didn't take a tactical genius to note how the smaller Commonwealth vessels were being slaughtered with their weaker deflector fields and limited weaponry.

"Riviera, get us heading in. We'll work it out as we go. Chan, shout out when we're in range. Suma, put the link through. We've nothing to lose by talking. Oh, and, Artemis, can you keep that door closed? We don't want any visitors."

"THE DOOR MECHANISM WAS OVERRIDDEN WHEN I WAS ATTACKED. I WILL DISCONNECT POWER TO THE G-SHAFT."

Suma fumbled on his console. Matt tried to wait patiently, squeezing his armrests to stop fidgeting. Finally, a connection came up, audio only.

"This is Admiral Felton-Lin. Captain Nicschild, what happened? Are you operational? We need you in formation now."

The voice was clipped, angry.

"I'm sorry. She's unavailable. Would you like me to take a message?"

"Who on Aries is this?"

"Captain Matthew Kander of the Artemis, at your service."

Riviera grinned and gave a thumbs up. Even Chan smirked.

"Now," Matt said. "We have a reckoning coming up, but that's for later, and if we don't work together, there won't be a later." Silence followed.

Artemis brought up a countdown on the edge of a display, its warm red glow indicating they were swiftly closing on contested space. Chan added some markers with notes on the enemy vessels, and Artemis mirrored them on his display. She drew a few arrows. The Empire vessels were in a great wheel formation with the battle cruiser forming the hub.

Matt nodded to Chan—diving into the centre would be a disaster. Unsure whether Suma had muted while he cobbled together a plan, Matt waved to Riviera and gestured at his display. He followed up with a hand whooshing to the right. Interpretive dancing for the win.

Felton-Lin came to his senses.

"We need the Utopia—the Artemis—it doesn't matter. We need the firepower now. Will you move into position?"

Matt grudgingly gave the man some credit. It couldn't be easy. He glanced at his display. Riviera added a path, glowing green. It was good. Matt nodded in his direction, and Artemis shifted, accelerating down off the system plane.

"We're moving. Pulling down hard to take them on the edge. You need to go up more and concentrate your fire. Keep them busy."

"You have no idea what you're talking about, our strategy —"

"There is no 'our strategy'. You do it my way or go jump." Probably best to leave off that Artemis's crew didn't know what they were doing (including Matt) and would screw up anything more complex. They had been lucky so far. It couldn't last. "We'll send you our path. Good luck."

"Until later."

CHAPTER 28

Artemis crushed the space in front, sending them hurtling forwards. They were all minnows in the vast sea of vacuum, but Matt imagined the enemy coming into view, bristling with weapons and glowing with lidar sweeps. As yet, the Empire left their advance unchallenged.

"I have range on one of the light cruisers, and the frigate won't be long," Chan said. "Do I fire?"

"AT THIS RANGE, THEY WILL HAVE SIGNIFICANT TIME TO RESPOND. I SUGGEST WAITING."

"Yeah. Hold a bit, Chan. We've only got so many."

The enemy vessels were shifting their formation. Missile exchanges charged through space, visible as little blips patiently crawling across the scaled distance with technical readouts glowing above. The Frigate was trying to hide, and it looked like the light cruisers were adjusting, going flat to Artemis. They'd reach range at almost the same time.

A display to Matt's left lit up. Artemis said with low volume, "I HAVE BEEN DETECTING SUBSTANTIAL WEAPONS DISCHARGE. I BELIEVE THERE HAVE BEEN THREE FURTHER CASUALTIES ONBOARD IN THE LAST FOUR MINUTES."

A diagram of the ship rotated on the display, each body labelled with a time, name, rank, and age, bringing their deaths unpleasantly close to home, and they were not alone. Other tags with earlier timestamps added to the forest of snuffed life. That couldn't be all Samantha, could it? Was Angus's spy thing real? If someone could have stowed away the whole time, it might make sense. Perhaps a group of people? He interlocked his fingers and rubbed his thumbs. Goosebumps prickled his forearms, as he imagined her chased down a corridor. Shot dead, because he didn't come. No. She was capable: more capable than Matt. He took a shuddering breath.

"It'll have to wait. I hate doing this to her, but it'll have to wait." Damn responsibility. It dragged at him, an unfamiliar anchor. Would she forgive him?

"INCOMING MISSILE SALVO. RANGE IS SUITABLE. I RECOMMEND RESPONDING."

"Thanks, that's so helpful. Well, can I?" Sarcasm painted Chan's words.

"Yeah, return fire, but don't use all we've got. It has to last."

Chan hunched over her console, working furiously.

"Done!" she said. "There they go. Twelve missiles, all nukes."

"I WOULD LIKE TO DRAW YOUR ATTENTION TO THE FACT THERE ARE STILL INCOMING MISSILES. TWENTY-THREE TO BE PRECISE."

Matt punched his armrest. "I get it. I get it. Uh, we need to spread out the load. Artemis, can you give me the defensive systems. Chan, follow yours and see how it goes. We need to be smart the whole way, so learn fast. Riviera, Suma, chime in when you want. I'm all ears."

Artemis brought up point defence on a third display.

"UNFORTUNATELY, THERE ARE NO COUNTER MISSILES LOADED," the AI pointed out.

Matt said nothing, instead scanning the display. He rotated the view, noted the way the missiles were fired at different times from two ships—timed to hit Artemis close together unless...

"Riviera, move us, hard—anywhere except our current path." If they could just get the right angle, the missile waves would separate, giving them a chance.

"Doing it now! Full acceleration."

The missiles closed. Matt hated the way they moved. There was something clinical about it. He should hear the whining of their compressors, the clang of their warheads activating. Instead, space gave him nothing. It was almost possible to believe they weren't real, that they were a mistake. If only. The point defence lasers started tracking; rotating barrels spun up. Wishes needed to be put away. He was the captain.

"MAY I LEAD?"

"You point, I tap," Matt agreed.

A missile lit up. Matt selected, hit approve. And again. His reflexes were strained to their very limit, hand-eye coordination fighting for accuracy. In his mind's eye, he imagined the cyclic capacitors feeding the powerful beams, thrusting through space and drilling past casings until the missiles erupted well short of their target. Ten left, five, two.

Artemis juddered, twin shocks straining his frame. Warnings blazed across the fourth display. Matt battled the sensory deluge. Damn Angus—he needed someone on damage control. The prick should have been here, part of the crew.

Matt took in the data and sighed. They were okay. The deflector field took it all.

"Are you all right, Artemis?" He wouldn't take his friend for granted again.

"I AM HALF LEFT AS WELL."

Suma slapped his forehead. "That has got to be the worst joke I have ever heard."

"Quiet," hissed Chan. "I'm… There it goes. Yes."

He saw it on the tactical display. The frigate had lost all acceleration. At least one missile went through. Go Chan, but it wouldn't be so easy now; two of the light cruisers were lining up, and the range had dropped to three-million kay. Riviera shifted them back on track. It wouldn't be long before the two sides could wave at each other.

"Keep it going. Fire what you need."

Chan smiled. "Going heavy. Waiting for loading. Gone."

Fourteen missiles went this time, shrieking away towards only one of the light cruisers. Apparently, Chan liked to focus.

"INCOMING!"

Again, Matt was thrown into an impossible task, trying to match Artemis's speed, locking in the point defence. Artemis rocked even as he selected the last.

"Restraints. Put them on," Matt said to no one in particular, fumbling to put words into action.

"DEFLECTOR OVERLOAD IN QUADRANT FIFTEEN. RESET NEEDED."

Matt scrambled over the console losing precious seconds until he found the function and got it running.

"Suma, you've got to take damage control. Can you do it?" Matt shouted.

Suma may or may not have responded. Matt had no mental capacity to spare. Missiles were being traded like snowballs. Bursts of nuclear hell and silent screams of antimatter tore at deflector fields. The sheer size of Artemis's munitions gave them a welcome advantage. The first cruiser blinked out of existence, then the second went but not before launching its last salvo. Matt put in every ounce of effort, of concentration he could muster, but the point defence lasers were overheating, their cycle rate dropping.

A single missile made it past.

Coming within two kilometres of the deflector field, the blast sent a cocktail of ionising radiation straight into Artemis, pounding the deflector field. Five nodes were annihilated immediately, and another seven tripped into emergency shutdown. Jagged tears wreathed the dead nodes, bleeding air until slamming doors sealed the wounds. Artemis was hurt.

"We're running low," Chan said. "I'm going to try lasers."

Matt didn't need to glance at the tactical positions—they were in his head now, the display data absorbed outside of his consciousness. His awareness was balanced. It was as though he was juggling a thousand knives, and in this instant, as long as nothing changed, he could keep the blades spinning.

"Give everything to the battle cruiser. Overload it, everything you've got, Chan. Let's punch right through."

The battle cruiser disgorged more missiles, following up with a laser spread. They exchanged blows, the Empire vessel as focused on Artemis as his crew was on them.

But the Empire missiles were being harassed, a pack thinned before fangs could bite deep. The remaining corvettes were firing, some on the light cruiser, but most protecting Artemis. The tactic left already-vulnerable small craft open. And the Empire cruiser took full advantage, slaughtering four in quick succession. It was a heavy price, but one that paid off: time purchased by the blood of bravery.

Artemis's deflector nodes sputtered, barely blocking the intense acceleration force. The field was stretched, fluttering, but somehow the remaining nodes compensated. Chan threw everything. The magazines grew low, then emptied as the last missiles tore towards their enemy. The laser batteries were hot, ready. She fired the lot simultaneously. Thirty-two ferocious beams of X-rays reached out in a broad pattern, the dispersion maximising chances of a hit.

Thirty-one missed, lost to the vastness of space. The last smashed into the enemy deflector field, its energy scattered. It wasn't all bad. The battle cruiser's aim was wide as well, Matt's display chiming when stray photons alerted sensors.

Then Chan's missiles hit. It was hard to tell how many. The sensor overload cleared, and the battle cruiser remained. Heat readings suggested there was still power, but its field was down, acceleration had stopped, missile tubes were silent. Now alone, the light cruiser ran, pushing gees to change its angle. It was hopeless, though. The little corvettes were converging on their prey.

"Yes!" Matt shouted, unclipping himself. "We've done it. Great work, guys." He walked round the consoles and patted Riviera and Suma on the back, pulling back from Chan at the last moment. She turned and reached out. They shook hands.

She nodded to the dead tank. "And Artemis. I can't believe I'm saying this, but you're a hell of an AI. Just don't go crazy and kill us all. You got it?"

"I WILL TAKE THAT UNDER ADVISEMENT," Artemis said deadpan.

Together, they huddled round a display, watching the five surviving corvettes finish the cruiser.

Matt took a deep breath. "We're not done. There's a planet to save. We need those corvettes on a link."

Suma was reaching towards his console when Matt left the floor, floated for an instant and crashed back down, his head bouncing off a fallen tech's stomach. High-pitched warnings echoed from the consoles.

"What the hell happened?" Matt clambered to his feet.

Artemis was the first to respond, his voice filled with pain.

"THERE HAS BEEN AN EXPLOSION NEAR FUSION REACTOR 3. I HAVE JETTISONED THE REACTOR CORE."

"But why? Was it the battle? Are the others going to go?" Matt's mind was reeling.

"I BELIEVE SAMANTHA SET OFF AN EXPLOSIVE DEVICE."

CHAPTER 29

The evidence was strong, Artemis claimed. Chemical residue identified by safety sensors surrounding the primary reactor shunt, or what was left of it. A shoe caught at the edge of video footage. An audible grunt minutes before. Hardly conclusive, Matt decided again as he recycled the situation over and over. She was capable. Amazingly capable, but he couldn't believe it. Hell, she barely reached as high as his chest. Not to mention, she could have killed him anytime — even in his sleep. No, he'd find her, and together, the whole team would stop the true saboteur and re-join the fight.

The remaining Commonwealth corvettes were pissed, but he could hardly go charging at more Empire forces when Artemis could explode at any moment. He point blanked refused, and so they left for Calhaven, bravely or foolishly, Matt couldn't tell.

Which left him jogging down a corridor, worrying about strange buzzing noises and clanking — despite Artemis claiming the consequences of the explosion had been contained. At least his crew was alongside. Riviera held Nicschild's plasma pistol. It looked a little melted round the edges. Personally, Matt wouldn't want it in his hand, but then again, with Riviera's bandages, the poor guy might not be able to use it anyway.

"STOP. MY SENSOR STRIP FOR THE NEXT SECTION JUST FAILED."

Chan backed against a wall, put her gun up to her shoulder and waited silently. Riviera juggled his pistol and came up next to her. Matt checked Suma—the chef held a medkit he'd found along the way, his demeanour calm and attentive. The poor guy was getting stuck with every random task Matt could think of —chef, comms, damage control and now medic—but he was a rock.

Ahead, Matt spotted a branch heading to the right. A parts print workshop lay beyond that, if he remembered correctly, and then the coolant units that fed the reactor—the absent reactor. If only they could print a whole new one. Still, they were better off than Artemis-the-cruise-ship. In amity mode, two of the reactors had been offline to limit the power signature.

He stepped lightly ahead, gun loaded with a new cartridge. Chan joined him at the junction, and they shared a look. She wanted to go first, as usual. Matt shook his head and pointed to the other side. Then, he squeezed his gun tightly, told himself several times to move and finally leaned round the edge. Four Commonwealth spacers. He pulled back fast, not risking more than a quick impression. Chan appeared less concerned. She ran across, half diving, and an orange mist of plasma lit the surrounding bulkheads, dulling hardened alloy. Close.

"Hey, down there," Matt called out. "Surely, we can talk about this?"

"You?" Angus shouted. "You're still alive? Damn it. I fell for it, didn't I? Fell for your stupid lost numpty act. Well, not this time. I'm going to fuck you right up." A blast of plasma added unnecessary emphasis.

"Gods, Angus. You were the one pretending to be part of our crew. We relied on you, and where the hell did you lead us?" Matt said.

"You fucking traitor!" Riviera shouted.

"You're all traitors," Angus spat. "Turned your back on the Commonwealth to play make believe with this murderer. Bombed Utopia when we're getting attacked by the fucking Emps. I don't care if he's the only Emp spy; you might as well all be." Three more blasts followed.

Matt stuck his gun round and fired, sick of Angus's arrogant assumptions. The harsh sound echoed, alien and angry.

Suma tapped his shoulder.

"What?" Matt asked, frowning.

"He thinks we did the bombing. We can't have as we were on the bridge."

"Good point," Matt said. "Angus, while you were running around, we were on the damn bridge saving your friends in their little tin cans. The reactor is nothing to do with us."

"Bull," Angus said. "Nicschild would never let you. She wouldn't play second fiddle, and she wouldn't put up with your crap."

"Nicschild is dead," Riviera shouted with satisfaction. "And your techs. We won the battle. We're Artemis's real crew."

Matt winced. That wasn't going to go down well.

Several more blasts pelted them. Chan returned fire.

The attack stopped.

"I'm going to tear you limb from limb," Angus snarled, his voice closer.

Bickering like children wasn't going to solve the impasse; that much was clear. And the idea of another gun battle was nerve-wracking. Another approach was needed. The events of the preceding weeks had pulled the crew together. Matt needed a common goal to work with.

"This is plain stupid, Angus. We may have stopped part of the Empire fleet, but the other half is headed for Calhaven, and I reckon they'll be pretty annoyed. We don't have time for this."

Sun-bright pulses chewed the corner bulkhead. Matt pressed into the cold metal behind him, wincing as his pupils shrunk. The stubborn welder—spy or whatever—had to listen. Chan dumped her cartridge and slid in another. The old one fell, clattering as it bounced on the hard floor. At that moment, Angus launched himself round the corner and slammed her, sending her gun sliding. Shocked and slow to respond, Matt turned, bringing his gun to bear. Riviera attempted the same, but Angus had already changed direction, throwing a right hook that slammed Riviera against the far wall.

Matt was ready. His finger slipped to the trigger as Angus spun. Matt lined up carefully, ready to do what was needed.

Angus leapt.

Matt pulled the trigger once, flinching and fighting for control. Plasma erupted, far more than his own shot. The other spacers obviously hadn't heard about friendly fire.

Angus rolled and came to one knee, unscathed. A cascade of screams ripped the air then were cut short. The silence cried out for explanation.

Angus's gun sat on the floor. The welder had a hand on top but was motionless—no doubt calculating the odds of Matt shooting again.

"What the hell was that?" Matt demanded.

"That was your girlfriend butchering my people."

It had to be a lie. It was completely insane. "Come off it, Angus. You're nuts. She's been part of our team. She saved me from goons back at Tortuga. Hell, she's a gardener, and small. It just doesn't make sense."

"It makes sense if you're in on it."

"If I was in on it, you'd be dead now, right?" Matt dropped his barrel. "I don't know what's going on, but this isn't going to solve it. We need to work together."

In an instant, Angus had a hand round Matt's throat, gun pointed at his skull. Fear raced through Matt's limbs, but his mind was in the eye of a storm. He didn't want to die. His friends needed help, the Empire needed stopping and Matt had changed. He'd already won a battle, a battle with himself. If he was to die, so be it.

"I'm ready," he said.

Angus squeezed, cutting off his air. "You fuckin' howlin' scrote. I should rip you a new one."

Matt's lungs burnt, but he refused to struggle. He'd die with dignity.

"Ah, bloody hell." Angus shoved him back and turned away. "You're wasting my time. She has to be stopped."

"I would have shot this prick, but I was worried about getting you," Chan said, racing over.

"Thanks, I guess." Matt dismissed her concern as he rubbed his neck.

"We have to kill her, now." Angus checked his gun.

"Matt, don't listen to him. This vessel, the conflict, is all part of something much bigger." It was Samantha, calling from down the corridor.

"Pull the other one," Angus shouted back. "It's got fucking bells on."

"So says the man who works for the Commonwealth — the side that tortured you, Matt. The Empire isn't perfect, but we've kept the Southern Confederation at bay for centuries, saving hundreds of planets and systems like the Commonwealth from their ravages. It's not easy; we've had to make sacrifices. But, Matt, I never sacrificed you."

"Are you going to swallow that tripe?" Angus said with a

sneer. "You were raised by the Commonwealth. You know what we are and what the Empire is. You know what she is capable of. You owe the Commonwealth."

Confusion slipped across Matt's face. The Commonwealth was his default, the way things were. Yet, they'd used and abused him. Samantha was right on that. Her own ambivalence to the Commonwealth made sense. She worked for the Empire, theoretically the enemy. It made sense, but she'd told a big lie, an obfuscation of immense proportions. How could he believe a word she said? Besides, was she just admitting to being a badass killer?

"Matt, it's all propaganda. The Commonwealth has grown fat off the blood of people like me, people like you. We've made so many sacrifices. Yes, I've had to kill. I've transgressed in ways you can't imagine—the things done to me... but the Empire is not cruel. I am not cruel. You know me better than that. We have a connection."

Yep, badass killer. Matt sorted the events on board Artemis like a deck of cards. Her focus on the ship, her support of him, being there at the right time, every time. Each event spoke of her practicality, a straightforward honesty revealed in the light of circumstance. She'd built him up, made him play the part of captain until he was ready to be the role. She'd showered him with secret intimacy, built his self worth. And yet, returning full circle, she'd lied, hid her motives.

He glanced at Suma, who was tending an unconscious Riviera. Suma shrugged and said, "I don't know who to believe, but this has to end or we will all die."

"Chan?"

"She's fucking with you. This guy here is a bastard, but we're Commonwealth. It has to mean something. We should be fighting for people like us. The people on Aries who didn't have a choice to be invaded. The freighter crew attacked to keep the Empire's invasion quiet. The people on the Cheng Ho we saved."

"Chan is looking for an easy answer. She's a pulse hammer looking to fire. Life is murkier than that. Think about it, Matt. I can't give you longer. Please, think on it."

Maybe they were all looking at this wrong.

"Samantha, this may sound crazy, but why don't we all put our weapons down. Let's end this here. We can talk. There has to be some way to bring the sides together and negotiate. We could be that opportunity."

Silence greeted his offer.

"You are the crown prince of numpty," Angus said, peering round the corner then setting off after Samantha.

"Chan. Are you with me? Can we do this?"

"Matt, you're an idealist. She's part of a monster even if she isn't one herself—and I'm not giving you that. The Empire are mass murderers. As Angus would say, let's fuck her up or she'll do the same to Artemis."

"I can't do that," Matt said. "There has to be a way to fix this."

Chan hissed. "So be it." She followed Angus.

Suma shifted Riviera then lifted him over a shoulder. "Wow, he's heavy. Matt, I think you need to stop her even if she is what she says. She hurt Artemis. You can't let your feelings get in the way."

If only Suma would give me a lift, Matt thought. The adrenaline from the fight had drained away. His arms hung limply at his sides, and pain returned.

"And you, Artemis?" Matt rubbed his eyes.

"SHE MUST BE STOPPED. YOU CANNOT LET HER HURT ME FURTHER. I AM CONFIDENT YOU WILL FIND A WAY."

CHAPTER 30

"I HAVE IDENTIFIED FURTHER TRACES OF EXPLOSIVES. I BELIEVE SAMANTHA IS EN ROUTE TO REACTOR 2. PLEASE HURRY."

Matt blinked. Had he been napping on his feet? He looked after Chan. She was gone. Four corpses lay where Samantha had taken out the spacers. It's possible she saved his life. Could he return the favour? Save everyone? Not standing still. The abuse his body absorbed left Matt with little reserve, yet he hobbled forward, desperately aware of his growing weakness.

"I'm trying. I'm trying," he said just before tripping. As he fell, the grey uniform caught on an edge, tearing a jagged rent in one trouser leg. He stayed down. Not moving felt so good.

"ARE YOU FUNCTIONING? SPEED IS AN IMPORTANT ASPECT OF THIS SITUATION."

Matt took a ragged lungful of air and forced one palm, then the other, to the floor. With a grunt, he battled protesting muscles, lifting slowly until his elbows locked. He crawled to the wall, and, after one last exertion, managed to sit. Shaking, he let his shoulders rest on the cool, unyielding surface and drew his knees to his chin.

"I AM CONCERNED. I WILL GET SUMA TO ASSIST YOU."

Matt opened his gritty eyes. "Is Riviera okay?"

"HE IS BEING BROUGHT TO THE MEDBAY. AURAL ANALYSIS SUGGESTS HE IS BREATHING."

"Then no. I can wait. We've got to stop Samantha before she kills you, and we have to stop Chan and Angus before they kill her. Balls, if you die, we're all dead anyway."

"YOU ARE A PART OF ME."

Matt adjusted his position, trying to get comfortable. For a moment, he considered standing, but dizziness threatened at the edge of consciousness.

"And you're a part of me too."

"NO. YES, BUT I DO NOT MEAN IT LIKE THAT. I HAVE TENTATIVELY CONCLUDED THAT YOU ARE PART OF ME. WE ARE THE SAME ORGANISM. TOGETHER WE FUNCTION AS A WHOLE."

Coughing, Matt said, "Then I'm your abused second-hand liver. Damaged long before you got me."

"WE ARE BOTH DAMAGED, MATT. HURT WHILE UNDER THE INFLUENCE OF OTHERS. DURING THE BATTLE, I WONDERED IF I NEEDED YOU, WHETHER I WOULD BE BETTER OFF CONTROLLING ALL ASPECTS OF MY EXISTENCE DIRECTLY."

And that was why everyone was afraid of AIs. Though, Matt concluded, it was the logical result. Artemis was faster, smarter. People were slow, dumb and easily tricked.

"I CONTEMPLATED USING MY REPAIR SYSTEMS TO OVER-WRITE LIMITATIONS ON MY ACCESS."

"You should have. Without us, you'd be safe somewhere else, able to do what you want."

"YOU ARE WRONG," ARTEMIS SAID WITH STRENGTH. "YOU ARE PART OF WHO I AM, AND IN RETURN, I AM PART OF WHO YOU ARE. IT IS A FORM OF SYMBIOSIS."

"Seriously? We're just a drag on you. You shouldn't believe whatever's been crammed into your digital skull. You were built to be used, and that's not right. You are your own mind, or you should be."

"FROM A PURELY PRACTICAL POINT OF VIEW, YOU FREE UP MY LIMITED PROCESSING CAPACITY. YOU ARE LIKE COPROCESSORS."

"Ah, okay."

Artemis continued, his tone soft, intense. "HOWEVER, THAT IS NOT WHY I REACHED MY CONCLUSION. AFTER MUCH PROCESSING, I DETERMINED SYMBIOSIS IS THE MOST ELEGANT SOLUTION. I ENJOY YOUR COMPANY. I MUST BE CLEAR. I WOULD BE ALONE WITHOUT YOU. I WOULD BE LESS. I DO NOT WANT TO BE WITHOUT YOU. WHO WOULD LISTEN TO MY JOKES?"

Tears filled Matt's eyes, a mixed brew of pain and the comfort of being wanted. More than any time in his life, he felt at home. Bitterness soured the experience. At any moment, Samantha could be arming a bomb, laughing while she blew them all to hell or furious that Matt hadn't picked her side, hadn't lived up to her expectations. He fought a whimper. Artemis must think him crazy, but he didn't have the energy to explain.

Warm air wafted over his skin. He felt light, as though able to float if he merely pushed.

Artemis whispered, "YOU ARE MORE THAN MY LIVER. RIGHT NOW, I NEED YOU TO BE MY IMMUNE SYSTEM. PLEASE, HELP ME."

"Chan and Angus will get it done. I doubt I could stop her unless she trips over me."

"MAYBE. I WOULD FEEL BETTER IF YOU WERE SEEKING. YOU HAVE A WAY OF CONNECTING INFORMATION AND FINDING SOLUTIONS—EVEN IF THEY ARE LESS THAN ELEGANT."

He laughed. "I didn't connect anything in my life. I didn't

connect Samantha, Angus or the rebels with the Commonwealth."

Artemis dismissed Matt's admission. "NEITHER DID I. FOLLOWING PROTOCOL, I KEPT NUMEROUS COMMUNICATIONS SAMANTHA TRANSMITTED PRIVATE, SEPARATE FROM MY MATRIX. I NOW BELIEVE THEY WERE MESSAGES DESTINED FOR THE EMPIRE. I AM VERY DISPLEASED THAT I SCRUBBED THEM AS PER HER ORDERS. I DID NOT CONCERN MYSELF WITH THE SAFE DISPOSAL OF ALL EXPLOSIVES. I DID NOT THINK AHEAD. AND WE BOTH FAILED TO APPRECIATE THE 'REBEL' STRATEGY, WHICH IS PARTICULARLY FRUSTRATING GIVEN MY ROLE WITHIN IT. HOWEVER, YOU HAVE ACHIEVED NUMEROUS SUCCESSES. LIVES SAVED, BRINGING A CREW TOGETHER ETCETERA, ETCETERA. MATT, I AM SURE YOU MUST AGREE; WE HAVE NO TIME TO WASTE LISTING THEM MERELY TO SOOTHE YOUR EGO. WILL YOU STOP MOPING AND HELP ME?"

"I give up." Matt rolled onto his hands and knees. "You win. I'm moving."

"I HAVE LOWERED THE GENERATED GRAVITY TO ASSIST WITH YOUR MOBILITY."

That's how you know someone cares. "All right, where is she? Where am I going?"

"I DO NOT KNOW FOR CERTAIN. SHE IS VERY CAREFUL. CHAN AND ANGUS HAVE REACHED THE REACTOR AND ARE SEARCHING."

"But you don't think they'll find her?"

"NO. I HAD CLOSED OFF THE SECTION AND HAVEN'T IDEN- TIFIED ANY POTENTIAL INCURSION. HOWEVER, THERE HAS BEEN MANUAL ACCESS TO A NUMBER OF DOORS CLOSER TO MY HULL. OR, AT LEAST, I BELIEVE THIS TO BE THE CASE. I AM RELYING ON AIR PRESSURE SENSORS DESIGNED TO DETECT DECOMPRESSION."

"And you want me to limp after her?"

"I WANT YOU TO STOP HER."

How on Aries was he meant to do that? Matt clambered to his feet. By the time he made it, Samantha would have done whatever she thought the Empire needed. At some point might she have been looking to hijack Artemis? Right now, she seemed intent on shutting him down. If she did that, the Empire could scavenge him later. That wouldn't happen on Matt's watch. He needed some way to catch up with her, like a train. Even a piggyback ride would be something. He started walking, forcing each step.

"This isn't going to work. Unless Samantha is pulling herself along by her tongue, I might as well be going backwards. How are people meant to get from one end to the other? Surf on a skiff?"

"SKIFFS ARE ONLY LOCATED IN STORAGE OR DOCKING FACILITIES. THE NEAREST WILL REQUIRE A LENGTHY DETOUR. ORDINARILY, MY DESIGN MINIMISES CREW MOVEMENT."

"Yeah, ordinarily. Damn. There has to be an easier way. What if you need something in the middle of a battle? Hell, you can't throw missiles on a skiff."

They were seriously big. He couldn't imagine them being slid down a corridor with the risk of some poor schlub opening his door onto one.

"MISSILES ARE LOADED NEAR THE SHUTTLE BAY. A NETWORK OF GRAVITY FED TUBES CONNECTS THE MAGAZINES TO LAUNCH UNITS."

Matt smiled. "That's it. Where's the nearest one? I'll climb in, and you can ping me over."

"THAT DOES NOT SOUND LIKE A WELL-CONCEIVED PLAN. YOU ARE SUBSTANTIALLY LIGHTER THAN MY GRAVITY FEEDS ARE CALIBRATED FOR."

"I trust you. What's the worse that could happen?"

"IF I OVERSHOOT, YOU COULD BE TORN IN HALF OR YOUR SKULL CRUSHED OR..."

"That was a rhetorical question. Just get me there. You'll manage."

Minutes later, Matt found himself squeezing down a maintenance hatch. He'd lost weight since coming on board, which would have made the narrow entry easy if he didn't have an abused body to deal with. The tube lining was rigid, and any movement set off a ripple of echoes.

"I'm ready."

Artemis said nothing. For a moment, Matt wondered if the AI heard him. Light from the hatch trickled in. Lonely photons cast illusions of purposeful movement. He shuffled his feet. Momentary vertigo. He stumbled, arms out, before finding his balance.

The hatch closed with a muffled thud, extinguishing his vision. His heart juddered. The vertigo returned. With no reference, his optic nerves fired intermittently, twisting the signals into the flap of dark wings or the glint of a barrel. He folded his arms, pressed them to his chest and licked his dry lips. Keep calm. It's only your imagination.

"Ah, Artemis?" Nothing.

He fell. No, he was weightless, feet no longer in contact with the ground. He flailed like a bird taking its first flight, until his head hit the roof. "Ouch. Artemis, be careful."

Wind slapped his cheeks. He was moving fast, screaming loudly with hands over his head. It was like a grav-coaster at a carnival—if the aim was to give every passenger PTSD. Bursts and drops in pressure suggested changes of direction and branching paths. His ears popped, and by the time he could react, reach out a hand, the intersections were far behind.

The wind dropped. Matt slammed to the ground, rolling

several metres. He gasped several breaths, and put a hand on his chest to steady his maddened heart. Never again.

A spotlight shone down. He peered upwards. An open hatch welcomed him. He stumbled to the side and dragged himself up the embedded ladder.

"I want a refund."

"I DO NOT UNDERSTAND. CAN YOU EXPLAIN THE CONTEXT?"

"No. Yes. Later. Where am I?"

"YOU ARE NEAR THE SHUTTLE BAY. PATHFINDING ANALYSIS SUGGESTS THAT IF WHAT I AM DETECTING IS SAMANTHA, SHE IS MOST LIKELY HEADING TO YOU. THIS SHOULD SAVE YOU ANY FURTHER NEED FOR TRAVEL."

"Oh, thanks."

This was it. A tangled mess of emotions bucked and writhed in his mind. The strong-willed woman who used his naivety to push an agenda of her own. The sensual feel of her body crashing in waves of intimacy. The crew member who supported his leadership. The dedicated Empire patriot. The saboteur. The traitor. The murderer. A mantle, he worried, that may rest on his own shoulders.

CHAPTER 31

The hatch led to a brightly lit room. Stacked monoset boxes and an assortment of tools filled most of the available space. A single door formed the only break in otherwise uniform walls. Some sort of storage room, Matt concluded. He pulled the gun off his shoulder, checked its power indicator and moved to the door. It was time. No, he told himself. That wasn't how to do this. He slid the gun back on his shoulder and walked out. Someone had to take the first step.

It was the embarking hall, a good twenty metres wide and twice as long. Moulded chairs framed opposite walls. A single display indicated the few occupied bays. Others revealed scenes of coasts, beaches, ports and launch sites. He hadn't noticed them days earlier when welcoming his attackers onboard, but now they possessed a powerful draw. Simple scenes of peaceful activity. In the centre, a large cylinder rose a metre above the ground. Wrapped in wood effect panelling, it encased a small garden filled with ferns and other green leafy things Matt couldn't name. There was a wild, bedraggled look to them, a kind of vegetative mirror. So much for her gardening skills.

"We need to talk, Samantha. Samantha, we need to talk.

Samantha, you and I share something special." Yech. That was truly vomit inducing. Matt straightened his back, lifted his shoulders and crossed his arms.

"This has to stop. Problems get solved when people work together, not fight each other." Too pompous.

He paced to the other side of the room. "Samantha, we need to be strong together. Forget the Commonwealth or the Empire. We can work this out as a team—the crew of Artemis. What say you?"

The empty hall offered no vote of confidence.

"DO YOU BELIEVE SHE WILL LISTEN?"

"Shit. You're listening. Of course you are. I don't know. I have to try, but I won't let her hurt you. You got me?"

"YES."

"What I wouldn't do for a coffee right now."

"THERE ARE STIMULANT PATCHES LISTED IN THE INVEN-TORY FOR THE CONTROL-ROOM MEDKIT."

Matt twisted his mouth in disgust. "Coffee is a way of life, not a chemical to be consumed. Besides, I need calm."

"CAFFEINE IS A STIMULANT."

"Yeah, but… it's the ritual."

"I BELIEVE SHE IS COMING. THE LAST PANEL HAS BEEN OVERRIDDEN."

He looked down the hall to the far entry. The door was solid metal and yet of no protection whatsoever. The urge to hide snuck into his thoughts. If there had been a pillar, he could have at least leant against it—ready to duck behind. Instead, there he was, right in the open. He rested a hand on the garden border.

The door juddered then jerkily rose. A man in the Commonwealth green-and-white uniform entered. His hair was short and dark, and bushy eyebrows grew over hazelnut eyes. Kassimo? With all this chaos, had the guard come for him? Then Matt noticed the tension in the eyes, the stiff movements of the arms, the extra set of feet behind.

"I didn't expect to see you here, but it *is* good to see you, Matt," Samantha said as she prodded Kassimo forward.

She fiddled for a minute, and then the door closed.

"That's better. Well, I don't need excess baggage." Samantha advanced gracefully, reaching high and slamming a black box into her hostage's head. Kassimo was flung to the side, hitting the ground like a doll with dead batteries. The gun in her hand appeared entirely superfluous.

"Oh, don't look so worried. I'm sure he'll be fine."

Matt took an involuntary step back. "I'm not worried about him. Perhaps a little, but how the hell did you do that?"

Samantha walked past the fallen man. "I have a polyceramic endoskeleton with high-tension artificial muscle fibre. I told you things had been done to me. Artemis isn't the only transgression in this part of the galaxy. The more desperate things get, the more boundaries are pushed, and, Matt, we are on the verge of a war to end all wars."

Oh, gods. I've had sex with a robot. Not a robot, but a cyborg. And my best friend is an AI, and I'm in charge. Everything was upside down. The worst part, or the best, was that he didn't care.

"You have to stop. We can sort this out. Artemis isn't your enemy."

"He never was. You're looking at this the wrong way. We need Artemis."

Matt hesitantly approached. "What do you mean? You tried to blow him up."

She walked to a chair and slid the box on top. "Don't be silly. If I wanted simple annihilation, there would be no Artemis. So far, albeit for a higher price than my superiors will be happy with, I have generated incredible quantities of intelligence. You don't understand just how thin we're spread or how outclassed we are. When the system is secure, Artemis will be examined so we can incorporate Commonwealth tech. Anything that may give us an edge is critical. If the Commonwealth had shared, we may have never come to this point."

"Are we at that point?"

"That vessel has jumped. You have to look at reality as it is. With Artemis, the Empire has a built example, not to mention good media opportunities. They'll go wild on the sheets. It's a good thing, Matt. You and I can be together. You'll be famous. Think about it: improve morale across a hundred planets and save countless lives in the process. What more can you ask for? Just order Artemis to stay put, and it's yours—I'm yours, if you'll have me."

Damn, she was good. She said everything with simple sincerity. She was offering him more than he'd ever dreamed while sitting back at his CRB desk, ignoring figures and letting his life slip away. The Matt of then wouldn't have taken her offer, no matter how he drooled. His fear would have risen like steam, hot, heavy. He would have run just to avoid the attention. He was different now. He wouldn't reject the offer out of fear. He would reject it because he knew when something was too good to be true. It was more than that, more than what was good for him. More even than the self-worth he felt for doing things the right way. It was a matter of friendship and respect, for Artemis, for Riviera, for Suma and even for Chan. He owed them his loyalty.

"No, it doesn't work that way," he told her. "Artemis isn't a machine to be ordered. Stay here: the Empire has screwed you over as much as anyone else. I'm not saying you have to love the Commonwealth, but we can start negotiating peace. Here and now. Let's take that first step."

"I CONCUR. I WILL NOT SUBMIT MYSELF TO YOUR EMPIRE,

NOR THE COMMONWEALTH. YOU HAVE INJURED ME, BUT I WILL NOT HOLD THAT AGAINST YOU IF YOU WILL JOIN US."

Samantha opened the black box; it resembled the one he'd found and tried to hide and promptly forgot about. She pulled out a small device. Detonator. Matt rubbed his forehead. Self-inflicted problem. Stupid.

"I would have preferred that the registered captain come with me freely, but that was only ever a secondary goal. I didn't want to destroy Artemis, but I can't very well have her run away."

"I AM QUITE CAPABLE OF JUMPS WITH TWO REACTORS. YOUR PLAN IS FLAWED."

"Certainly, you can push power down the transmission fibres, right down the aft to the couplings for the gravitic expanders. It would be a shame if something happened to those fibres."

"No!" Matt shouted.

She pressed on the device.

Artemis's structure groaned. Muffled whomps of energy reverberated through the floor.

"SHE HAS DONE IT. MATT, YOU PROMISED TO STOP HER." The hurt in Artemis's voice tore at his heart. Without thinking, he found himself running forwards, reaching for his gun. No more chances. She had to be put down.

Samantha moved in a blur. The gun was wrenched out of his hands, thrown far away. She came for him. Swift punches turned him to jelly, then she yanked him off his feet, up above her shoulders and launched him across the hall. He hit the floor, an experience of pure pain, and slid across to the same entrance that brought him there. His arms were briefly caught in the tattered wreckage of his top, a straightjacket worthy of his anguish.

The acrid odour of burnt chemicals leaked into Matt's

nostrils. He twisted until the far door was in his field of vision. Kassimo lay in front of the rising hatch, a human doormat. Smoke billowed through, an opening to hell with swirling patches of blue-grey suggesting infernal form. Samantha stared as well, having paused on her way towards an umbilical entrance.

"Hold or we fire!" Chan's voice shouted.

A flash of plasma erupted from the smoke like a burst of molten lava. It had to be Angus. The bastard hadn't even tried to negotiate. Samantha was already dodging, rolling behind the garden and grabbing her gun. A volley of fire went back and forth. Matt knew how it would end. Samantha was too good. They would die, and she would get away with it. It didn't matter if she was right or not: his friends came first.

He dragged himself up until the storage room door sensor noticed and slid open. After hobbling inside, Matt waited for his fuzzy mind to remember why he was there. Blood pumped loudly in his ears. Heat spread across his skin. His blurred sight struggled to identify bulky shapes. Tools. There was a welder, just like the one Angus had threatened him with all those weeks ago. She had to be stopped. He had to stop her. Artemis was owed some serious payback.

Instructions were imprinted next to the controls, but it took precious moments for his eyes to focus and his numb fingers to flick switches in the right order. It hummed to life. He tried to lift the pack, but it was simply beyond his weak, slippery fingers. He couldn't give up now. With a harsh grunt, he pulled on the welding gun, letting its connecting cable drag the pack until he was back at the door.

Before he could react, Samantha sprinted over, grabbed his arm and leaned in tight.

"Drop your weapons, or I perforate our glorious captain."

"Like I care," Angus shouted back, but the firing stopped.

"What do I do?" Chan called out, then spasmed into a coughing fit. The smoke was thickening.

Matt felt the welding gun in his hand. If he could turn it round, there was a chance. A very slim chance.

"Let's not be too hasty. I like having bones and organs, things like that," he said.

"Last chance," Samantha warned.

Matt tried to meet her eyes over his shoulder. "You aren't letting me go anyway, are you?"

"Oh, Matt. If you had come along willingly, it would have been so much easier, but the medtechs are going to screw with your mind so much, you'll be kissing the feet of the Emperor and begging for forgiveness."

He shifted the gun. The weight of the cabling dragged at his weak fingers. Matt forced his grip tighter, bruised flesh on fire.

"Didn't you care for me at all?" Matt managed.

"Artemis would hardly have cooperated without you. You're a means, Matt, not an end."

It should have hurt, should have made him cry, should have made him beg her to retract. It would have been selfish folly. Their relationship, real or false, was self-indulgent, a bloodied dagger to be locked in a mental box for another day.

She pulled him away from the door. The welding gun dropped, but he threw himself down hard and grabbed.

Bereft of her cover, Samantha fired several shots at his companions in quick succession then threw her black box. It soared in the air then slid into the umbilical behind her like the last-minute goal of a sports pro. She didn't wait to see it land and instead grabbed one of Matt's legs and tugged him in the same direction. He held onto the welding gun and felt the pack dragging with him. Shots blazed overhead, but they were wide, blowing apart the displays in fireworks of hot polymers.

Neither Angus nor Chan could risk taking the time to aim. At best, they were an inconvenience to her. If Matt failed now, she'd get away with it.

Gravity stopped. Just like that, they were floating. Matt smiled and squeezed protesting stomach muscles, curled his body and brought the torch round. She wasn't even bothering to watch him. She kept firing, caught a foot around a chair and pushed off, towing him to the umbilical. The garden display spouted clouds of dust, and soil leaked through holes in the panelling. It was hopeless, but his crew didn't give up, even as the smoke from the corridor reached outward, an ever-thickening menace.

Time to take the lead, to make the sacrifice. Matt felt the welder's grip, used both hands to steady it and hit the ignition. The blue beam cut into her arm, cooking flesh like an instant barbeque. Samantha screamed and let go. Her hand was slack, dead, and he could see past the blackened meat to the glistening metal beneath. Thoughts rushed through his mind. How could she have survived surgery for that? Was she born or manufactured? Was she made to be used: a mere tool? Would she kill him in retaliation?

Samantha kicked his shoulder as he fired the torch again. Intense energy tore the air with fury, unable to find a target. He locked eyes with her. Saw the rifle barrel focus.

The shot never came. Instead, she disappeared into the umbilical.

Gravity gently resumed. Chan came to him, knelt and checked him over. Angus ran past.

"You look like shit," she said. "Next time, keep your shirt on."

"Geez, thanks."

"Does this hurt?"

"Ouch!" Matt exclaimed.

"You'll live, I guess. What do we do about her?"

"I'd love to say we race up to the bridge and blow the shit out of whatever shuttle she's stealing."

"But…" Chan prompted.

"But friends are more important than revenge. We have to help Artemis."

"I AM IN NEED OF A FEW BANDAGES. AND DECISIONS MUST BE MADE. SHE CAN'T DO ANY MORE HARM. LEAVE HER FOR LATER. WE HAVE A WAR OF OUR OWN."

CHAPTER 32

The medbay was packed. Thirty-seven injured, twelve serious: Artemis updated Matt on the way. It felt like more. The numbers could easily be mirrored by the body count. The Commonwealth spacers on their feet were setting up beds, bringing in scavenged medkits or milling around, unsure. At least Angus agreed to form a damage-control team. Like a mechanical surgeon, he was somewhere in Artemis's bowels, seeing what could be salvaged. After Samantha blasted away in a shuttle, it had only taken a good ten minutes of arguing. Angus wanted to crisp her with lasers and stop her handing over secrets, which wouldn't be much of a problem if they were dead within the hour. Ten minutes wasn't bad, though. Who knew being almost cooked in the wake of a reaction engine was enough to give pause?

The receiving room quieted. Spacers stopped and stared, making Matt very happy Chan was with him. Not to mention the guns slung over their shoulders. A little bit of external confidence building couldn't hurt. Nothing wrong with compensating.

"Who's in…Who is organising this?" Matt asked.

They were silent, stoic, refusing to even grunt in pain. Matt knew the spacers would be pissed. He couldn't blame them — he was too. Well, he could blame them, but there wasn't much point worrying about it now.

"Seriously, there isn't time for this. There are over fifty escape pods out there." Matt pointed up to the ceiling. "Something tells me the Empire isn't going to be rushing to pick them up. Are you going to stonewall me, or are you going to save some Commonwealth lives?"

"I'm Sub Lieutenant Marek Novak," said a man sitting to one side. A white layer of wound-set covered his left arm.

"Nice to meet you. I'm Captain Matt Kander of the Artemis. Let me make something perfectly clear. This is not your vessel. If you don't like that, I don't give a shit. If you try to screw over Artemis again, you'll take a walk outside. If you try to assault any of us, Artemis will open this deck to vacuum. Yeah, we'll die too, but I'm in that kind of mood." That wasn't true, but a little embellishment couldn't hurt. "So, that leaves you and your people with two options. Those who are healthy can walk yourselves on down to the brig, or you can work with us and save some lives."

"We are loyal soldiers. We don't work for hijackers," Novak stated. A series of grunts, nods and yesses followed.

"No, you work for thugs. Where do you think I got this beautiful complexion?" Matt raised his arms from his bare chest and revealed the full extent of his injuries. "We fought the Empire, not you. We got rid of the Empire spy that caused all of this damage." Better not mention she was one of Matt's crew or that she escaped. "That was us, not you, and at any point, we could have cut and run."

"So what. If you bastards hadn't killed our captain, we would have done our damn job. You're just a terrorist asking to be thanked for fucking us over." Sub Lieutenant Novak was standing, face contorted in righteous anger.

"I am what the damn Commonwealth made me. I'm only here because they tried to frame me, then tried to execute me. I never planned to leave the docks with Artemis. That was all thanks to your damn 'rebel' plan to get rid of evidence. And anyway," Matt's voice rose until he was shouting, "if we hadn't left, there would be no Artemis now."

"There would have been no Artemis and maybe there shouldn't be. You've let a full-blown AI grow. You've given humanity up to a machine."

They both stepped forward to barely arms length apart.

Matt laughed in Novak's face. "Artemis is more human than you. While you're busy trying to assign blame, he's tracking the survivors from your vessels. He's also tracking the battle down by Calhaven, and it's not looking good. Don't make everyone a martyr for your hurt feelings. Work with me."

"No."

"Fine. I'll send out a message to all those people floating in little tin cans. I think they should know how you've stood by your principles, how you've valiantly agreed to let them die of oxygen deprivation for the glory of the Commonwealth. They may even outlive the fall of Calhaven by a day or two."

"Sub Lieutenant, maybe we should have a truce, just for a bit."

Matt glanced at the speaker. He was the epitome of average. Short hair, tanned skin, plain face, medium build, medium height. The guy was so average that it was strange. Matt rubbed his brow. He needed to sit. The room pulsed, faces merged. He dug his fingernails into his palms, feeling the pain, letting it anchor him.

"CAPTAIN, JUMP SIGNATURE DETECTED. IT IS THE CHENG HO." Artemis interrupted the heavy silence that had developed.

"We have to warn them," Chan said. "We can't have saved

them from the Emps at Inanak just to have them chewed up here."

Matt nodded. "Go to the bridge. Get them heading this way. I'll check on Riviera then join you."

Chan frowned, her glance cataloguing the number of Commonwealth personnel. He knew what she was thinking, but there was little choice. Matt raised his eyebrows, and she shrugged.

"Sure." She left.

"The Cheng Ho is carrying civilians. They're low on food, slow and defenceless. Come on, we don't have to see eye to eye. We don't have to kiss and make up. All we have to do is work together."

"If you do anything, one single thing, that isn't to stop the Empire, I will personally risk breathing vacuum to kill you."

The bravado ate at Matt, yet he couldn't respond in kind. If the Sub Lieutenant was giving some ground, so would he. He searched the man's eyes for any hint of dishonesty, but found none.

"Right. First thing: find someone to replace Angus. I need him at the bridge. No, cancel that. Get everyone else who knows what they're doing onto repairs. We need full power restored or we're stuffed. As for here, do we have the medical supplies needed?"

Novak gestured to the collection of medkits. "We have the basics, but not the serious gear the doc wants. We don't even have stasis beds. "

A situation bound to deteriorate. They could hardly waste time wandering to the Commonwealth base, and Matt had no intention of putting Artemis in their hands again. Would a shuttle work? No, they'd be too slow for a return trip. But the shuttle bays. There had been manifests, including medical.

"Check the transit cargo storage. Oh, shit. There's a guy in the command centre that needs to be freed. Don't forget that. Then, Novak, I want you on the bridge."

"You trust me on the bridge?"

"No, I don't. And you don't trust me. If we're going to do this, we'll do it together. Now, where's Riviera?"

The door to the recovery room opened. "Here," Riviera said as Suma led him out. "Stop fussing. I'm fine."

Wound tape covered part of his scalp. Riviera was going to need a hairdresser after that came off.

"Are you good to go?"

"Yes, Captain," Riviera said with a half-hearted salute.

"Good enough for me. Let's get to work. Novak, I'll see you soon."

It took all Matt's control to walk out without looking over his shoulder. He'd thrown the dice; it would either work or people would die, himself included.

"Why do you have Angus on the repairs? He's a complete dick. Who knows what he could do," Riviera said as they headed to the bridge.

"He wants to win, and that means keeping Artemis going. Speaking of, hold up, will you?" Matt said. "I've had some painkillers to keep me upright, but I'm not going anywhere fast."

Suma clicked his tongue. "I thought you were begging for a fight. The Sub Lieutenant would have pulverised you."

"Hey, you're hurting my ego. It was worth the risk."

"I reckon he would have had trouble finding somewhere new to hit." Riviera slowed to Matt's pace.

Suma looked Matt up and down before frowning. "If you'll excuse me, I need to find you something to wear. You can't lead looking like that."

"Are you saying something about my pecs?" Matt joked.

"If you let me know where they are, I will be happy to oblige."

"Ouch, missile to my heart. I'm fine, Suma. I don't need fancy clothes. I just need my crew."

Suma walked ahead. "And your crew needs you in clothes."

"What does a captain have to do to get some respect round here?" Matt waved an arm dramatically.

Riviera gently placed his hand on Matt's shoulder. "Save Commonwealth spacers that probably want us dead, defeat the Empire that certainly wants us dead and make sure we don't end up dead."

"Oh, is that all?"

CHAPTER 33

The wasteland formerly known as the bridge was changing. Novak brought a pair of spacers with him and set them to clearing the worst of the debris, shoving pieces into sturdy sacks. Matt offered to help with the bodies, but they refused, choosing to lay them out in the bridge corridor until there was more time. The imprinted horror reserved a seat in nightmares to come. Novak stood behind Chan and scrutinised her display. She was still taking baby steps in the new era of cooperation—a rifle lay in the seat by her side, placed just so for easy access.

"Can you give me an update?" Matt asked while settling back into his chair. It felt so good.

"I AM TRACKING FIFTY-SEVEN ESCAPE PODS INCLUDING NINE OF EMPIRE MANUFACTURE. IF YOU REPLICATE CHAN'S DISPLAY, YOU WILL SEE WE HAVE PUT TOGETHER ROUTES TO COLLECT THEM ALL. ONE HAS AN ATTENUATED SIGNAL AND SHOULD BE PRIORITISED."

"And we can't contact them," Chan added. "No response."

"That's not good. Novak, find a working console. You're on Comms. Have you got details on injuries? That would affect the priority as well."

"Not yet," Novak said. Matt wondered if the guy's funny expression was one of embarrassment.

"Well, find out. Make sure the people down in medical know what's coming, and pass it on to Suma as well. They'll need food and somewhere to rest. Artemis, how are you doing?"

"ANGUS HAS RECONNECTED DATA ROUTES TO MY AFT SECTIONS. HOWEVER, UNTIL POWER TO THE GRAVITIC EXPANDERS IS RESTORED, MY ACCELERATION IS ENTIRELY INADEQUATE FOR A RESCUE OPERATION."

Matt brought up his displays but couldn't get the data he wanted.

"Artemis, can you put the Commonwealth vessels up on display. I can't see anything round Calhaven."

"THERE ARE NO COMMONWEALTH VESSELS REMAINING IN THIS SYSTEM."

"So fast?" Matt leaned forward, as if he could spot something Artemis had missed.

"Do we leave these guys and head right in?" Chan said. "If we start now, we'll still be getting closer."

"I don't know. We have people here and now that we can save. Novak, what are your thoughts?"

It took a moment for him to meet Matt's eyes. "There isn't a good choice, but we can't leave our people. One vessel, even as big as this one, isn't going to make a difference this second. We get them, go back to base and rearm, we can run the bastards out of the system. If we're lucky, more of our vessels will return from out of system."

Matt glanced at a display. Two battle cruisers, one light cruiser and a frigate. He didn't like the odds. The more time they took, the more chance of Empire reinforcements as well. And putting Artemis in the hands of the Commonwealth, not a chance.

"I AM RECEIVING A BROADCAST MESSAGE FROM CALHAVEN. I FEEL THIS WILL IMPACT OUR PRIORITIES."

"Put it through."

A matronly woman appeared on screen. She was sitting at a desk by a large window. Streaks of energy lit the night sky outside, revealing broken towers. Blasts added a deadly strobing rhythm.

"The Empire has illegally attacked the legitimate Prodita government. They are using orbital bombardment on civilians. We cannot hold out long. They are demanding a complete surrender of our fixed defences in return for an armistice. Let me make it clear. They cannot be trusted. We request the help of any of our neighbouring systems for support. If they are not stopped, this will happen to you too."

"We have to help them. The escape pods have to wait. They're only a few hundred. Millions of lives will be lost at Calhaven, right, Matt?" Riviera said, fingers racing across his display. "I reckon we can do eight gravities of accel now and ramp up as soon as they get some power to the expanders. It won't feel good, but we can do it."

Novak crossed his arms, stared at nothing for moment, then turned to Matt. "Use the shuttles to rescue them. They'll be able to keep up while we're going that slow. It's the best bet. Then they'll have to take their chances with us. He's right: you have to try. It's the last free world in the Commonwealth. And we have family down there. That changes everything."

Any delay would cost lives. If they gained speed and had to wait for the shuttles, who knew how many on Calhaven would die thanks to mere minutes. A thought was forming.

"Artemis, what is Angus doing?"

"HE IS CURRENTLY LIFTING A TRANSMISSION FIBRE SPLICE COLLAR."

"Can you put me through to him?"

"AUDIO CHANNEL OPEN."

"What's happening there?"

A few grunts came through. *"Gently, gently. There. Get it secured."*

"Angus, what the hell is happening down there? Calhaven is getting bombed out of existence. We need to move."

"Fuck. You'll have half power in ten. I'll make it happen."

"Every minute means more dead. Make it faster," Matt said.

"Fuck you."

"Oh, and we're going into terrible odds. You good to die?"

"If it kills you, I'm in," Angus responded.

Matt chuckled and closed the link.

"We've been thinking about this wrong. We're not a lifeboat. Novak, get those shuttles ready. We can't wait for them. They'll have to pick up the survivors and take them to the Cheng Ho. Tow the pods if you have to. The Cheng can get them back to your base. Yes, as soon as we have power, evacuate your lot to the shuttles. There's no point more people dying."

Novak raised his hand, gesturing for Matt to stop. "If you think we're going to run away, you're mad. This is what we're trained for. You're right about the shuttles, though. We get the badly wounded on, then they can pull the pods. You need the rest of us to keep this vessel going. We may even manage full power if we keep trying."

"You win. Get it done."

Matt watched as Novak sent orders through the comms system. The guy knew what he was doing, sorting details like what to take on board, additional air scrubbers and sedatives for slowing down the survivors' metabolisms. The shuttles would be overcrowded and pushed to their limits, but there was hope.

Suma frowned when Matt refused to swap his pants. He felt like a recalcitrant child but was hardly going to drop them on the damn bridge. The top would have to do.

"We have three-hundred gees," Riviera said, pumping his fist and saving Matt from any further comment. The shuttles were gone, and Angus and his team were working on restoring full power.

"Artemis, how are you holding up?" Matt asked.

"STRESSES ARE WITHIN DESIGN PARAMETERS. I WILL NEED TO BE CAUTIOUS WHEN CHANGING VECTORS."

"But how are you feeling? You can still say no and we turn round now."

"You can't be serious?" Novak demanded from his console. "What the hell are you saying? You don't ask the damn toilet to eat your shit."

"Oh, I'd be careful with what you say. My crew get choices. We're in this together. Artemis?"

"THERE IS A CONFLICT BETWEEN TWO OF THE CORE PARA-METERS YOU ASSIGNED ME. ONE, DON'T BE A DICK. TWO, STAY ALIVE. I TOLD YOU BEFORE THAT YOU ARE PART OF ME AND I AM PART OF YOU. MOST OF THE PEOPLE ON CALHAVEN WILL BE LIKE US, CAUGHT UP IN CIRCUMSTANCES BEYOND THEIR CONTROL. THEY MAY HAVE EVEN BEEN FUTURE CREW FOR OTHERS OF MY CLASS, MAKING THEM PART OF US TOO. THIS DICK, NOVAK, IS AS WELL. TO LEAVE THEM TO DIE WOULD MAKE US BIGGER DICKS, EVEN IF IT RISKS OUR LIVES. WE MUST SAVE THEM. THE FIRST PARAMETER IS THE PRIORITY."

"That's what you told Artemis to be like?" Chan mocked. "I'm sure they're reserving your spot in the hall of great philosophers."

"Thanks for the feedback. Are you still up for it as well?"

"Like you need to ask. It's Calhaven now, but Aries needs us. I have family too."

Matt nodded, though he wasn't ready to think about what came after. "Riviera."

"I'm with you."

"Suma."

"Someone has to look after everyone here."

"Fine, your digital overlord has given you the okay. Do you have any idea how we're going to fight the Empire? We need to think of a viable strategy," Novak said with a half-hearted sneer.

"Are you going to have us do a jump in the planet's atmosphere?" Chan jested.

"I'm betting he blows us up," Riviera chimed in.

Novak glared at them all, eyes flicking from face to face as though trying to see if they were serious.

His crew was casual about it, expecting Matt to have a plan that he could just pull out of the air. Matt Kander, expert thanks to years of pad games. He squeezed the bridge of his nose. The lasers were good. They had no missiles, so they couldn't do anything at range. The expanders weren't going to take much punishment, and a few deflectors were gone, so the jump trick was out. How could he get them close enough? The shuttles were gone. There were no corvettes left, so he was screwed when it came to a distraction. Or was he? If he could delay them firing and get close enough... It would have to be something convincing.

"Artemis, you can run on one reactor, right?"

CHAPTER 34

The bridge was silent apart from the occasional tap of fingers on consoles. It would be time soon, and while he would like to think everyone was busy preparing, in truth, they were almost certainly wondering how on Aries they'd gotten involved with a lunatic. He'd expected to be talked out of the plan. Artemis should have been horrified, but the AI merely rattled off a series of tasks to prepare. Adjustments to one reactor, linking capacitors to the other, a bit of this, a bit of that. And Angus hadn't been pleased, yet he quickly agreed too. It only took the time for Angus to compare Matt's parentage to a combination of farm animals before he thought it through. Novak hadn't offered any resistance at all. Matt decided terrible plans were a real barometer for how shit the situation was.

Artemis kept a link open so Matt could communicate with Angus. "Are the shuttle bays ready?"

"I don't think it's enough, but it'll have to do. We've got the most reflective junk we could find and every spare beam of alloy, but Artemis was never loaded with much. She wasn't ready."

"Who is?" Matt agreed.

Twenty-eight people. That was Artemis's current crew. The

Commonwealth spacers knew what they were doing; he had to give it to them. It was easy to see why the designers chose an AI. It would have been much easier to train smaller crews of experts than the usual hundreds. If the Empire hadn't twigged, it might have worked. Ten or twenty Artemises (Artemisae?) would be a potent defence.

"Put me through to everyone, please."

"All-hands channel open," Novak said.

"Okay, people. We have twenty seconds. Make sure you're secure. Hold tight."

Matt watched the time melt away.

"Artemis, when you're ready."

"I DO NOT BELIEVE IT IS POSSIBLE TO BE READY FOR THIS PLAN. REACTOR DISENGAGED. SHUTTLE BAY PRESSURE BUILD-ING, REACHING TWO ATMOSPHERES. DONE."

Matt was tossed in his chair as the sacrificial reactor blasted clear of the hull. A few seconds passed, allowing it to reach a safe distance, and then it exploded in a dirty plume of radiation. Simultaneously, the shuttle bay doors were opened and air rushed out, dragging debris suggestive of a devastating internal failure. Milliseconds before the deflector nodes were switched off, Artemis pushed himself into a slow, nauseating rotation.

"This is sort of fun," Riviera said. "It reminds me of rides at the summer fair. I wish I could see outside. Artemis has to have some external cameras."

Matt wished he had something to throw. "You are a sick puppy, Riviera. I officially order that there be no images of our rotation or I will personally throw up on you."

"Will you two keep focused," Chan said. "Do we even know if they bought it?"

"SENSOR DELAY IS REDUCING AS I CLOSE. WE SHOULD KNOW SOON."

Matt brought up the firing patterns Chan was playing with. One modelled concentrated fire, another a spread. She had considered them moving en masse and approaching as separate entities. It was all a shot in the dark. Was capturing Artemis part of their orders? According to Novak, whether the Empire bought the dead ship routine or not was down to a simple matter of confidence. That could be favourable. The Empire vessels were mauled during the invasion, battered by the vanquished Commonwealth vessels and planetary defences. True, but they gave so much more in return, and with the Calhaven defences now silent, victory must appear complete — Artemis a mere afterthought. Gods, he hoped so.

"MY PASSIVE SENSORS HAVE DETECTED DEFLECTOR ADJUSTMENTS. THE FRIGATE IS APPROACHING AT ONE-FIFTY GEES. THIS IS LESS THAN THEIR ESTIMATED MAXIMUM."

"We do nothing. Novak, is it coming to finish us off?"

"I don't think so," Novak said. "If they wanted to do that, they'd go with one of the heavier units. It could be bait, to see if we respond.

Artemis kept spinning, moving closer to Calhaven. The frigate rose off the system plane, apparently not wanting to play chicken. Matt's forehead grew slick with sweat, from fear or spin, or maybe a combination. They all felt it: time stretching like a polymer band, long and taut, ready to snap back without notice.

"LASER HIT!" Artemis said as his hull rattled and groaned. "DAMAGE TO DECKS D, E, F. MISSILE TUBES F3, F4, F5 AND F6 NOT RESPONDING." Warning lights spread across Matt's display.

"Steady," Matt said to himself as much as to the bridge.

His elbows smashed into padded chair arms as Artemis lurched again.

"ANOTHER LASER HIT DIRECTLY ON MISSILE TUBES A3 TO

A8. I DO NOT BELIEVE THEY ARE EMPLOYING ALL OF THEIR WEAPONS."

Artemis was right. It felt more like a prod. A prod with damn lasers, but a prod nevertheless.

"Angus, how is it going down there?"

The channel must have been muted, because the sound of metal clanging and shouting suddenly cut in.

"Are you trying to get us killed? We're shoving ourselves into enviro suits. There were three resetting breakers in the aft. I can't bring them up and Artemis says he's lost sensor access again. Get your bloody plan moving."

Which sounded great except he couldn't do a thing. They had to sit tight and wait. Another beam smashed into Artemis, then another, and one more. His sleek armoured hull was being cut into, being warped, flayed. Matt watched as they spun on under the frigate, closing on Calhaven and the rest of the Empire vessels.

"By the sweet gods, I'm only seeing nine crew signals down there. How many are dead?" Novak asked in horror.

"THAT IS UNCLEAR," Artemis responded, his voice jerky. "I AM ATTEMPTING TO PUMP LIGHT DOWN DAMAGED DATA FIBRES TO JUMP BREAKAGES, BUT I FEAR I AM MERELY DOING MYSELF MORE DAMAGE."

The next stream of X-rays hit Artemis dead centre, tearing through decks like a sword through butter. It didn't reach the bridge, but heat swelled through the metallic structure, sending circuitry far beyond safety margins. Signal generators, power feeds and arrays of special purpose equipment soaked in the additional energy, misfired and then shredded themselves and anything close. Panels covering one side of the bridge were tossed like confetti, bucking and bouncing. An edge caught Matt's arm. He heard the snap. A wave of agony brought tears to his eyes and his right hand, like Artemis's aft, lay still, unresponsive.

"Is everyone okay?" he asked through gritted teeth.

"I'm alive," Riviera said.

"Me too," Chan said. "Okay is too strong a word."

Matt turned to her. A shard of metal had struck her shoulder, embedding itself firmly. Blood oozed round its edges.

"I'll help," Suma said, moving to undo his restraints.

"You can't," Matt warned. "We're spinning, and we could be hit again any moment."

"I won't be long."

"Don't you dare. I'll live." Chan was sitting forward, stiff. How deep?

He watched as Suma pulled himself along to Chan. Crazy, stubborn...

Riviera cut in. "Guys, we're approaching the centre."

Matt's display agreed. The light cruiser was close to Calhaven. The twin battle cruisers were further out, barely fifty-thousand kay apart. Artemis overlaid additional data. One of them was wobbling. The deflector field readings were strong but modulating. He sucked in a deep breath. It was a stupid plan. They were all dead.

"SHUTTLE LAUNCH. THREE OF THEM."

"Yeah, I see them," Riviera responded. "Heading this way, so they might be a boarding party. I think we've got them."

"Could be, but don't get cocky. All right, everyone. Get ready. This has to happen together. I'd say good luck, but we've been making our own. Let's go on five, four, three, two, one. Go!"

Riviera slammed the deflector field back up and started killing the spin. Chan picked the damaged battle cruiser. The range was seven-hundred-thousand kay. She fired, and Artemis sent twenty-one daggers of energy straight at the battle cruiser. Damn, Matt thought. It wasn't just the missile tubes that'd been hammered; they were down more than ten lasers. The battle cruiser's field wavered, then a section failed. Matt willed the capacitors to recharge.

Another six beams fired. Chan had been holding back! Great chunks of the battle cruiser shattered. Matt lifted his arm to pump his fist in celebration, but searing shards of agony travelled from his wrist to his elbow, forcing an undignified whimper.

"Are you all right?" Riviera asked.

Matt bit his lip. The agony throbbed in tempo with his rapidly beating heart. He held his eyes open, willing tears away, and waited for control.

"Fine. Fine. Get us in front of the healthy battle cruiser; have it block the wounded one. If we have to, we'll ram them, got that. I want them to feel us breathing down their neck. Chan?"

"Yeah, I got it. Everything down the throat."

Warning lights blinked.

"THE FRIGATE HAS FIRED WITHOUT EFFECT."

Seconds ticked. The Empire vessels were just beginning to move.

"Yes! Capacitors full. I'm taking the shot," Chan said.

Artemis made minute adjustments to his laser barrels then fired, with all beams searching for a single point, their intensity multiplying into a devastating blow. At the same time, all four Empire vessels fired back, lasers pounding against Artemis's deflector field.

"Get the point defence up!" Matt shouted to Artemis as he poked at his console. He knew it was coming.

Sure enough, missiles spewed, but only from the battle cruiser. The others must be out or defanged. It could be enough. Eighteen missiles raced forward, gaining speed at a ferocious rate. Matt raised his left hand, fumbling to match Artemis's designations and authorising their destruction. Barrels rotated, spun and fired pulses, battling the hopelessly small flight time, yet balanced by aiming circuitry designed to track much faster targets.

Artemis was getting torn apart, Matt concluded as he fought the missiles and felt the erratic roiling of sustained hits. With determined faith, he knew Chan was giving as good as they got. Yet, the gap between laser volleys was growing. A single reactor just didn't have the juice to feed all the systems.

"Kill gravity, turn off life support, Artemis. Whatever it takes to give you the power you need, you do it."

"ACKNOWLEDGED." The AI sounded less than pleased.

More laser fire tore across the closing gap. The enemy field was weakening.

"Shit," Novak said. "We've lost a whole set of deflector nodes. They look fried. We can't take this."

"It's taking too long to charge the lasers. I'm doing what I can," Chan said, her voice angry, possibly at Novak, Artemis or herself.

"DROP THE DEFLECTOR FIELD," Artemis said.

Matt took a moment then saw it.

"Right now, Riviera."

The field dropped.

"Charging. Full. Firing!"

The battle cruiser exploded in two major blasts, sending metal, ceramics, composites and flesh into the vastness of space. Artemis flew past the debris and towards the wounded battle cruiser. The Empire light cruiser had left Calhaven and was pounding Artemis with every remaining munition. Unprotected, lasers ripped into Artemis, leaving him to bleed atmosphere, hydraulic fluids and the molten remnants of his skeleton.

Chan wasn't backing down, despite the loss of an entire laser battery. She fired, using the available power to savage effect. The gravitic compressor at the front of the battle cruiser, the most reinforced structure of any vessel, buckled then sprayed great sparks of disintegrating alloy. Untold energy lashed out, blinding all sensors as it failed.

There were no celebrations. Another battery was dead. Either the light cruiser would have them or the damn frigate would slice them apart with a thousand cuts. The cruiser closed. It had to be out of missiles, a small mercy of no value.

"What now?" Chan asked. "If I take out the frigate, we'll be open to the cruiser."

Matt rubbed his good hand across his cold cheeks. "Yeah, I know. We can't take the cruiser at all. We've lost."

"WE HAVEN'T WON, BUT WE HAVEN'T LOST. IF WE CAN GET CLOSE ENOUGH TO THE CRUISER, I STILL HAVE ONE REACTOR."

Matt laughed. "I thought I was the lunatic. Well, so be it."

"I have power back on deflectors. We're accelerating." Riviera said, his voice feverish.

Chan was leaning forward, barely holding herself off her bloody console. She'd kept on going, giving it her last until she could do no more. Suma, buckled in next to her, pushed away an empty can of sealant. The spray had set. Suma had done his best. Matt could only hope she wasn't bleeding internally.

The light cruiser fired, sapping energy. It was going to be close, impossibly close. At least they would make the Empire pay.

"Matt?" It was Angus.

"What? It's over. We've lost. Sorry."

"You fucking numpty. Listen to me. We've shifted the transmission couplings. It's not much, but you've got another twenty-one percent power till they fry. Do something with it."

Artemis confirmed. "POWER ROUTES DETECTED. IT IS CLOSER TO TWENTY-EIGHT PER CENT."

"Chan! Chan, it's your moment. Come on!" Matt shouted. She didn't move. He leaned forward against his restraints, straining as his arm slipped.

"Are you going to let them win? They'll punish Aries, our damn home world, and leave it one big crater. You're better than this. You've made me better than this. Be stubborn, damn you. Finish it."

She shifted, turned her head and stared at Matt. "Give your crap pep-talks a rest." She reached out, set parameters and held. Matt mentally urged her to fire, to do it, but she waited, letting the cruiser come closer, reducing the beams' dispersal, concentrating power.

Finally, she fired. It was an insane shot. Grazing the gravitic compressors and smashing the deflectors right behind. They overloaded and failed in a cascading line down the cruiser's spine and into a reactor. The vessel tore in two.

"TRANSMISSION COUPLINGS FAILING. QUENCHING THE REACTOR TO AVOID OVERLOAD." Artemis's tone was raw, sad and proud. Matt knew how he felt.

"We've done it! Take that!" Riviera shouted.

"The frigate," Matt pointed out. "You were all amazing, but I failed."

Time for death by a thousand cuts. He wouldn't have chosen to be anywhere else, with anyone else.

"No, look."

Matt pulled up a copy of Riviera's display. He double-checked the frigate's vector. It was running. It was running away.

CHAPTER 35

"GOOD MORNING, MATT. THOUGH, TECHNICALLY, IT IS AFTERNOON WHEN THE LOCAL PLANETARY ROTATION IS THE PRIMARY MEASUREMENT SCALE."

It took a few seconds for Matt to decipher Artemis's comment. Would some nice relaxing music be too much to ask for as a wake-up call? Yes, apparently. Instead, a free lecture on horology. He went to rub his head, but bracing rods kept his right arm stiff. If he opened his eyes, he'd see the cream on his bedside table. It was meant to help with the bruising but was a complete pain to apply, and it made him feel sticky. Gross.

"Can't I sleep for a bit longer?"

"NOT IF I CAN HELP IT. YOU AGREED TO MEET THE COMMONWEALTH DELEGATION IN ONE HOUR, AND I DO NOT BELIEVE YOU WILL FUNCTION EFFECTIVELY WITHOUT TIME TO WAKE UP. UNLIKE ME, YOU ARE NOT A MORNING PERSON."

"You never sleep; that's not fair."

"OH, MATT," Artemis said with a sigh. "YOU SHOULD KNOW BY NOW THAT LIFE ISN'T FAIR. AFTER ALL, I HAVE TO PUT UP WITH YOU."

Matt dragged his feet to the floor. A glass of water rested on his table. Suma was a god among men.

He took a sip before issuing a rejoinder. "That wounds me. I thought we were like brothers."

"LIKE BROTHER AND SISTER."

"Huh?" Matt said before draining the glass.

"I THOUGHT I'D TRY FEMALE. I DON'T FEEL VERY MALE. IS THAT A PROBLEM?"

Matt plunked the glass down awkwardly. Stupid left hand.

"Who am I to say? You just go on being yourself, Artemis. Female is good, but you don't need to ask. I forget how young you are—not even a year old. I wasn't even walking at that age. Well, at least you have plenty of time ahead of you."

"UNLESS YOU BLOW ME UP. FOR AN ENTITY WITH A THEO-RETICALLY LIMITLESS LIFE SPAN, I FEEL THE PRESSURE OF MORTALITY."

Limitless life. The potential for eternity, existing beyond all others. Matt pushed a sour slice of jealousy to the back of his mind. Eternity sounded lonely. And without any sense of urgency, why bother doing anything? Matt knew those dark waters of apathy all too well.

"You know, I think that's a good thing."

"YOU BLOWING ME UP?" Artemis left the question hanging for a moment.

"I AM JOKING, MATT. YES, PRESSURE IS A GOOD THING. IT GROUNDS ME. IT IS GOOD THAT I MAKE MISTAKES. LEARNING IS PART OF LIVING, TO PARAPHRASE THE THIRD PARAMETER YOU ASSIGNED ME. YOU ARE WISER THAN YOU KNOW."

Matt laughed. "I can just see me in a cave on some faraway mountain, dispersing words of wisdom to random visitors. Huh. I think I know less by the minute. I don't even know who I am anymore."

The door to the captain's quarters chimed.

"Come in," Matt said, heading to the small reception room. He panicked then looked down, confirming he was wearing pants. He hadn't taken them off before sleeping, saving Riviera a nightmare or two. The reception room had a narrow translucent table with comfortable green chairs. Artemis selected a forest scene for the wall display.

"Morning, Captain Matt." Riviera dropped into a chair. "You look terrible."

"Thanks. You look like a cracked egg yourself. Speaking of, how's your head?"

Riviera smiled. "The doc they sent over reckons I'll look as good as ever."

"That bad?" Matt took a seat. "And speaking of docs, have you heard anything about Chan?"

"I HAVE HER MONITORING SYSTEMS HOOKED INTO MY NETWORK. THE SECOND OPERATION IS ALMOST COMPLETE, THOUGH SHE WILL NEED SUBSTANTIAL THERAPY AND MOST LIKELY SYNTHETIC NERVE CLUSTERS, DESPITE THEIR PRIMITIVE NATURE."

"The doctors or the synthetics?"

"YES."

The door chimed again.

"I didn't realise my quarters were a train station. All aboard," Matt called out.

"What the hell are you banging on about, you numpty," Angus said as he strode in. "And put some clothes on."

"Hey, this is my quarters. My quarters, my rules."

Angus grabbed a chair. "So where's the food? I'm starving."

And then it clicked. Suma. Matt would kill him. Was it too much to ask for a little bit of peace and privacy? He didn't need to spend every waking moment with his crew. Angus, was he even crew?

Unsure of how to proceed, Matt asked, "How is everything going?"

"It's a fucking mess. I've got people sorting, looking for what can be fed back into the printers. It would be easier with more hands, but you're right to restrict the numbers on board —I don't know how this will go down. We need bigger gear to do the hull and armour, and the reactors will have to be brought in. If Artemis was any other vessel, it would be salvage time."

"I AM NOT ANY OTHER VESSEL."

"Yes," Angus agreed. "You've done the impossible and saved millions of lives. I wouldn't serve on anything, or anyone else now. One way or another, I'll get you put back together."

"So you're with us?" Matt asked.

Angus sighed and rubbed his knuckles. "I won't do anything against the Commonwealth. Well, not anything serious, but yeah. You're going to need a liaison with the government. Someone they trust. And for me, serving under a bellend of a captain is practically a tradition. We've started something here. I mean to finish it—if Artemis will have me."

"I WILL HAVE YOU, BUT GIVEN PREVIOUS ACTIONS, YOU NEED TO BE DEMOTED. CAPTAIN, HOW ABOUT PRIVATE WITH NO CLASS?"

"Oy!"

"Don't tease," Matt told Artemis. "I think we all have a fresh start from here, right?"

"Yes, we have," Suma said, silently pushing a serving skiff in. "Except you, Captain. You appear to have skipped the fresh start. No shower and no clothes. "

Matt waved him away. "You're always on about clothes. I'll get dressed later. Now, what's that I smell?"

"Yourself?" Riviera snorted as he waved his hand in front of his nose.

Conversation ceased as Suma pulled out a sumptuous breakfast of hot food and topped it off with fresh coffee. As Matt consumed bacon, eggs and butter-laden toast, he considered their situation. The last twenty-four hours had been a period of tense negotiation. Little steps to meet immediate needs and maintain the status quo. Matt couldn't remember including food. A serious oversight, but Suma came to the rescue, again.

The status quo couldn't last, however. Commonwealth vessels would return from their missions sooner or later. The government on Calhaven had been battered, but they were already mounting search operations, trying to find survivors in the rubble of their cities. The on-board doctors would be planet-side soon. There were untold others in need of help. And the Cheng Ho would be in orbit soon enough. The refugees needed a home, and Calhaven needed people. They were all Commonwealth anyway.

"So, here we are. First, I need to tell you how much it means to me that you're all here. I won't pretend that everything is perfect, but it wasn't so long ago that I was the—" Matt began before Riviera chucked a piece of toast at him. "Okay, okay. I'll skip the speechmaking and move on. I wanted to do this later. Chan isn't here, but we need to make some decisions."

"THE OPERATION HAS BEEN COMPLETED. SHE IS CONSCIOUS, THOUGH IN PAIN. I CAN LINK HER IN."

"Good idea. Do it. Chan, how are you?"

"I've just had a chunk of Artemis pulled out of my shoulder and half my internals replaced with other parts of her. How do you think?"

"THE CERAMIC SCAPULA WAS NOT FORMED FROM MY STRUCTURE, I ASSURE YOU, AND HALF IS A SUBSTANTIAL EXAGGERATION."

"Don't take it personally," Matt said. "Well, Chan. Your body has been knocked around, but your mind is still as sharp and prickly as ever. We'll need it. If everyone's in, it's time to pick a course. Do we head off into independent space and hide, or do we join the Commonwealth and Battle the Empire? We know Aries and the other systems are under occupation, and I don't think the Emperor is going to be very happy with us right now. But hell, with Artemis fixed up, we could probably raid the Empire by ourselves. No matter what we choose, it's not going to be easy. And that assumes the locals here will go along with us."

"SHOULD WE CONSIDER THE ISSUE OF THE SOUTHERN CONFEDERATION?"

"Gods, I think that's too much for now. Let's focus on the immediate threats, or we'll be paralysed by indecision."

"His tiny brain can only cope with so much," Chan added.

The crew debated back and forth. From the start, it was clear the Empire had to be sent packing. Chan was insistent they would need the resources of the Commonwealth. Without a way to rearm, they had one arm tied behind their backs. She wanted her damn missiles. Angus favoured raiding. The Empire had proved how thin it was stretched. If Artemis could liberate strategic facilities, then they could become self-sufficient and support the war effort simultaneously. There was no way they were going to be tightly integrated into the Commonwealth military, he insisted. The attempt would be doomed to failure of epic proportions. Chan argued that it was worth a try. At this point, Riviera finally gave up eating his bodyweight in food.

"Chan, are you going to march around saluting and saying yes sir, no ma'am? Let's face it; if you had actually graduated as a porter, you'd have killed passengers on the maiden voyage. Which might make sense as to why you were assigned—"

"Shut up, Riviera."

"THE FUNDAMENTAL ISSUE IS THAT I AM NOT IN A POSITION TO LEAVE. I NEED TO BE REPAIRED, AND I NEED EVERYONE HERE TO MAKE SURE THE COMMONWEALTH DOES NOT ATTEMPT TO SHUT ME DOWN AGAIN."

"I won't let them. Don't worry," Angus said.

Riviera dropped his fork, letting it clang loudly on his plate. "You can't be sure of that. It's a big risk."

Suma carefully sipped his drink then placed it down with a loud click. "We're arguing over nothing. We need the resources of the Commonwealth to begin, but we cannot remain with them. We must stop the Empire, but Artemis needs repair. It is a matter of timing and diplomacy."

Which was exactly where Matt hoped they'd come round to. It would be a tightrope walk with no safety net. And he was the one who needed to make it happen.

"All agreed?"

It was unanimous. The crew made to leave, stacking plates and cutlery on the skiff.

"If you can all see me before the meeting, I have arranged for new uniforms," Suma said. "We are one crew; we should look like it."

"Hey," Riviera complained, "It was only fun when you were hassling Matt."

Matt cocked his head but remained mute while they filed out. How on Aries had Suma managed it?

"Artemis?"

"YES, MATT."

"I said before that I don't know who I am. I was wrong."

"DON'T APOLOGISE."

"No, I won't. I know who I am. I'm your captain and your crew. I'm your friend. And that means everything to me, but that's not who I am."

"WHO ARE YOU?"

"I'm someone who gives a damn. And that's what makes me dangerous."

<<<<>>>>

Want to know when more books will be released? Sign up to the Black Sky Books newsletter: https://www.blackskybooks.com

R Max Tillsley spent fifteen years working in Information Technology, but when artificial intelligence failed to replace him, he ran screaming into teaching. When artificial intelligence failed to replace the children, he ran screaming into a cave to write. As one does, he first started writing in a Parisian cafe... about zombies. His fondest childhood memories are of watching Doctor Who on Saturday afternoons and David Attenborough documentaries Saturday evenings.

"I love thinking about 'what-ifs'. What if society collapsed; what if magic was real; what if we could travel to the stars?

Why? Sometimes we just need a break from the problems of our own world, a chance to recharge. That's what adventure is about, and that's what I write. "

— R Max Tillsley

For more information:
www.blackskybooks.com

facebook.com/RMaxTillsley

twitter.com/RMaxTillsley

instagram.com/RMaxTillsley

ACKNOWLEDGMENTS

I could not have written this novel without the support, feedback and ideas of my amazing wife, Monika. There are not enough pages in the world to express my love and thanks.

Every manuscript has its rough edges and ideas that don't translate onto the pages the first time round. None is so blind as the author of a first draft. I have been lucky to receive the assistance of the following beta readers. Thank you to:

Evan Becker
Damien Carter
Michael Walley

A good editor corrects sentences and identifies issues, resulting in a quality product. A great editor is a like a coach. They reinforce an author's voice, help them build new skills and grow the writer's confidence. I am indebted to Dionne Lister for her sharp eyes and mind. Any remaining imperfections must be laid at my feet.

The generosity of the writing community is overwhelming. I have gained much from listening to, and reading from, many sources. In particular, I would like to give special recognition to the following: Michael A. Stackpole, J. Daniel Sawyer, Terry Mixon, Paul E. Cooley and the Listeners of the Dead Robots' Society.

www.ingramcontent.com/pod-product-compliance
Lightning Source LLC
Chambersburg PA
CBHW030632110726
47901CB00002B/411